The Sheriff's Irresistible Love

Deacon and Candy

The MacFarlands
Book Three

By SJ McCoy

A Sweet n Steamy Romance

Published by Xenion, Inc

Published by Xenion, Inc.
First paperback edition August 2022
www.sjmccoy.com

Editor: Kellie Montgomery
Proofreaders: Aileen Blomberg, Traci Atkinson, Becky Claxon.

Cover Design by Dana Lamothe of Designs by Dana
Cover Image by Jean Woodfin of JM Photography and Covers
Cover model: Brady Cyphert

ISBN: 978-1-946220-96-7

Dedication

This one is for Brady.

Folks need heroes, Chief, to give 'em hope.

So, smile, would you?

While we've still got something to smile about.

I'm so happy to have your image grace the cover of this book.

And thank you for adding a little something to Deacon's character.

I think we made 'em smile.

Love

J

oxo

Chapter One

"Hey, buddy. How was your day?" Deacon asked as soon as he let himself in through the door.

Clawson replied with his usual scratchy-sounding meow as he rubbed around Deacon's legs. Deacon squatted down to pet him, and the big, orange tomcat butted his head into Deacon's hand before fixing him with a baleful stare.

Deacon had to laugh. "Don't look at me like that; I already told you that you have to stay inside when I'm not around – at least, you do until someone shoots that damn coyote."

Clawson didn't look impressed with his explanation and headed straight for the back door. Deacon followed and let the cat out into the back yard. He shouldn't feel guilty; he'd locked the cat flap to keep Clawson inside for his own good. Several neighbors had complained about a coyote prowling around over the last few days.

There was a litter box in the mudroom; it wasn't as though Clawson had to wait for Deacon to get home before he could take care of his business. No, he just liked to make his point. The cat was worse than a damned woman; when he didn't like something, he made his point with passive-aggressive behavior instead of just coming out and saying something. Although, to be fair, as a cat, it wasn't as though Clawson could sit him down and talk about it.

Deacon took his hat off and leaned back against the kitchen door as he watched Clawson putz around the yard. They wouldn't be out here for long – the cat would be more interested in getting his dinner than prowling the yard. Deacon was looking forward to his dinner, too. Rocket had dropped him off a big dish of his special lasagna this morning. That was some good eating.

"Oh, no, pussy! You're not supposed to be out!"

Deacon almost choked at the sound of a woman's voice. What the hell?

"Stay there. I'll come and get you. Grumpy the sheriff is not going to be happy with you."

Grumpy the sheriff? Deacon looked up to where the voice was coming from the window above his head. It was Candy, the woman who was renting his upstairs apartment. He pursed his lips. He tried to avoid her as much as possible, but as he heard the window close, he realized that he wasn't going to be able to avoid her tonight.

He glanced at Clawson, who was strutting toward him with his tail in the air and what looked like a smile on his face. Deacon narrowed his eyes at him. "Is this your payback for me keeping you inside all day, you little shit?"

Clawson rubbed around his legs and purred loudly.

A few moments later, he heard the door on the side of the house open, and Candy started talking before she appeared.

"You be a good boy, Clawson. Don't you run off on me, you hear? Grumpy the sheriff isn't going to be happy with either of us if I can't get you back inside, and we don't want that." As she rounded the corner of the house, Deacon stayed quiet. He should have let her know he was there, but he was curious to hear what else she might have to say – especially about him. Grumpy the sheriff, huh?

When she rounded the corner of the house, Candy stopped and looked around the yard. "Clawson? Come on, help a girl out, would ya? Don't get me in trouble with –" She stopped dead when she saw Deacon standing there, her eyes widening in surprise.

"With Grumpy the sheriff?" Deacon asked. He wanted to be pissed, part of him was, but another part of him wanted to laugh, especially at the shocked look on her face.

"Oh, shoot!" She folded her arms across her chest, and Deacon couldn't help watching. Her arms didn't cover her breasts – instead, they rested under them, pushing them up higher and … He shook his head and forced himself to look away.

When his gaze came back to her face, she raised her eyebrows, and he knew that she'd caught him checking her out. Damn. He prepared to go on the offensive, hoping to end this encounter as swiftly as possible, but she beat him to it.

"I didn't know you were out here with him. I just knew – from your lecture about the back door – that you don't want him outside by himself. I swear, I didn't let him out. I haven't been out here."

She was only a little thing, maybe five-three, but she had a powerful personality, nevertheless. She was all bubbly and outgoing – everything that drove him nuts. Deacon had been about to question her as to why she was referring to him as Grumpy the sheriff, but he didn't really need to. He knew the answer – that was exactly who he was. Most people wouldn't dare say it, but it was true.

He held his hand up to stop her from trying to explain further. "I brought him out myself. I just got home."

"Oh."

She stared at him, her light green eyes assessing him. He stared back at her, feeling like he should say something. Maybe he should apologize, but after hearing what she called him, he didn't feel much like doing it. From the look on her face, she wasn't going to apologize either.

After a few moments, he nodded curtly and bent down to scoop Clawson up to take him inside.

"Goodnight, then."

He turned back to look at her over his shoulder. She looked … he didn't know what. Lost, maybe? She hadn't been here long. She'd moved up here to help at the bakery. She didn't know anyone in the valley except for Spider, who owned the bakery, and Rocket, his buddy who worked there with him. She'd been a foster mom to both of them when they were kids, and that was as much as he knew about her.

He felt bad, leaving her standing there like that, but what else was he supposed to do? It'd been a long hard day and he was ready to kick back and relax; he needed to feed Clawson, then take a shower and get some dinner himself.

Candy might look a little lost, she might be looking to chat for a while – she was a chatty kind of woman from what he'd seen, but … But he didn't have the time for that.

"Goodnight."

He nodded again, and took Clawson in, closing his kitchen door behind him.

He felt like a shit as he listened to her come into the house through the side door and then make her way up the stairs to the apartment. He blew out a sigh. She wasn't his problem. He still wasn't sure how she'd even ended up renting from him. Well, he knew how; Rocket had been living up there, but he'd moved in with Janey MacFarland. When Candy came, Rocket had let her stay at, what was at the time, his apartment. When it turned out that she was staying in the valley, to work at the bakery, the apartment was perfect for her – since the bakery was just across the road. And since she was a single woman, here alone, it was better for her to be at his place rather than …

He set Clawson down and got his bowl ready. He needed to stay focused on feeding the big, orange furball, and keep his mind away from the fact that he had a single, very attractive woman living upstairs.

She was better off being here than somewhere else. But him? He'd be better off if she were where he didn't have to see her, or hear her, or smell her. When she cooked, the smell of it always drifted down to him and made his mouth water. And every time he stepped out into his hallway, which she shared, he'd catch a hint of perfume or whatever it was she wore – and that made his mouth water, too.

He set Clawson's bowl down in front of him and went to get himself a beer from the fridge. He needed a cold one before he took his shower – and unless he could stop his mind from straying to Candy, the shower would need to be cold, too.

~ ~ ~

Candy closed the door to the apartment and closed her eyes as she leaned back against it. "Hell's bells!" she muttered. "Why, oh why, oh why?" she asked the ceiling as she shook her head. "When am I going to learn to keep my mouth shut?"

She let out a short laugh and stepped away from the door. Probably never was the honest answer to that question. If everything that had happened in the last year and a half hadn't taught her to not run her mouth, then slipping up in front of Grumpy the sheriff wasn't going to do the trick.

She went to the kitchen and looked around. There was nothing to do. She'd already had dinner and cleaned up after herself. She'd learned to eat early since she'd started work at the bakery; she needed to go to bed early if she wanted to be up at four-thirty and not be yawning all day.

She went to the cabinet and took out flour and sugar before turning to the fridge for eggs. People might assume that she'd be sick of baking after spending all her days making cakes, and pastries, and doughnuts, but she loved to bake. For years, she'd had no one to bake for, and now she had a whole valley full of people who depended on her. She loved that even more. She loved to feel part of a community, to feel like she was contributing, and if she was honest, she loved to feel needed.

She'd felt all of that and more – so much more – when she was younger and had been part of the foster care system. She'd opened her home and her heart to those kids. Her smile faded. She'd had to give it up because of Len. Her husband hadn't been the kind of man who … She pulled herself together and got the mixing bowl down from the shelf. She didn't need to be thinking about him. He was gone, dead and buried. It had taken some adjusting to, but she was out the other side now, and she wasn't looking back. Well, she still looked over her shoulder sometimes, afraid that his past might catch up with her.

But tonight, she wasn't going to think about any of that. All she was going to think about was the batch of muffins she was going to bake for Deacon. He came into the bakery every day for his coffee before he started work. He always ordered straight, black coffee and a scone. One day, before she'd admitted defeat and given up trying to break through the walls he kept up, she'd commented that he was the scone guy.

She smiled when she remembered his response. He'd actually laughed – and that was a sight to behold. He told her that he wasn't a scone guy; it was just that scones were the least messy thing to eat on his drive up to town. She'd felt brave that day and asked him what his favorite pastries were. He'd laughed again when he told her that he was a muffin guy. When she pushed, he'd cited banana-nut as his favorite, but claimed that he was happy with any muffin he could get. That had been the cause of much teasing from his friend Ace, and she'd left them to it.

But she was glad that she'd stored the information away. She was going to make him a batch of banana-nut muffins tonight and leave them with a little apology note when she left for work in the morning.

She frowned. That wouldn't work. If she left them outside his door, he wouldn't see them until he left, and the whole point was for him to be able to have one before he went out – so that he didn't have to eat it in the car.

She blew out a sigh as she set the oven to preheat. First to bake the muffins, then she'd figure out if she was brave enough to take them down to him. She'd been planning to leave a note that just said *sorry* with them. If she took them down to him, she'd have to *explain* that they were an apology offering, and she didn't particularly want to remind him that she needed to apologize for calling him Grumpy the sheriff! She wasn't even that sorry for calling him that – the name suited him. She was only sorry that he'd heard.

By the time the muffins were done, the apartment smelled wonderful. She tried not to eat too much of whatever she made; she'd never been slender, even when she was younger. But she'd made the proverbial baker's dozen tonight. She took one from the rack where she'd set them to cool. Grumpy the … no, Deacon, she should probably start using his name even in her head. That way she'd be less likely to slip up again. Deacon wasn't going to be the only one who got to enjoy a muffin for breakfast in the morning.

With starting so early at the bakery, she usually waited and had her breakfast after she'd been at work for a while and had gotten the first batches of bread and pastries in the oven. Tomorrow, she'd have a little treat with her coffee before she went out.

She paced the kitchen, eyeing the muffins. She'd rather not have to go down there and face him. But since she'd gone to the trouble of baking for him, she wanted him to be able to have one before he left for work. The only way that was going to happen was if he knew that he had them.

She took a Tupperware container down from the cabinet and carefully placed them inside. She'd been telling herself that she was waiting for them to cool, but the truth was that she was putting it off. It'd be better to get it over with, then she could come back up here and get into bed. It was early, even for her, but she'd just started a new book and she loved to read in bed. She'd just need to be careful to not get lost in the story and stay up too late reading. That was a habit she'd had to break herself of since she'd started working at the bakery.

She picked up the container and took a deep breath before she headed for the door. She could do this. Hopefully, he wouldn't be able to stay mad at her for calling him names once he saw the peace offering.

She made her way down the stairs and took another deep breath before she tapped on his door. All her breath got stuck in her throat when the door opened, and he stood there, bare-chested.

Wow! He was a good-looking guy, no question about it. His brown hair had a generous sprinkling of gray, as did his beard, and … she couldn't help letting her gaze rove over his bare chest. The dusting of dark hair there also had silver highlights. She pulled herself together – silver highlights? She could just imagine what he'd have to say if he could hear what she was thinking. Silver highlights weren't words that went well with all that muscle that he had on display.

He cleared his throat and she remembered to look up at his face – his rugged, handsome face, and his gray eyes that were boring into her from under his furrowed brow. Shit! She needed to say something, not just stand here eyeing him up!

"Um." She thrust the muffins toward him. "These are for you."

His hands closed around the container, and he frowned as he looked down at it before looking up at her again. "What is it?"

"Muffins."

He cocked an eyebrow. "Muffins?"

"Yes, muffins." Damn, she needed to pull herself together. "I … they're … it's." She closed her eyes and sucked in a deep calming breath. She wasn't some stuttering idiot, and she wasn't going to let him turn her into one. When she opened her eyes, she made herself smile and meet his gaze. Damn, he had beautiful eyes. Stop!

She gave him a rueful smile. "They're a peace offering. An apology. I know you heard what I called you earlier. I … I'm sorry."

He looked down at the container again. When he looked back up at her, the corners of his lips were turned up in the ghost of a smile. "What flavor?"

She felt her shoulders relax. If he wanted to know the flavor, hopefully, that meant that he wasn't going to give her a hard time.

"Banana-nut. Since that's your favorite."

He looked at her more closely, and she felt a blush creep over her cheeks – great!

"You remembered that?"

"Of course I do. I had you down as a scone guy, but you said that you're a muffin guy, and that banana-nut is your favorite."

She couldn't figure out the expression on his face, so she pushed on, hoping to get this over with so that she could go back upstairs and hide under her covers with her book. "You said that you only get scones in the mornings because you can eat them as you drive without making a mess. I … I made you muffins so that you can have one before you go out. It doesn't matter if you drop crumbs …" She trailed off.

Deacon's face had lit up with a smile. It was the most friendly and approachable she'd seen him look since she met him. "Thank you."

She nodded rapidly. "You're welcome. I … I'm sorry." She didn't want to remind him that they were an apology for what she'd called him. She didn't want to do anything that might cause that gorgeous smile to disappear.

He chuckled; it was a low, deep sound that seemed to echo in her chest. Wow!

"No problem. If this is what I get when you call me Grumpy the sheriff, keep it up!"

She stared at him for a moment, not understanding. She wrung her hands together, thinking that she'd messed up, made things worse somehow. But when she dared to look at his face again, he was smiling big, and he winked! It was so unexpected and so sexy it took her breath away,

"Wow!" She let out a short laugh. "If I'd known this was all it'd take to make you smile, I would have brought you muffins weeks ago."

He let out another low chuckle and shook his head. "You brought them now, that's what counts. Thank you, Candy."

She nodded, her smile fading as she realized that she should go. She'd delivered the muffins; she didn't need to hang around outside his door any longer – no matter how much she might be enjoying both his smile and his naked chest.

"You're welcome." She pointed at the stairs. "I should go. I … I'll leave you to it. I … hope you enjoy them."

She turned and almost tripped over her own feet as she headed for the stairs. Of course, he was still standing in the doorway watching her. Way to go, Candy!

"Goodnight, then," she muttered as she dashed up the stairs.

"Goodnight, and thanks again," he called after her.

Chapter Two

Deacon smiled to himself as he eyed the muffin sitting on his desk. He'd had one this morning with his coffee before he left the house. It was delicious. It was so good that he'd put another one in a baggie and brought it to work with him.

"Hey, Deacon. Are you …? What's that?"

He looked up when Luke stuck his head around the office door. "Am I what?"

Luke came into the office, grinning as he edged closer to the muffin. Deacon snatched it and dropped it into his desk drawer.

"Am I what?" he asked again.

Luke laughed. "I was going to ask if you're going to eat that, but I can see that the answer is yes."

"It is. But what were you going to ask before you saw the muffin?"

"Oh, yeah, right. I was going to ask what time you're headed home tonight."

"The usual time, barring anything unexpected. Why?"

"Can I catch a ride with you?"

"Sure. Why'd you need one?"

Luke shrugged. "I left my truck outside Chico."

Deacon narrowed his eyes at him. "Because you were being a responsible deputy and caught a ride home with a friend after you had a couple of drinks?"

"Yes, Sheriff. That was it, Sheriff." Luke grinned at him.

Deacon blew out a sigh. "I don't want to know what else it was."

Luke laughed. "That's fine because I don't want to tell."

Deacon held his gaze for a moment. "When are you going to man up?"

All the humor left Luke's face. "Don't. Let's not start that shit right now. I was just asking my brother for a ride, that's all. I don't need to get into the lectures about … *her*."

"Okay. Fine. I won't say a word. Come find me at the end of the day and I'll give you a ride back to your truck."

"Thanks. Want me to buy you dinner while I'm down there?"

"Sure, you can do that."

"Okay, I'll get back to work." Luke glanced at the desk. "Unless you feel like telling me where you got the muffin from?"

Deacon frowned at him. "You can't have it."

Luke laughed out loud. "I know. I'm just curious."

"About what?" Deacon wasn't sure why he felt so defensive. He shouldn't have a problem telling Luke about the muffins – other than knowing that Luke would no doubt wangle himself an invitation into the house later and want to eat half of them.

"Well, if you got it from the bakery, it'd be in a brown paper bag, not a Ziplock. If you bought it from the store, it'd be packaged up. So …" Luke met his gaze. "I'm guessing that it's homemade."

Deacon rolled his eyes. "And? What, Detective? What's your point?"

"My point is that we don't know many people who bake. In fact, with Andrea gone to Billings, the only person I know who bakes just happens to live upstairs from you. What I want to know is if you have your own personal muffin maker now?"

Deacon scowled at him. He should have known that Luke would figure it out. "What's the big deal? Yes, she made them for me."

Luke's eyes gleamed, just like they used to when he was a little kid and was about to play a prank on him. "Want to tell me about it? Candy's sweet."

Deacon blew out a sigh. "There's nothing to tell. You're right, she does live upstairs, that's no secret. She gave me some muffins."

Luke threw his head back and laughed. "Sorry, that just sounds so wrong."

Deacon shrugged and managed to contain his smile – he knew how it sounded.

"But why? She's been living there a while now. From what I've seen, the two of you barely even speak. I mean, I've talked to her more than you have, and that's just from going into the bakery." Luke raised his eyebrows. "Has anything changed? Has something happened that's led to her baking for you?"

Deacon decided it'd be easier to tell the truth than to try and hide anything. The more he tried to hide, the nosier his younger brother would get. "What happened was that she was talking to Clawson when she didn't know that I was there. I overheard what she said, and she felt she needed to apologize. The muffins were a peace offering."

"What did she say?"

Deacon laughed. "I don't think I want to tell you."

"Why? Was it bad?"

"No, it was funny. The trouble is, I know that you'll think it's funny, too. And if you start giving me any shit, you'll be pulling all the worst shifts for the next month."

Luke smirked. "I get the feeling it'd be worth it. Go on, tell me what she said."

"Like I said, she was talking to Clawson, thinking that I wasn't home. She called me ..." Deacon cleared his throat, knowing that this was a bad idea. "She called me Grumpy the sheriff."

Luke threw his head back and laughed. "That's awesome! I really like her. She's a lot of fun, don't you think?" His smile faded when he met Deacon's gaze. "What? She is."

Deacon shrugged.

"You are one stubborn asshole." Luke shook his head.

"What? I don't know the woman. I can't agree or disagree with you. I don't know her."

"Exactly! And you could, you *should* know her. She is a lot of fun. It seems like everyone in the valley has taken to her, accepted her as one of us. Everyone knows her, everyone likes her – everyone except you. She's living right there in your house; you should know her better than anyone but you're too damn bitter and stubborn."

Deacon sat back in his chair, surprised by Luke's outburst. "What brought that on?"

Luke shrugged. "Sorry. I just get frustrated with you sometimes. You're my brother, and I'd like to see you happy. But you just won't allow that to happen, will you? Candy's awesome. But never mind. I'm sure it won't be long before someone comes along who sees her for what she's worth – and snatches her right out from under your nose."

Luke pushed away from the wall where he'd been leaning and headed for the door. "I'll come find you at six."

Deacon stared after him, not understanding what had gotten his younger brother so rattled. He knew that Luke had gotten friendly with Candy. It was true that she was friendly with almost everyone in the valley, and that she'd been accepted and welcomed. That was a rarity for a newcomer. But he didn't understand what Luke thought she could have to do with him being happy. Deacon had given up on women a long time ago. Luke knew that and he knew why.

He pushed his chair away from the desk and headed for the break room to get a cup of coffee to go with his muffin. Maybe Luke was taking his own frustration out on him. Who knew?

"You want me to bring you a coffee, Miss Candy?"

"I'm good, thanks, Rocket." She had to smile when he came back into the kitchen and put his hands on his hips. "Don't even try it, sweetie," she said with a laugh. "You don't seriously think that you can boss me around, do you? I want to get finished with my cleanup for the day. Then, if you still want to make me a coffee, you can. In fact, you can bring it out and sit with me while we're quiet for a bit. I'll have a coffee with you, then I'll head home."

"Okay." Rocket continued to stand there with his hands on his hips. He no longer looked stern, but he did look … concerned?

"What's up, my little Rocky?"

He chuckled. "You're the only one who ever got away with calling me Rocky, you know."

She laughed. "I know. You can face down all the big, bad guys in the world, but you won't even say boo to me."

He smiled through pursed lips. "You're right, I won't. But I do worry about you. We both do."

Candy put her hand over her heart when Spider came through the door from the front of the bakery and stood beside Rocket. "Aww."

They gave her matching puzzled looks.

"Aww, what?" asked Spider.

She had to swallow before she explained. "I'm just so damn proud of you both. I remember when you were just little boys. Look at you now."

She chuckled to herself when the two men exchanged a smile. She knew that to the rest of the world they might look like tough guys; between all their tattoos, and Spider's mohawk, and Rocket's sheer size, they didn't look the kind of men you'd want to run into in a dark alley. But they were good men, both of them. They were kind souls and always had been. Some of the kids who had been placed with her had been trouble through and through. Some of them were simply a product of their environment, others had convinced her that in some cases nurture would never win out over nature – some people just had evil inside them. But Rocket and Spider, they had goodness inside them, and it spilled out wherever they went.

Spider shook his head at her. "Never mind trying to distract us. What Rocket's trying to get you to do is take a break. You work so damn hard. And you know how much I appreciate it, but you don't need to be cleaning up. You need to let us do that. You're saving our asses just by being here. But all I need you to do is bake – nothing else."

She shrugged and laughed. "What else I am going to do? You know I've always kept a clean kitchen. And I'm glad to see that what I taught the two of you stuck. You keep this place nice."

"We do – which should tell you that we're capable of doing it – and that you don't need to."

"I don't mind. It's not like I've got anything to rush home for."

They exchanged another look at that, and she felt bad. She wasn't complaining. She was fine. She didn't want them thinking that she needed their time and attention outside of work.

"Frankie asked if –"

"Nope!" She cut Spider off before he could finish. "I'm not coming down there to see you guys. You have your own lives to be getting on with." She looked at Rocket. "Same goes for you and Janey. I wasn't complaining that I don't have anything to rush home for. I have plenty to do. And if I wanted company, I'm more than capable of going out and finding some. So don't either of you go feeling that you need to include me in anything, or I'll get mad. You hear me?"

"Yes, Miss Candy."

She had to laugh. They sounded like the pair of little kids they'd been when they were first placed with her. She took pity on them.

"If it'll make you feel any better, you can make me a nice vanilla latte, but only if we can all go and sit and have a break together. It's quiet out there." She nodded through the door to the bakery, which was empty, as it tended to be this late in the day. "We can sit and have a break. Then if it bothers you that much, I'll go home and put my feet up, and let you two finish off. How about that?"

They both grinned and she made her way out to one of the big comfy booths on the back wall while Spider made their coffees, and Rocket filled a plate with pastries.

She smiled to herself as she watched them. She might not have achieved much in her life, but these two men were her pride and joy. She had to blink away the tears that pricked her eyes as she watched them.

She blew out a sigh of frustration when the front door opened. The only reason she'd agreed to leave her cleaning was that she'd wanted some time with her boys. Between working so hard in here, and them having their girls to go home to, she didn't get to spend nearly as much time as she'd like with them. This had seemed like the perfect chance for the three of them to have a little catchup – for her to enjoy having them to herself for just a little while. She loved Rocket's new wife, Janey, and Spider's fiancée, Frankie. She'd come to love them almost as much as her boys. She wasn't greedy for the boys' time, she was thrilled that they were happy in their lives, but she did cherish the moments that she got them to herself.

She frowned at the door, wondering who had come in to intrude on their special time. Her breath caught in her throat when she saw Deacon. He hadn't seen her yet, but Luke had. He grinned and lifted his hand as he came over to the booth.

'Hey, Candy. It's good to see you."

"Hi, Luke, sweetie. How are you?" She loved Luke. He was a sweetheart. It was hard to believe that he and Deacon were brothers. They were like night and day. Where Deacon was taciturn and … grumpy, Luke was friendly and outgoing.

"I'm good, thanks."

"What brings you out here at the end of the day? Are you still working?" She jerked her chin toward Deacon, who had spotted her now and lifted his chin in greeting but turned back to the counter to talk to Spider.

"No. We're done for the day. I just rode down here with Deacon." He had a weird glint in his eye that Candy wasn't sure she liked.

She raised her eyebrows at him, but he just shrugged.

"I'm going to buy him dinner at Chico. Do you want to come?"

"What?" She liked Luke, and they always chatted, but they hadn't socialized outside the bakery before. She hadn't really socialized with anyone, other than Rocket and Spider and their girls.

Luke smiled. "I just wondered if you wanted to join us."

Candy glanced over at Deacon, but he had his back to them and seemed determined to stay that way. If she'd thought for a split second that the invitation might be coming from him, her hope was snuffed out. No. It wasn't hope. What was she even thinking? Why would she …? She couldn't even go there.

She smiled at Luke. "That's sweet of you, but no, thanks."

Luke's smile faded. "Okay. Maybe next time."

"Maybe." It was better to go with non-committal than to give voice to the *hell no* that had bubbled up. She wasn't even sure where that had come from. She wouldn't mind having dinner with Luke. And Deacon? Yes, he could be grumpy but … She bit down on her bottom lip when she realized that it wasn't his grumpiness that put her off – it was her reaction to being around him – especially when the memory of his naked man chest flashed through her mind.

A shiver ran down her spine when she looked over at him again. He was something, all right. His broad shoulders might be covered by his uniform right now, but she knew how they looked bare. Her gaze dropped to his backside, but she didn't allow it to linger there – and no way would she allow herself to entertain thoughts about getting to see *that* bare! He was smiling at something Rocket was saying to him. She should probably ask Rocket how he'd managed to win him over.

"Are you sure you don't want to come?"

She looked back at Luke, who was watching her with that same glint in his eye. She shook her head rapidly. It was bad enough that she was realizing what her reaction to Deacon meant; no way did she want Luke figuring it out, too!

It had been a long time since she'd felt attracted to a man. Len had died eighteen months ago, but there'd been nothing left between them for at least a decade before that. That was a sad confession to make, even to herself. But it was true.

"… you think?"

She made herself focus on Luke, but she had no idea what he was asking. She'd been too lost in her thoughts to focus on whatever he was talking about.

"I'm sorry?"

Luke smiled through pursed lips. "The yard sale. At the school. Do you want to come?"

She frowned. She'd obviously missed a lot; she hadn't heard a thing about a yard sale. "When did you say it was again?"

"Saturday afternoon."

"And it's at the high school up in town?"

"No. The elementary school. You have Saturday afternoon off, right?"

"I do."

"So, you should come."

"Okay." She didn't see any reason not to go. She wasn't thrilled about the thirty-mile drive up the valley to town yet. But she'd get used to it. And as much as she loved hanging out at the bakery, she wanted to broaden her horizons. "What time?"

"It starts at two-thirty, but I'll pick you up just before two."

"Oh." She must have missed the part about Luke giving her a ride there. "Okay, then. Thanks."

Luke grinned and straightened up. "You should give me your number so that I can call you if anything changes."

He took out his phone and just as he was tapping her number in, Deacon turned to look in their direction and scowled. "Are you ready to go, Luke?" he called.

"Be right there." Luke winked at Candy before putting his phone back into his pocket. "I'll call you."

"Thanks."

He tipped his hat at her before turning back to his brother saying, "Hold your horses, would ya? I'm coming."

Candy watched them leave. Despite what had to be at least ten years between them, and despite the difference in their attitudes, there was no mistaking that they were brothers; they carried themselves the same way, had the same walk. She smiled to herself at the image of Luke as a young boy following his big brother around, trying to emulate his mannerisms. She couldn't deny that Deacon would be a good role model. Though no way should she be thinking wistfully about the impression he could have made on Spider and Rocket when they were younger.

When they reached the door, Luke went straight out, but Deacon paused and looked back at her. She had no idea how, but it looked like she'd managed to annoy him again. She gave him a bright smile, hoping that he might smile back. He didn't; he gave her what she was coming to think of as his trademark curt nod and then followed Luke outside.

Rocket and Spider slid into the booth, sitting across from her. Spider set her vanilla latte in front of her, and Rocket raised his eyebrows.

"Was I seeing things, or did Luke Wallis just ask for your number, Miss Candy?"

She laughed. "He did, but not like that – and you know it."

Spider gave her a stern look. "We know nothing of the kind. What's he after?"

She couldn't help laughing again, loving that they wanted to look out for her, but knowing how ridiculous it was to think that Luke might want her number in the way they meant.

"He's not after anything. Apparently, there's a yard sale up at the school in town on Saturday. He offered to give me a ride up there."

Rocket's eyebrows drew together. "That doesn't make sense."

"Why not?"

"Because he lives close to town. Why would he come all the way down here to pick you up?"

"Unless he has an ulterior motive," added Spider.

She shook her head at them. "Don't be silly! Luke's a boy – he's like the two of you. He could have been one of my kids. He's probably the same age as you."

"So?" Rocket's blue eyes looked stormy. "He could have been one of your foster kids, but you're not old enough to be his biological mom. There's not that much of an age difference between us."

"And you're a good-looking woman, Miss Candy. Don't you go believing that guys aren't going to hit on you," said Spider.

Candy just laughed. "You two are so funny. Luke's not interested in me that way. He's just trying to help me find my feet here and get to know people, that's all."

"We can do that," said Spider with a scowl.

"Would you drop it? You're being silly and we all know it." She gave them a stern look. "Now tell me something fun. Tell me what the girls are up to."

Rocket smiled through pursed lips. "Janey's off this weekend. I'd guess that she'll want to go to the yard sale at the school."

"Fine! I'll see you there, then. And perhaps Janey will be able to convince you just how ridiculous it is to think that Luke might …" She shook her head. She couldn't even finish that sentence.

She wasn't stupid. She knew that people had relationships with age gaps much wider than the fifteen or so years that there were between her and Luke. It wasn't so much because of his age that she knew he wasn't interested. It was because his heart was already taken, and she'd assumed that Spider and Rocket knew that as well as she did. If they didn't, Janey would be able to set them straight without Candy having to go talking about things that were none of her business.

Chapter Three

Deacon glanced at the bakery as he pulled off the highway and headed for home. Spider and Rocket were coming out and locking up. It made Deacon smile to see them, which was something he wouldn't have believed not so long ago. Seeing a couple of big, muscular, tattooed, strangers like them in town, would have had him on edge – it *had* set him on edge until he'd gotten to know them. Now, strange as it may seem, he considered them his friends.

In fact, more than that, he considered them to be part of his extended family. He'd known Rocket's wife, Janey, and Spider's fiancée, Frankie, their whole lives. They were the kid sisters of men whom he considered to be his brothers; Cash and Maverick MacFarland. He'd grown up with those guys and later served with them. Part of him wished that he'd stuck with them when their team had chosen to not reenlist. But that was only a small part of him. He'd always known that he needed to come back to the valley. Luke was here, and he had work to do here – a mission that he'd set his heart on when he was just a little kid.

He raised his hand when Rocket waved at him. He considered stopping to chat, but they were on their way home. The girls wouldn't thank Deacon if they knew he'd held their men up.

He blew out a sigh when he pulled up in the driveway next to Candy's little Nissan. He didn't know who had advised her to buy that thing, but he didn't like it. She was going to need four-wheel drive when winter rolled around. Even if she only had to go across the road and back for work, she'd still need to get up to town for groceries and … and what the hell did it matter to him?

He shrugged as he cut the ignition. It didn't matter to him. Well, maybe it was just that since she was staying at his place, he'd no doubt be the one who had to help her out. He scowled to himself. Why would he have a problem with that? He helped anyone and everyone who needed it. He blew out a sigh and got out of his truck, wondering why he was giving the woman so much headspace. Hell, she might not even be here by the time the snow flew. A lot of folks loved the idea of living out here in the summer but hightailed it back to wherever they came from once the reality of the harsh winter set in.

That thought stopped his hand in mid-air as he reached out to unlock the front door. His heart raced. He couldn't imagine her not being here anymore. He might bitch to himself about all the ways she encroached on his life; the smell of her baking, the smell of her perfume, her cheerful smile every morning when he went into the bakery for his coffee, but the thought of not seeing her anymore?

He shuddered and unlocked the door in a hurry, letting himself in and hurrying down the hall to his own door. He didn't know what had gotten into him, but he needed to get it out again – fast. If she left, she left. She was just one more of the many tenants who'd rented his upstairs apartment over the years. He didn't miss any of them; he wouldn't miss her, either.

"Hey, buddy," he called when Clawson didn't immediately come to greet him. "Where are you, big guy?" He frowned as he hurried to the bedroom. Clawson had been known to make himself a nest in the clothes that overflowed from the laundry hamper and fall so deeply asleep that he didn't wake up when Deacon called him.

He wasn't there. Deacon checked the bathroom, remembering the one time that Clawson had managed to lock himself in there. He'd clawed the hell out of the linoleum floor around the door before giving up and somehow pulling all the towels down from the rail. Deacon had found him sleeping in his towel nest when he came home. But the bathroom door was open, and there was no sign of Clawson.

"Where are you, buddy?" Deacon's heart began to pound as he headed to the kitchen. The cat flap was locked. He knew it was. He'd flipped the little catch down a couple weeks ago when he'd first heard about the coyote in the neighborhood. Clawson was a smart cat, but there was no way he could have figured out how to unlock the flap.

Deacon checked it, and he was right; it held firm when he pushed. His heart sank and he tried pulling it inward, but it didn't budge in that direction either – reassuring him that some predator hadn't come inside and made a meal out of the cat. He let out a short laugh. As if! Any creature that was small enough to fit through the cat flap wouldn't stand a chance. There'd be blood and fur everywhere; Clawson was a badass.

Deacon took his hat off and ran his hand through his hair as he looked around. Where the hell was he?

He jumped at the sound of a knock on his door. Who the hell was that? Well, he knew the answer, since the knock was on his living room door and not outside, it could only be one person: Candy. He'd done his best to avoid her since the muffin incident, and he really didn't want to see her right now. He was tempted to ignore her knock, but he couldn't. He'd have to go outside next to look for Clawson. How the hell the orange furball could have gotten out, he had no idea. But he must have. That was the only explanation.

He hurried to the door when the knock came again and pulled it open. He was in a hurry to get rid of Candy so that he could get out and find Clawson.

"What?"

Candy took a step back

Shit. He didn't need to take it out on her. "Sorry. I –"

She held her hands up and started to back away from him. The look in her eyes slayed him. She was afraid – afraid of him. What kind of asshole was he? "I'm sorry." He could see her swallow before she continued, "I can see I'm disturbing you. He can stay up there as long as you like."

Deacon frowned. "He can what? You mean Clawson? He's upstairs?"

She nodded rapidly, still backing away from him before turning when she reached the bottom of the stairs. "But it's fine. He's fine. I …"

Deacon blew out a big sigh as worry turned to relief, then he sucked in a fresh breath when relief turned to anger.

"What the hell is he doing up there? How did you –?"

It was amazing how quickly Candy's fear turned into anger of her own. She stopped cowering and pulled herself up to her full height. When she realized that she was still at least half a foot shorter than him, she stepped up onto the first stair.

"That's exactly what I came down here to ask you! I don't mind him being up there. I'll watch him any time you want me to, especially with that coyote prowling around. But you should ask first. And there's no way that you should use your key to my apartment and just let yourself – and him – in like that."

Deacon stared at her. "What the hell are you talking about?"

She glowered at him. "I think you know damned well what I'm talking about. I came home from work, let myself in, and then had to scrape myself down from the ceiling – I jumped that high when I sat down on the sofa and realized there was already someone sitting there – that someone being Clawson."

Deacon ran his hand through his hair. "I just got home. I've been looking for him. How … how did you get him?" He'd heard what she said – that Clawson had been in the apartment when she got home, but he wasn't buying it. It wasn't as though the cat could just let himself out of Deacon's place, wander upstairs and unlock Candy's door.

He didn't know what her game was, but she had to have come and taken him.

She put her hands on her hips. "I just *told* you! He was in the apartment when I got home."

Deacon shook his head. Maybe she was a little unhinged. It was probably best if he just went and got Clawson and hoped like hell that she didn't take him again.

"Can I come get him?"

She nodded curtly and when she turned to go upstairs, he followed. This really was the worst time to be looking at her ass, but he couldn't help it. It was round, and it seemed to taunt him as it swayed from side to side with every step.

She opened the door to the apartment and her whole demeanor changed as she approached Clawson, who'd made himself a nest in a blanket on the sofa.

"Hey, Clawson, baby. It's time to go home now. Your daddy's come to take you."

Deacon clenched his jaw. What was wrong with him? He should be worried about getting his cat and getting away from her. He should not be loving the sound of her sweet sing-song voice. And his dick should *so* not be twitching at the sight of her ass as she bent down!

He forced himself to focus on Clawson. "Come on, buddy. Let's get you home."

Clawson gave him his signature scratchy-sounding meow in greeting but didn't shift from his spot on the sofa.

When Deacon approached, he head-butted his hand but didn't get up. As soon as Deacon reached for him, the furry, orange traitor shot off the sofa and ran straight up the curtains until he was sitting atop the curtain rail, purring down at them.

Deacon cursed under his breath and refused to look at Candy. "Come on, buddy. Let's go."

He held his arm up, hoping that Clawson would walk right down it like he did with Janey, but the cat didn't move. He just sat there, purring.

Deacon scowled up at him, but Clawson just kept on purring, the expression on his face looking for all the world like a smug smile.

"Clawson, get down," he ground out.

Candy shook her head at him. "I don't think that'll work."

Deacon scowled at her, but she shrugged. "I wouldn't want to come anywhere near you if you growled at me like that, either."

"I'm not growling. I'm trying to get the damn cat to come down so that we can get the hell out of here."

"Mind if I try?"

"Be my guest."

She turned to look up at Clawson, and Deacon couldn't stop himself from watching her as she spoke in that soothing, sing-song voice again.

"Come on, Clawson, baby. Come on down. You're a good boy."

All of a sudden, the ridiculousness of the situation hit Deacon and he let out a short laugh.

Candy raised her eyebrows at him. "What?"

He shook his head but couldn't stop himself from smiling. "Sorry. It just hit me that in the same way that you just said you wouldn't come anywhere near me if I spoke to you like I spoke to Clawson, I wouldn't be able to stay away from you if you spoke to me like you're speaking to him."

Fuck! What the hell had he just said?!

Candy obviously didn't understand what he meant any more than he understood why he'd said it. She cocked her head to the side and gave him a puzzled look.

Candy felt as though she was desperately playing catch up, but she wasn't getting there. She'd come home from work and startled badly when she realized that Clawson was sitting on the sofa. She'd gone from startled, to puzzled, to angry when she figured that Deacon must have let the cat into her place for some reason. She didn't mind him being there – she was happy to cat sit, whenever. But she didn't like that Deacon must have let himself into her apartment without asking or even letting her know.

Deacon had scared her when she'd gone downstairs to let him know where Clawson was. She would have brought the cat down with her, but he hadn't wanted to budge. Instead of admitting that he'd let himself into her place, Deacon had acted as though she'd somehow managed to kidnap Clawson; he'd been angry. It didn't make sense – any of it. But the thing that made the least sense was what he'd just said – that he wouldn't be able to stay away from her if she spoke to him the same way she'd spoken to Clawson.

She fixed him with a puzzled, and still wary, gaze as she thought back to what she'd said. She'd called Clawson baby, asked him to come down, and told him he was a good boy. She swallowed and took a step back. Deacon must mean something else. He couldn't mean that he'd like her to talk to him that way. She frowned. She didn't get it – didn't get any of it.

Why was Clawson in her apartment? Why was Deacon denying that he'd let him in here? And why was he looking at her like that?

She had no idea what to say to him. So instead, she turned back to Clawson. "Come on down." She spoke more sternly this time and, apparently, the cat didn't like it. He shot down from the curtain rail and disappeared into the bedroom. Candy hurried after him, aware that Deacon was close behind her.

When they reached the bedroom, there was no sign of Clawson. She got down on her hands and knees and looked under the bed. He wasn't there. As she got up, her breath caught in her chest when Deacon caught her elbow and helped her.

She bit back a laugh at the wild thought that he might be some kind of weirdo who'd planted his cat in her apartment as a means to get into her bedroom.

She stepped away from him again as soon as she was on her feet. "Where the hell is he?"

As Deacon looked all around the room, Candy was glad that she'd put her laundry away earlier. Her cheeks heated at the thought of him seeing all her delicates that she hand-washed and which, up until an hour ago, had been strung around the bedroom and bathroom anywhere she could hang them up to dry.

Deacon frowned and stalked over to the hatch in the wall. She didn't know what its original purpose might have been, but she'd found that it let in a bit of outside air, so she'd gotten into the habit of sliding it open a little whenever she had laundry hung up to dry.

Deacon slid the hatch door all the way up and then stuck his head inside. "Clawson?"

Candy's eyes widened in surprise when she heard the familiar scratchy-sounding meow come from somewhere below them. She hurried over to join Deacon and stuck her head through the hatch next to him.

She hadn't bothered to look at what might be inside there before but now, she saw that it was a chute. It wasn't a sheer drop but went down at a steep angle toward a square of light maybe fifteen feet below them.

Deacon pulled his head back out, and when she joined him, he said, "Mystery solved."

"It is? How? I don't get it. What is that?"

"It's a laundry chute. At least, it used to be. I bought this place from a family. They were … strange. The house has a bunch of quirks like that. There's the laundry chute, and there's even a tunnel from the basement out to the shed at the back. Anyway, enough about the house. The point is …" He gave her a wry smile. "The point is that you didn't kidnap Clawson. I didn't let myself into your apartment and dump him here. He found his own way up the laundry chute and let himself in." He glanced at the hatch. "I thought I'd closed that door off."

Candy blew out a sigh, relieved that he wasn't mad at her anymore. "It wasn't locked or anything. It was a bit stiff, but I didn't realize that I wasn't supposed to open it. I use it when I'm air-drying laundry; it lets some fresh air in."

Deacon frowned. "You can use the dryer any time you like, and there's a line in the backyard if you want to use that."

Candy nodded. She did use the dryer for most of her things. She appreciated that Deacon hadn't enclosed the laundry room into his own apartment but had made it part of the communal space at the end of the hallway. "I do mostly. I just … some things are more delicate."

She had to hide a smile at the way a hint of pink spread up his neck and ears. "Ah. Right. Okay. Anyway. Sorry about that.

I should …" He headed for the door and Candy followed. She almost walked into the back of him when he stopped suddenly and turned around.

She knew that she should take a step back – she was in his personal space, and he was in hers, but as she looked up into his stormy, gray eyes she didn't want to. So, she held her ground and waited to see what he had to say.

"I … Do you want to come downstairs and see the other end of the chute? I can close it off down there so that he doesn't come up again."

She wasn't sure why he was offering, but this felt like the first real chance to break the ice between them, so she nodded. "Sure. Although, I don't mind him coming up if you don't. And I promise that I won't let him outside."

Deacon held her gaze for a long moment. It felt like he had a bunch of questions, but he didn't ask any. He just nodded and turned away, heading out of her apartment and down the stairs.

Chapter Four

As he trotted back down the stairs with Candy following, Deacon questioned why he'd asked her to come down. He didn't need to show her the chute. He didn't need her in his space. But he didn't regret asking her to come.

When they reached his door, he opened it and gestured for her to go in ahead of him. He did a mental run-through of the state of his place. It wasn't untidy. It was clean. And why the hell did it matter? He pulled himself together as he closed the door behind them. Then he led Candy to the hallway to the bedroom. The bottom of the laundry chute opened here. He'd put this wall up when he'd partitioned the house off. He'd been in two minds about making the laundry room part of his personal space but had decided against it. He hadn't wanted to have to do all the plumbing and venting that it would have taken to put a washer and dryer in upstairs. And he knew it'd be a pain in the ass for renters to have to use the laundromat up in town.

He pointed the hatch out to Candy, and they both dropped to their knees at the same time. Now that he knew what was going on, Deacon wasn't surprised to see that Clawson had dragged himself a towel in there and made a nest at the bottom of the chute.

He turned to smile at Candy, but all his breath caught in his chest when she turned to him at the same time. Their noses were only inches apart. He could smell that sweet, vanilla perfume or whatever it was. He froze, his heart thundering in his chest as he realized that it would only take leaning forward slightly for him to be able to kiss her.

Her pupils dilated, and he wondered if she'd realized the same thing. A rush of warmth filled his chest when she didn't immediately pull back, she just smiled.

"Mystery solved," she agreed with what he'd said earlier.

Deacon nodded and got to his feet before offering her a hand up. Her hand felt small and soft inside his and he held on to it for a moment too long once she was standing.

He gave her a wry smile. "I'm sorry. I'm not going to make any excuses. I shouldn't have been so harsh with you."

He felt his shoulders relax when she smiled. "No problem. You were worried about him."

He nodded. "Still. I apologize."

She let out a chuckle and the sound of it reverberated in his chest. "Really, there's no need. I'm just relieved that there's a reasonable explanation." Her green eyes shone as she looked up at him. "And I like this explanation much better than any of the ones I could come up with."

He raised his eyebrows, and she chuckled again. "All my explanations involved you letting yourself into my apartment, planting your cat in there, and then denying it."

He had to laugh with her. "Yeah. And the only explanations I could come up with involved you kidnapping my cat and denying it."

She smiled and sucked in a deep breath before blowing it out. "Okay, then."

"Okay."

She turned to head back down the hallway, and for the life of him, Deacon didn't want her to leave.

"Do you want to stay for a drink now that you're here?" He swallowed as she slowly turned back to face him.

She looked as shocked as he felt.

He shrugged. "I … I might be Grumpy the sheriff, but I'm not *all* bad."

She dropped her gaze. "Sorry. You shouldn't have heard that."

That made him laugh. "Maybe not, but I like that you didn't apologize for saying it – only that I heard it."

She slowly lifted her head again and gave him a wry smile. "I tend to call it as I see it."

Deacon liked that. It wasn't something he was used to, especially not from women, but he liked it. "And you have a point. But as I said, I'm not all bad. And I think this little drama with Clawson tonight showed that I need to prove that to you. I mean, you live here. We share a house. I hate that you think I'm an asshole."

"I don't." Her hand reached out and touched his arm. Her hand was small, like the rest of her. But it still sent a powerful jolt through him.

Before he allowed himself to wonder about that too much, he made himself smile at her. "So, stay and have a drink with me. If you like, we can sit out back while Clawson prowls for a while."

She held his gaze for a moment longer and then nodded. "Okay."

~ ~ ~

Candy sat back in one of the big log chairs next to the table on the back patio. She'd sat out here before when she knew that Deacon was at work and wouldn't be home. But she'd only sat on the bare wood. She hadn't known that he had big, comfortable cushions stashed inside the shed. Once he'd arranged them and brought her a rum and cola, she felt as if she'd found her new favorite place to be.

Deacon took the seat beside her and raised his bottle to clink it against her glass. "We probably should have done this as soon as you arrived. But … welcome."

"Aww, thank you." A rush of warmth spread through her chest at his words.

"Damn. We definitely would have done this sooner if I'd known that you'd look so happy about it."

She chuckled. "No. You didn't need to do anything. I know that you kind of got landed with me. What with everything that happened with Janey, and Rocket staying at the hospital with her. And me having just shown up out of the blue. You didn't really get much choice about me becoming your new tenant, did you?"

She knew from the way he shrugged but didn't answer, that he hadn't had any say at all – and he hadn't been too pleased about it. That made her feel bad.

She turned in the big seat so that she could see him better. "I appreciate it, I do. And if you'd rather I leave, I can find somewhere else to stay."

"No!"

She sat back at the force with which he said it.

He held his hand up. "Damn. I seem to screw up every time I open my mouth around you."

She had to laugh at that. "I feel exactly the same way. I feel like I piss you off just by being here. Then I went and called you Grumpy the sheriff."

She loved the sound of his laughter. Loved, even more, the way he looked when he threw his head back like that. When he turned back to her, his eyes seemed to twinkle, and she was hit once again with just how handsome he was.

"I love that you call me that."

"Yeah, right."

"I do. It's like you said – you call it as you see it. And you see me for what I am."

She had to ask. "Why, though?"

"Why what?"

"Why so grumpy?"

His smile faded.

She hurried on. "I mean, some people are just grumpy by nature. But you're not, not really."

"What makes you think that?"

"I don't know. You laugh too much for someone who's inherently grumpy. You're kind and considerate – and that's not something that comes naturally to grumps."

He chuckled. "I guess not. I haven't exactly been kind and considerate to you, though, have I?"

"We already covered that. I was an unexpected, and not particularly welcome, surprise."

"Yeah."

"Are you avoiding the question?"

He chuckled. "Most people would let it go."

She had to smile. "I think you've already noticed that I'm not like most people."

She couldn't figure out the look in his eyes as he took a long swig of his beer before nodding slowly and saying, "I have."

"So?" She knew she was pushing it, but the man sitting beside her was nothing like the one she'd gotten used to – the one she'd gotten used to calling Grumpy the sheriff. She wanted to hear why he acted that way. She didn't think it was *just* with her – at least, she hoped not – but at the same time, she already knew that he didn't act that way with everyone.

He sucked in a deep breath and blew it out slowly, staring out at the mountains. Just when she started to wonder if he wasn't going to answer and if she should move the conversation on, he spoke.

"I guess, if I'm honest, I get grumpy around women."

She raised her eyebrows but didn't interrupt.

"Well, not even all women. Just women I don't know."

She pressed her lips together to stop herself from asking why; he'd either explain or he wouldn't.

He turned to look at her. "I don't trust women. I haven't had great experiences with them in my life."

She nodded but still didn't interrupt.

The silence dragged on for a few minutes before he turned to her again. "I'm waiting."

"For?"

He chuckled. "The barrage of questions."

She chuckled with him. "Then you'll be waiting a long time."

"You don't want to know?"

"Of course I do. But I also respect that if you want to tell me, you will. If you don't, you won't. It was rude of me to push you as far as I did."

"How did you grow up?"

"What do you mean?" she asked, a little thrown by the abrupt change in direction.

"I mean, what was your family like?"

"Oh."

"Let me guess: your dad worked, and your mom was a housewife, and you had a yard with a white picket fence where you played with your dog?"

She let out a short bitter laugh at that. "Err, nope. You couldn't be more wrong."

"Really? Tell me, then?"

She sighed. "I have no idea who my dad was. I never knew my mom to work, but then I only knew her until I was eleven."

Deacon frowned. "She died?"

"No. She left me with her brother and never came back."

Deacon's eyebrows shot up. "So, your uncle raised you?"

"Wrong again."

"Who then?"

"I stayed with him for nearly two years, but eventually child services took me away and after that, I lived in foster homes."

"Shit!"

"I survived." She hadn't talked about her childhood in years. It was a long time ago. She'd left the worst of it behind her – with the help of years of therapy.

"You did more than survive. You used it to do good in the world, didn't you? Whatever you went through in those foster homes is the reason that you became a foster parent yourself, right?"

She nodded.

"Tell me something?"

She smiled. "Maybe. But if I do, you have to tell me more about you. This started out with me asking about why you don't like women, remember? I don't know how we got on to my childhood."

"Fair enough. What I want to know is why you wanted to foster other kids. Was it because of something good that happened to you in the system – that you wanted other kids to have that, too?" Deacon's eyebrows came down, and he looked as formidable as she'd ever seen him when he asked, "Or was it something bad – something that you didn't want other kids to have to go through?"

She held his gaze for a moment before she looked away.

"Thought so."

She shrugged. "It's not something I like to think about anymore – let alone talk about. Maybe one day I'll tell you." Even as she said it, she doubted that she'd ever tell him.

"My mom left me and my dad when I was nine." He surprised her again with the abrupt change of subject. "I don't blame her for leaving. The old man was a drunk. Well, not just any old drunk, he was the town drunk. And meaner than a rattlesnake."

Candy waited as he took another drink of his beer and stared out at the mountains again. She wasn't sure if he'd said as much as he was going to.

He hadn't. "I don't blame her for leaving, but I do blame her for not taking me with her."

She nodded; she could relate to that. For years, she'd hated her mom for not taking her with her.

Deacon blew out a sigh. "How anyone could leave a little kid with that bastard is beyond me, but how she could leave her own kid ..." He shook his head. "So, yeah. My first experience with a woman – the one who brought me into the world and was supposed to love me – didn't pan out too well. The second one was even worse."

Candy risked a peek at him. He must have felt her looking because he turned and gave her a wry smile. "How the old man managed to make a second woman fall for him is beyond me, but he did. Luke's mom. She hated me from the minute she saw me. The old man used to taunt her about how my mom did things better than she did. Anyway, life was no picnic with her. And maybe my dad had a point. My mom stuck it out till I was nine. Luke was even younger than that when his mom left."

"Oh, wow! And your dad kept you both?"

He let out a short bitter laugh that she understood only too well. There might be no such thing as a stupid question, but some questions seemed pretty dumb when you'd suffered the kind of hell that she – and she now guessed, Deacon – had.

"We grew up in his house."

"How old were you when Luke's mom left?"

"Sixteen."

"Damn!"

"Yeah. I don't suppose many boys become both a mom and a dad at that age."

"No."

Deacon drained the last of his beer and looked at Candy's glass. "You want a refill?"

She knew she probably shouldn't. She'd pay for it when she had to be up in the morning, but she had the feeling that Deacon rarely ever opened up to anyone. She was honored that he was talking to her, and more than that, she had the feeling that he needed it. So, she smiled and held her empty glass up with a smile. "Please."

Deacon grabbed another beer from the fridge and looked down when Clawson rubbed around his legs.

"Shit, I'm sorry, buddy. Let's get you fed. I figured you were hiding out in your nest because you thought I was mad at you."

Clawson looked up at him and meowed.

"Okay, so I was, at first. But by the look of it, you did me a favor. In fact, I reckon this weekend I'll have to see what I can do about getting you some fish as a thank you."

Clawson meowed again and went to stand beside his bowl, waiting for Deacon to feed him.

After he'd taken care of the cat, he fixed Candy's drink and headed back out, leaving the kitchen door open so that Clawson could come out when he was ready. The sight of Candy sitting in one of the chairs made him pause in the doorway. He didn't know what it was about her, but he was enjoying talking to her. He should have done it sooner. He'd been friendly to all of his tenants in the past, so why he'd been such an asshole to her, he didn't know.

She was looking out at the mountains wide-eyed, obviously drinking in the beauty. That made him like her more. Sure, everyone admired the beauty of Paradise Valley; it was breathtaking. But it took a certain kind of person to still appreciate it after they'd lived here for a while. It was too easy to get caught up in living your life and only focus on that – and let it taint everything around you. It seemed to him that the folks who'd grown up around here had a love of the place bred into their blood somehow, but most newcomers soon got over their initial wonder, focusing instead on the harsh environment and lack of conveniences and amenities compared with wherever they came from.

That certainly seemed to be the case with women, anyway. He brought himself back to the moment and took Candy's drink out to her. Maybe it wasn't that women, in general, were that way. Maybe that had just been Willa, and he'd painted all other women with the same brush ever since.

Candy smiled up at him as she took her glass. He sat back down beside her, deciding that he'd rather turn the conversation back to something lighter than tell her any more about why he didn't trust women.

She jumped in her seat when her cellphone rang and gave him an apologetic smile as she pulled it out of the back pocket of her jeans. She made a face when she checked the screen.

"Sorry. I need to take this."

"No problem." He wasn't sure if he should make himself scarce, but curiosity made him stay in his seat. If she needed privacy, she could always go inside.

"This is Candy."

It was a strange way to answer since she must know who it was.

"Yes … No, I told you. I don't plan on coming back down there anytime soon."

Deacon tried not to listen, but it was useless. He wanted to know who she was talking to and what they wanted. He wanted to know what they were saying that made her shoulders tense up. In fact, no, her shoulders had tensed as soon as she checked the screen. It wasn't just what they were saying, but who they were, that stressed her out.

It dawned on him that he didn't know much about her. He knew that she'd been a foster mom to Spider and Rocket when they were kids. She'd moved up here to help them out at the bakery. But he didn't know what kind of life she'd left behind. He frowned as he tried to recall what else he might have heard and paid no mind to.

Len, the name popped into his mind at the same time that he remembered Rocket and Spider talking about her before she came up here. She'd been married to a man named Len. The guys didn't like him – thought he was an asshole. He'd died – some time ago if Deacon remembered rightly. Before she'd moved up here, Rocket had spent a couple weeks trying to get ahold of her, and he and Spider had talked about how they were glad that she was finally shot of Len, but that they were worried about her being on her own.

He looked over at her again, she was still talking, still looking irritated – or stressed, he wasn't sure which.

"I don't care," she said. "Honestly, if I could just sign it over to you guys and be done with the whole thing, that would suit me just fine." She blew out a sigh. "Are they really going to need me to do that?"

He watched her press her lips together. Whatever *they* wanted her to do, was definitely more stressful than irritating.

"It's not like I'm just around the corner anymore. I'm in Montana. I'd need to book a flight and … yeah. Okay, but please try to give me as much notice as you can? I have a job here. People I don't want to let down." She sighed again. "I know!"

Deacon was more than curious now. He wanted to take the phone and find out just who was harassing her and what they wanted. Her next words made him freeze.

"I know they can subpoena me. Don't you dare threaten me. I'm not saying I won't come. I'm just saying that I'd like some notice. Jeez! You wouldn't even have a case if it weren't for me." She glanced at Deacon as if remembering that he was there but then turned back to look at the mountains, sounding resigned as she said, "I'll be there. I have to go. If there's anything else, you can call me tomorrow. But wait until the afternoon. I'm working in the morning."

She ended the call and put the phone back in her pocket. Then, she picked up her glass and took a long drink before setting it down and turning to him with a smile. "Anyway, where were we?"

Deacon smiled. "I take it that's your way of saying *don't ask*?"

"Yeah. If you don't mind. That's a long story, and not one I want to get into right now."

"Okay. But …" He probably shouldn't say anything, but he couldn't stop himself. "I know we didn't get off to the best start – and that's all on me, but if ever there's anything I can do; if you ever need my help, I'd be happy to."

She met his gaze and nodded.

But it didn't feel like enough. He had to make her understand what he meant. "I mean, I'm happy to help as a friend – if you want me. And it can come in handy to know that you've got the sheriff at your back, if you need him, too."

She looked into his eyes and nodded again. "Like I said, it's a long story. But … thanks, Deacon. I hope I won't have to take you up on your offer of help." She blew out a sigh. "But you have no idea how good it feels. I haven't had anyone at my back for …" She thought about it for a moment and then made a face … "Ever, if I'm honest."

Deacon reached across and touched her hand. "You do now." It was crazy that after all these weeks of avoiding the woman, he now wanted nothing more than to have her back. Well, maybe that wasn't true … he might want more than that, but he wasn't going to do anything about it. His history with women had taught him that it was better to steer clear.

He'd help Candy with whatever he could in his official capacity, but he couldn't allow himself to get too close to her in a personal capacity. He could be a friend to her. That should work out okay.

Chapter Five

Candy laughed when Luke grabbed her hand and dragged her toward a stall that was set up with rifles and targets. What he'd called a yard sale was more like a fair to her. Yes, there were rows and rows of tables set up where people were selling everything from clothes and household appliances to fishing rods and video games, but there was also a whole area with fairground games and even a few rides for the kids. She loved it.

Luke had already won her a teddy bear by throwing darts at cards pinned to a wall. He was so sweet, and a lot of fun. No matter what Rocket and Spider might have muttered about him bringing her up here, Candy knew that Luke wasn't interested in her in that way. He just wasn't. As she watched him pick up a rifle and take aim at the targets, she could admit that she'd be thrilled if he were. He was a good-looking guy, and more importantly a good guy. She might be in her early fifties, but she'd have no problem if a guy in his late thirties were interested in her.

She hugged the bear as she watched Luke shoot. He was good. He only missed one of his ten shots. He turned and winked at her before throwing more money down and asking for another ten. She was grateful to him for bringing her up here. This was fun. She was grateful that she could do something for him in return, too. She knew beyond a doubt that Luke Wallis had no interest in her in any kind of romantic way because she knew that he'd given his heart away more than twenty years ago.

Candy had never been a mom in the biological sense, but she'd mothered more kids than she could even count. She was happy to play that role for Luke. It wasn't as though he talked about it much. He'd opened up to her after Rocket and Janey's wedding. The girl he still loved had been here for that, and Candy had caught him in an off moment after he'd seen her, and he'd spilled everything.

She laughed when he hit every one of his second set of targets and threw more money down. He might be a respected member of the community, and one of the sheriff's deputies, but at that moment, he reminded her of a carefree little kid. She loved it for him. From what Deacon had told her the other night, she didn't imagine he'd had many carefree moments in his childhood.

"Hi, Candy!"

"Wade! Hello." She grinned at the sight of Janey's brother, Wade MacFarland. He had his arm around his fiancée, Sierra, and was holding the hand of their little girl, Maya. Maya's brother had hold of her other hand, and they both smiled up at her.

She immediately squatted down to get on their level. "And how are my favorite little people?"

Maya gave her a huge smile. "Hello, Miss Candy. We're going to win a goldfish!"

She laughed and looked up at Wade and Sierra. "You are, huh?"

Mateo nodded solemnly. "We are. Our dad said we can have goldfish if we take care of them. I will take care of them."

"I'm sure you will." Candy loved these two. They'd had a rough start in life but had fallen on their feet when they ended up with Wade and Sierra. Mateo was still super protective of his little sister, but even in the time that she'd known them, they were both starting to blossom into the carefree kids they should be at their age.

Luke came to join them with a big grin on his face. "Well, if it isn't the bravest, smartest kids I ever met. Are you guys having fun?"

They nodded up at him.

Luke winked at Candy and then held out the handful of prize tickets that he'd just won for his efforts with the rifle. "Do you think you can have more fun with these?"

"Yes!" Maya jumped up and down and grabbed them from Luke's hand while Mateo looked up to check with Wade. As soon as Wade nodded, he grinned at Luke and told his sister, "You can have them, Maya. You pick what you want."

Candy's heart melted. He was such a good kid. She just hoped that he remembered to have some fun himself sometimes, too.

Wade ruffled his hair. "You can share them, little man. Half each."

Maya was already holding the tickets out to him.

Candy smiled when Sierra squatted down beside her and took half the tickets and put them in Mateo's hand.

"It's like your dad's told you before, brave boy. You're an amazing big brother. But you're not just a big brother. You're our son, too. Just like you want to take care of Maya, we want to take care of you."

Little Maya put her hand on his arm. "And I want to take care of you, too."

Mateo grinned and nodded happily.

When Candy got back to her feet, Wade and Luke were talking, and Sierra linked her arm through hers and started walking toward the stall with the goldfish, "Don't worry, they'll follow," she said when Candy looked back over her shoulder.

Candy smiled. She loved Sierra. She was such a sweet soul. It was hard to believe that she was some kind of billionaire. To Candy, she was just a sweet girl with a big heart who'd had the good fortune to meet and fall in love with one of the MacFarland boys and to start building a life here in Paradise Valley with him and with the two children they'd taken in.

"Are you here with anyone else?" Sierra asked. "Or just Luke?"

Candy had to laugh. "Just him. I know it might seem strange, but we're friends."

"It doesn't seem strange. I know you're friends." Sierra's cheeks touched with pink as she met Candy's gaze. "I was just hoping that you were here with Deacon, too."

"Really? Why?"

Sierra laughed. "Because Deacon's awesome, and so are you, and I've kind of been hoping … You know, with you living in his apartment and …" She shrugged. "Sorry. I'm being nosey and gossipy and that's not like me, but …" She shrugged again. "Maybe it's because I found my happily ever after, I want one for everyone else, too."

Candy had to laugh. "You just get on with enjoying yours, sweetheart. Not everyone gets one of those."

"Aww. That's a terrible thought. I hope you're wrong."

Candy shrugged. "I wish I were, but I don't think I am."

Sierra squeezed her arm and jerked her chin toward the end of the row of the stalls they were walking down. "By the look on his face, I'm guessing that Deacon wouldn't be against the idea."

Candy's breath caught in her chest when she followed Sierra's gaze and spotted Deacon standing there with his friend, Ace. His arms were folded across his chest. He looked kind of formidable and decidedly sexy – as he always did in his uniform. His gaze was fixed on her. She couldn't read his expression. But no matter what Sierra might say, it didn't look like he was thinking about happily ever afters. He looked pissed – again. Oh, hell. What had she done now?

She'd thought things were going well after the debacle with Clawson and the laundry chute. She'd really enjoyed having a drink with him and talking and getting to know each other afterward. He'd been friendly every morning in the bakery since then. But she'd crossed paths with him in the hallway last night and he'd been short with her. She'd put it down to it being late, and he was just getting home from work. But if the look on his face right now was anything to go by, he was mad at her for something.

She sucked in a deep breath, wondering whether she could change direction before they reached him, but Luke came up beside her and threw his arm around her shoulders with a grin.

"Oh, look. There's Deacon. Let's go say hi."

For a second, she hoped that Luke's presence might help, but when she looked back at Deacon, that hope died. He looked even madder than he did before. In fact, he looked like he was about to explode. This was not going to be good.

~ ~ ~

"What's up?" asked Ace.

"Huh?" Deacon tore his eyes away from Candy – away from the way Luke had his arm around her shoulders. "Nothing's up, why?"

"You look like you want to kick someone's ass. You … oh!" Ace chuckled.

"What? What's funny?"

Ace grinned at him. "You are. You're mad at Luke, right?"

"At Luke? Why?" Deacon's heart hammered in his chest as he realized that Ace had hit the nail on the head. He *was* mad at Luke. It was stupid, but he wanted to yell at him to get his damned hands off Candy. He'd been mad at him in the bakery earlier in the week when he'd asked for Candy's number, too.

Luke had explained that he was going to bring her up here to the yard sale today, but that hadn't helped. If anything, it made Deacon madder. There was no reason for Luke to be taking her anywhere. Luke had laughed and said that Deacon could take her if he preferred. He couldn't. He was here working. But that wasn't the point. Why would he want to?

He scowled as they got closer. There was no reason for him to take Candy anywhere – and even less reason for him to be mad at Luke for doing so. But he couldn't shake the anger he felt seeing Luke's arm resting around her shoulders.

Ace chuckled beside him. "Don't pretend like you don't know what I'm talking about. I've been wondering what's taking you so long."

He turned his scowl on Ace. "What the fuck are you talking about?"

Ace laughed out loud. "We can talk about it later." He turned away from Deacon. "Well, hello, Candy. It's good to see you out and about."

Deacon didn't miss the way her gaze flickered toward him before she smiled at Ace. "It's good to be out and about. This is wonderful. When Luke talked about a yard sale, I imagined a few rows of stalls with clothes and bric-a-brac. Nothing like this."

Deacon scowled at Luke while Candy and Ace chatted. Luke just grinned at him – what the hell was he playing at?

He looked down when he felt a tug on his sleeve and smiled when he saw little Mateo looking up at him with his big, brown, serious eyes.

"Hello, Mr. Sheriff."

Deacon's scowl transformed into a smile without conscious effort. He loved these two kids. He squatted down so that he was at eye-level with Mateo. "I've told you before, you can call me Deacon."

Mateo shook his head rapidly. "You're the sheriff."

"That I am." Deacon knew there was no point in pushing it. They'd been through this before. The boy was in awe of him – at least, in awe of his position.

"I'm going to be the sheriff one day."

Deacon grinned. "I believe you will be, son."

"And I'll catch all the bad men and lock them away so they can never hurt anyone else again."

Deacon's smile faded. He knew what drove the kid's interest in becoming an officer of the law. There hadn't been any of them around in his old life – and both his parents had been killed. "You'll make a good sheriff."

Mateo put his hand on Deacon's arm. "Will you teach me?"

Deacon's heart felt like it melted in his chest. He hadn't had the opportunity to teach his own kids much of anything before Willa took them away from him. Missing out on their childhood was the biggest regret of his life.

He made himself smile. "I'll do what I can, but you know, I'm getting older now; you might want to get Luke to teach you. He's younger than I am, faster, and stronger."

Luke gave him a puzzled look but finally let go of Candy and squatted down beside him. "Don't you believe that for a minute," he told Mateo. "It's true that I'm younger, but Deacon's not that old. He's still way stronger than I am." He smirked at Deacon. "He might not be faster than me anymore, though. I don't know. But even if he's not, he's still the sheriff. I'm just one of his deputies."

Mateo looked from Luke to Deacon and back again. "You're the best deputy, but Deacon's the sheriff. He's the best one and the most important one."

Luke nodded and gave Deacon a weird look that he didn't understand. "You're right, Mateo. He is. He might think that I could step in for him, but I couldn't." Luke glanced at Candy, who was chatting with Ace and Sierra, then gave Deacon another weird look. "There are some things that only Deacon can do."

Mateo rested his hand on Deacon's arm. "Someday I'm going to grow up and be just like you."

Luke chuckled. "Me too."

Deacon got to his feet and ruffled the kid's hair. He felt like Luke had been trying to get some point across, but he had no idea what it might be. "You're going to grow up to be the best thing you can be," he told Mateo.

"The sheriff."

"No, well, maybe, but more importantly than that, you're going to grow up to be yourself. You're a wonderful young man, and the world needs you to be exactly who you are. I can teach you stuff. Luke can, too. And your mom and dad will teach you how to be your best self. The world needs you to be you – Mateo. Never forget that, son."

Mateo nodded solemnly. When he looked up, Deacon realized that both Candy and Luke were giving him puzzled looks. He shrugged and started to turn away. He knew that they weren't there *together* but something about Luke having brought her irritated the hell out of him. He didn't want to shatter little Mateo's illusions about him being someone worth looking up to by being less than courteous to his brother or a woman.

He froze when Candy caught his arm before he could move away from them. He clenched his jaw as he turned back to see what she wanted.

Her eyes shone with something that looked a lot like admiration when he faced her.

"Hi."

That one little syllable hit him right in the chest. And it proved that he'd already been less than courteous to her – he hadn't even greeted her yet.

"Hey." He didn't need to force a smile; it came naturally as a reflection of the one she was wearing.

She jerked her head toward Mateo. "I hope you will spend some time with him; he worships you, you know."

His smile faded. "I wasn't saying that I didn't want to."

"No! I know that. I just don't think you realize how he sees you – how people see you."

He frowned.

"You're not just the guy who wears the badge – you're the embodiment of everything a sheriff should be. I know I haven't been here for very long, but I see it. I see it in the way everyone treats you – and more importantly, in how you treat them."

Deacon didn't know what to say to that. He shrugged and took his hat off to run his hand through his hair. "Thanks."

She laughed. "You're welcome. Sorry if I embarrassed you."

He nodded and looked around the rows of stalls; the crowd was thinning out now. It had been a good afternoon, but things were starting to wind down. Not that he was too worried about the yard sale, he just didn't know what to say to the woman standing before him.

"I'm sorry. I shouldn't be chattering away at you. You're working, aren't you?"

As soon as Candy stepped away from him, he fixed her with his gaze as if that could stop her from leaving his side.

"I'm not." He checked his watch. "I was off the clock an hour ago, but I've been hanging around, showing my face."

Luke appeared at his side again with that same weird glint in his eyes that he'd had so often over the last couple of weeks. He punched Deacon's shoulder and grinned. "Did you just say that you're done for the day?"

"Yeah."

"Are you headed home?"

"Yeah, why?"

Luke looked at Candy, and then back at him. "Wade said that Ford, Tanner, and Tyler are all off tonight. They're on their way up into town now."

"And?"

Luke scowled at him. "And they asked if I want to join them."

"And what's that got to do with me?" Deacon wasn't following.

He noticed that Candy was shifting uncomfortably from one foot to the other. "It's okay," she said. "I imagine that Wade and Sierra will be heading home soon. I can ask if they'll give me a ride."

Deacon closed his eyes briefly when the penny finally dropped. Luke was trying to set him up so that he'd have to give Candy a ride home. He scowled at his brother before he thought better of it and realized his mistake when Luke glared back at him – Candy had seen.

She let out a short laugh. "Really. I'm fine. I can …"

Deacon caught her elbow and drew her closer to him before she took another step away. "You are fine; you're getting a ride home with me."

She looked down at his hand on her arm and then up into his eyes, and he felt himself smile. It wasn't to reassure her; it was simply the effect she had on him.

"Okay," she breathed.

Luke grinned at them. "Great, I'm glad that worked out." He leaned down and landed a kiss on Candy's cheek. "Sorry to abandon you, but we had fun, right?"

She laughed. "We did. It's not a problem. Thanks for bringing me."

"It was my pleasure." He turned to Deacon. "And now it can be yours." He started walking away but turned back and smiled at Deacon. "If you think about it, you'll see that it's the same thing I just told Mateo." Then he was gone.

Candy gave Deacon a puzzled look. "What did he mean?"

Deacon shrugged. He was trying to remember what all Luke had said to the kid. The two things that immediately came to mind were, *He might think that I could step in for him, but I couldn't* and *There are some things that only Deacon can do.* It finally hit him what Luke was up to. He glanced over his shoulder just in time to catch his brother wink at him before he disappeared between two of the stalls.

Chapter Six

Candy felt weird, walking beside Deacon back to the Sheriff's Office. She doubted that he would have offered her a ride home if Luke hadn't cornered him into it. She'd seen the evil look he shot his brother, and he hadn't seemed too thrilled about it as they'd said their goodbyes. He hadn't managed to hide his scowl when Ace had hugged her and leaned down to kiss her cheek, saying that he hoped to see her again soon, either.

She blew out a sigh, wishing that she'd driven herself up here. She was going to have to get used to the drive up to town at some point. She might not be comfortable with driving thirty miles all by herself, but she was even less comfortable with the awkward silence between her and Deacon.

"Are you okay?"

She looked up at him. He still had a half frown on his face, but the lines around his eyes only made him look sexy. Damn. She had to stop that. Ever since they'd sat outside and chatted the other night, she kept thinking of him that way – as a man, and a very attractive man, at that. She'd probably be better off if she went back to thinking of him as Grumpy the sheriff – at least that way she wouldn't be so focused on just how good-looking he was.

"I'm fine, thanks."

When they reached the Sheriff's Office, he led her across the parking lot to his truck, surprising her when he went straight to the passenger door and held it open for her.

The corners of his lips twitched up into the hint of a smile when he took her arm and helped her up.

"Thanks." She waited for him to close the door, hoping for a second to pull herself together while he went around to the driver's side. He hadn't done it often, but each time he put a hand on her, she felt like she needed a minute to recover.

Instead of closing the door, Deacon braced his arms on the frame above his head and smiled at her. "I know you think I'm an asshole, but I know how to treat a woman."

Her breath caught in her chest as she stared back at him. Had he somehow read her mind? Could he tell somehow that she'd been thinking about him that way? Not as an asshole, but about how he might treat a woman – in every sense! She felt the heat in her cheeks but there was nothing she could do to hide the blush.

He gave her a wry smile. "Yeah, I saw how surprised you were that I opened the door for you."

"Oh." That was the only word that would come out; she was so relieved that he hadn't been mind-reading.

He chuckled, and the way his eyes twinkled only made him more attractive. "You could have denied that you think I'm an asshole."

She had to laugh with him. "I don't – think you're an asshole, that is. Not that I don't deny ... I … well, shoot!" She laughed again and pushed at his arm. "I can't deny that you throw me off."

His smile faded and he cocked an eyebrow.

Why had she said that? What did she want him to think? She needed to keep her mouth shut. Telling him that he was someone she admired – as the sheriff – was one thing. Telling him that he affected her the way he did was another.

"I throw you off, huh?"

She nodded, hoping that he'd leave it at that.

He held her gaze as he nodded slowly. Then he pushed away from the door and said, "You throw me off, too, darlin'," just before he closed the door and walked around to the driver's side.

Candy's heart raced in her chest as she watched him go. He couldn't mean it the same way she did – could he?

~ ~ ~

As he pulled out of the lot, Deacon's mind was racing. He was still trying to figure out how he'd ended up on his way home, on his night off, with Candy riding beside him. He scowled through the windshield as the light changed to red just before he reached it.

He knew how he'd ended up here – Luke had put him here. What he needed to figure out was what he wanted to do about it. He might have been a bit slow on the uptake when it came to the woman sitting beside him, but he wasn't a complete idiot. He might not have had time for a woman in years. He might have told himself ever since Willa left that women couldn't be trusted and that he had no interest in having one in his life, but the little lady sitting beside him had him questioning all of that.

Both Luke and Ace seemed to have recognized it before he had, but that didn't mean he couldn't play catch-up. He was attracted to her. As soon as he allowed himself to admit it, he could feel himself smile, and could also feel a stirring in his pants that hadn't happened in a while.

He glanced at Candy out of the corner of his eye. Her admission that he threw her off had made something in his mind snap. He probably shouldn't have admitted that she did the same to him, but he was glad that he had.

She turned toward him with a frown. "I know I keep annoying you and I'm really sorry. I don't do it on purpose, you know."

He hated that her voice wavered when she spoke; that wasn't like her. She was a little spitfire. She laughed and joked much of the time and didn't seem afraid to speak her mind – except with him.

As the light changed, and he pulled forward, he reached across to touch her arm. He miscalculated though and somehow ended up with his hand resting on her thigh. Shooting a glance at her, he could see that her cheeks were bright red, but she didn't complain or brush him away. So, instead of pulling back, like he knew he should, he left it there as he spoke.

"When I said that you throw me off, I didn't mean that you annoy me."

"Oh."

He shot a quick grin at her before turning his gaze back to the road ahead of him. He couldn't resist giving her thigh a squeeze. "Okay, if I'm honest, I have been getting annoyed when I'm around you. But it's not at you – it's at me."

"Why?"

He let out a short laugh. "Because I couldn't figure out what was going on."

They rode in silence for a few moments before she asked, "And what *was* going on?"

"What was going on, Candy, was that I was doing my damnedest to avoid you. When I was around you, it meant that I hadn't succeeded in avoiding you, so I was annoyed with myself."

"I see." The way she said it made it clear that she didn't see at all.

He glanced over at her again. "I don't think you do."

"You're right. I don't. I'm confused."

"What I'm saying is that I've been trying to resist you, but it turns out that you may just be irresistible."

He heard her sharp intake of breath and brought his hand back so that he could grip the steering wheel tight while he waited for her rejection. Why the hell had he opened his big mouth?

"I …"

He blew out a sigh, hating that he'd made her uncomfortable. "It's okay, darlin'. You don't need to say anything. I don't know why *I* said anything. All we have to do is get through this ride home and then we can go back to staying out of each other's way as much as possible."

He tensed when she turned toward him and then put her hand on his arm. He could feel the touch of her fingers burning through his shirt – and the way the interest stirred in his pants more intensely than before.

"What if I don't want to stay out of your way?"

He swallowed, wondering if he was imagining things. Was he hearing what he wanted to hear instead of what she was really saying? He glanced over at her again; her cheeks were still red, but her eyes were shining, and she smiled.

"What do you mean?"

"I mean that I … I don't know how to say this, and I have a feeling it might be a mistake, but … well, I … think you're a very attractive man, Deacon."

He couldn't have stopped his grin if he tried.

"And more than that, you're a man I respect and admire."

He swallowed.

"I … if you don't want to avoid me anymore. If you don't want to … resist me. Well, I don't want to resist you either."

All Deacon's breath came out in a rush. This wasn't a conversation that he wanted to continue while he was driving. He flicked on his blinker when he saw the turn-off for the fishing access coming up.

Candy's fingers tightened on his arm, and he realized that she was waiting for him to respond. He smiled and gripped the wheel tighter as the truck bounced over the rutted gravel road. "Looks like we might be getting somewhere, then, darlin'."

He was relieved to see that there were no other vehicles parked in the small gravel lot next to the boat ramp. He parked the truck under a stand of cottonwood trees and cut the engine before turning to face her.

"I stopped because I think we need to finish this conversation now. It's not fair to either of us if I can't give you my full attention. Want to walk by the river?"

Her eyes were huge in her pretty face as she nodded at him.

"Wait there, then."

He jogged around the back of the truck and went to open her door for her. He didn't know what it was about her that made him want to do that. He did know how to treat a woman, but he didn't think that little gentlemanly gestures like that were his thing.

When he opened the door, she sat there smiling at him, and he couldn't help it; he set his hands at her waist and lifted her out, setting her down between him and the truck before reaching to close the door again.

As he looked down into her eyes, he was reminded again of just what a little thing she was. She sucked in a deep breath and then blew it out again, then licked her lips before she asked, "What are we doing, Deacon?"

He put his hands on her shoulders and held her gaze. One part of his mind – the rational part – wanted to say that he had no clue what they were doing. Another part of him – a part that had been dormant for years – was too focused on the way her lips glistened, and on wanting to taste them. That part won.

"This," he answered, as he lowered his head toward hers. He had to bend to reach her. Something about her being so small just did it for him. He hadn't thought that he liked short women in the past. But she seemed so tiny. She wasn't delicate, but her size made him want to hold her against him and protect her.

Her green eyes shone as she held his gaze and lifted her lips to meet his. His hands rested on her shoulders until he brushed his lips over hers. She grasped his shirt at his sides, and that was all the encouragement he needed. His hands came up to cup the sides of her neck, and he pressed her back against the side of the truck.

"Deacon," she murmured.

He loved the way his name sounded on her lips, and he dipped his head, taking advantage of the moment to take the kiss deeper. Her whole body shuddered against him, and her arms came up around his shoulders, pulling him down to her as she greedily sought more.

Deacon wrapped one arm around her back and crushed her to his chest, loving the feel of her against him as their tongues tangled. His breath hitched in his chest when one of her hands came down and gripped his ass, urging him forward until his hard-on pressed into her belly. They both let out a moan at that.

Jesus! He knew that he should back off, tone it down. He'd brought her down here so that they could talk – not so that they could make out like a pair of horny teenagers. If anyone came by, it wouldn't do for them to find the sheriff with a woman pressed up against his truck, but damn, that thought just made him kiss her more deeply and grind his hips against her a little harder.

She moaned into his mouth, and he couldn't resist bringing both hands down to hold her ass. He let out a moan of his own when he did – her ass was round and soft and … and he had to lift his head before he took this too far.

When he lifted his head, the look on her face made him want to move back in for more. It made him want to get her into the back of his truck so that … but he was too old for that – they both were.

He gave her a wry smile and traced his fingertips over her pink, kiss-swollen lips. "Damn!"

She chuckled. "Yeah, damn! Where the hell did that come from?"

He shrugged. "You saying it was a problem?"

She shook her head rapidly. "My only problem is why it took us so long."

He had to laugh. "I think you can blame me for that. I …" He frowned as the truth hit him. "I don't do this."

She frowned back at him. "I know. Neither do I."

He nodded; he knew that, too. She'd been living in his upstairs apartment and had never had a man come over. She hadn't spent the night anywhere else since she'd been living there either.

He leaned in and pressed three short kisses to her lips. They were supposed to have stopped the kissing, but he just couldn't resist.

"I'm sorry that I haven't been the most welcoming. I'm not normally an asshole."

She nodded.

"It's just. I don't know … I … I think you threw me from the first time I saw you. I didn't know how to handle you – how to handle the way you make me feel. So, I guess I figured that it'd be easier to just avoid you."

She nodded, but she didn't look as thrilled as he felt to discover that what was going on between them was attraction rather than irritation.

He cocked an eyebrow. "Are you mad at me?"

"No. I …" Her green eyes seemed to shimmer as they looked up into his. "I guess, I'm just wondering what happens now?"

He smiled. "Whatever you want to happen."

She smiled back at him. "That's what I don't know."

"Yeah." He pressed another quick kiss to her lips. "I don't either, but I figure we can make it up as we go along."

"Okay."

"How about we start off with dinner?"

She raised her eyebrows.

"Tonight. Have dinner with me?"

He felt his shoulders relax when she smiled. "Okay."

~ ~ ~

Candy was still trying to figure out what had just happened as Deacon pulled the truck back onto the highway. When they'd left town, he'd been scowling away to himself, and she'd been convinced that she was somehow managing to annoy him again. Then he'd pulled off the road, taken her down by the river, and kissed the heck out of her!

He looked over at her and smiled. "You okay?"

She let out a short laugh. "I think so."

He laughed with her. "You will be. I'm sorry. I know that wasn't the most subtle way to let you know what's been going on with me – to let you know how I feel, but …" He shrugged and reached across the console to take hold of her hand. "Now that I've figured it out myself, I had to see how you feel."

She smiled down at their hands as she watched him lace his fingers through hers. "I'm not complaining. I don't mind admitting that I've been … hoping."

He grinned. "You have, huh?"

"Yeah. There's no need to smile like that, though. Don't let it go to your head. You're a handsome man, Deacon. I'm sure you have women after you all the time."

His smile faded. "I wouldn't know about that. I'm not exactly … open to it."

She gave him a puzzled look.

He shrugged. "I told you that I'm not comfortable with women. I …" He shrugged again. "I'm not interested. Well," he squeezed her hand, "I haven't been. Not until this little lady came to stay in my upstairs apartment."

She couldn't help smiling at that. "Well, given how friendly you've been toward me when you were interested, I'd hate to know what you're like when you're not."

He smiled through pursed lips. "With most women, I'm just the sheriff. I'm courteous and that's about it. It seems that it's only you who brings out Grumpy."

She had to laugh. "You're not going to let me forget that, are you?"

All the muscles in her stomach and lower tightened at the heat in the look he shot her. "Just the opposite. I'm going to do my damnedest to make you think of me as anything other than grumpy."

She couldn't wait to learn what exactly he had in mind.

When they arrived back at the house, he came around again and opened the passenger door for her before helping her down. She loved the way he did that. For one thing, it was such an old-fashioned, gentlemanly thing to do. And for another, it was a long way down for someone her size.

He opened the front door and gestured for her to go in ahead of him. She waited awkwardly in the hallway until he joined her. Part of her felt as though she should head up to her apartment, but she didn't know what he was thinking, and she didn't want to just walk away from him.

He went straight to his door and unlocked that, too. "Do you want to come straight in? We can have a drink while I make dinner. Unless you need to upstairs first?"

She nodded. She'd thought when he asked her to have dinner with him that he meant they'd go out. But if he wanted to eat here that was fine, too.

He watched her face and seemed to understand what she was thinking. "I'll take you out if you want to go. It's just … if we go out, we won't get much time to ourselves. One of the hazards of this job is that everyone knows me, and everyone wants to talk to me. If they see you with me, they're going to be curious. And believe me, the people in this valley have no boundaries; they'll ask if we're on a date, and you can guarantee that before midnight, we'll be the source of gossip from one end of the valley to the other."

She nodded again, more slowly this time. She could understand that he didn't want to spend half the evening chatting with people – she appreciated that. At the same time, she hoped that he wasn't just hiding her away here – that he wasn't afraid, or ashamed to be seen out with her. The last thing she wanted was to be his … she didn't know what. She didn't think he was that kind of man, but she'd hate to be his dirty little secret or just someone convenient – someone right there on his doorstep when he wanted a woman but didn't want anyone to know what he was up to.

He came closer and put his hands on her shoulders as he looked down into her eyes. "I'm trying to give us a chance to get to know each other better without being on display for the whole valley. But if you'd rather go out, we will."

"No." she smiled up at him. "This is good. I'd rather stay here. It's more relaxed and …" She laughed when Clawson came out of the door and rubbed around Deacon's legs before coming and doing the same to her. "This way, Clawson gets to join in, too."

Chapter Seven

"There you go." Deacon set Candy's drink on the table in front of her and pulled up the seat next to her. There was something about seeing her sitting here in his backyard that felt good.

He had everything going for dinner and had a little while before he'd need to go back into the kitchen. Asking her to eat here with him had seemed like the best idea at the time but now, he was second-guessing himself. She hadn't seemed too thrilled about it, and now that he thought about it, it wasn't exactly a great first date.

He should have taken his time, asked her if she wanted to go out with him one night soon; planned to take her to the Valley Lodge or the bistro up in town. He should be showing her a good time, not just asking her to hang out at his place with him – especially since it was her place, too. She probably hadn't been anywhere much since she'd come to live here.

"Next time, I'll take you out someplace nice."

She met his gaze and smiled. "I think it's nice here."

He smiled back at her. He liked that about her; she wasn't picky or demanding. Even if she might have preferred to go out for real, she was making the most of this.

"I'm glad, but I do want to take you out, too." He smiled through pursed lips. "That is, if you want to go out with me again after tonight."

She laughed. "I think we're safe there. It's not like this is some blind date where we might discover that we have nothing in common, or that we don't even like each other."

"That's true. I already know that I like you – although … do you think that we have anything in common?" He wasn't sure that they did.

Candy smiled. "Maybe not. I don't know for sure. But we have friends in common. We know that we get along okay." She chuckled. "We know that we can argue and be okay with each other afterward."

"Hmm."

She laughed again. "I don't mind telling you that I was pissed at you when I thought that you'd used your key and let Clawson into the apartment."

He chuckled. "Understandably so. And I was kind of mad, and kind of freaked out, when I thought that you'd somehow managed to kidnap my cat and then claim that you thought I'd done it. I thought you might be one of those crazy ladies like in the Lifetime movies. You know, first, you kidnap my cat, and the next thing I know I wake up handcuffed to your bed."

She laughed out loud at that, and her cheeks flushed pink. "You're safe from me there – besides, I thought you were the one with the handcuffs."

He waggled his eyebrows. "Sure. I have handcuffs. What are you saying?"

When her cheeks turned crimson, he had to let her off the hook. He leaned in and pressed a quick kiss to her lips.

"I'm teasing you, darlin'."

"I know but …" She fanned herself with her hand. "You want to be careful with that. You could give a girl ideas."

He threw his head back and laughed, loving that she was happy to joke about it. "Are you only after me for my handcuffs?"

She laughed with him. "No. It's the uniform, too."

He shook his head as he looked down at himself. "Sorry, it didn't feel right for me to go and change, since you hadn't. I didn't give you the time to go upstairs and change, so it's not fair that I should. I can, though, if you want?"

She shook her head rapidly. "I wasn't joking." A small smile played on her lips as she let her gaze travel over him. "The uniform works."

He laughed again. "Good to know. I'll keep that in mind." He felt like he should probably steer the conversation back toward safer ground. With all this talk of handcuffs and her confession about how much she liked him in his uniform, it was far too tempting to try to talk her into the bedroom. But that was something that he didn't want to rush.

"So, what else do you think we have in common?"

She pressed her lips together as she thought about it. "Well, by the sound of it, neither of us had the best childhood."

He nodded, hating what he'd learned about her childhood. He didn't want to take her back to whatever it was that she didn't want to tell him about what had happened to her in foster care that she didn't want other kids to go through. "Yeah."

"And neither of us has kids."

He froze at that. That was something he wanted to talk about even less, but if they were going to start seeing each other, even if it was only casual, she should know that about him. He'd hate for her to hear it from someone else and wonder why he hadn't told her.

He blew out a sigh. "I do."

"You do? Oh! I'm sorry. I didn't … you never talk about them."

He made a face. "No. I rarely talk to them. There's not much to say."

"I'm sorry."

He shrugged. "It is what it is. Their mom left me when they were small. She didn't want me to be a part of their lives."

"I see."

He knew that she didn't. How could she? He didn't see, and it was his life; they were his kids.

She put a hand on his arm. "We can change the subject if you like. Leave it there and move on."

When he met her gaze, she smiled, and it sent a rush of warmth through his chest. She wasn't rejecting him or judging him. She was trying to make it easy on him. The trouble was, it wasn't easy, it never had been.

He blew out a sigh. "I was in the Navy when I was younger. I met Willa when I was stationed in California. We got married young, and we had Callum and Cadence within the first three years. Willa hated being a military wife. There were rumors that she was cheating on me while I was deployed, but I didn't want to believe it, so I didn't.

"After my service was up, we came back here. That had always been the plan. I … I always knew that I wanted to be the sheriff in this valley. Willa said that she was good with it. She didn't have any family, and I thought she'd find that here. Not that I have much family left; I only have Luke. But as you may have noticed, friends become family out here.

"It didn't work that way for her though. She didn't make friends. Instead, she looked down on everyone. She hated the winters, and she hated the summers. She hated pretty much everything about Montana. I tried. I used to take the kids horseback riding and hunting and fishing – everything that kids do here. Willa hated it. She stopped them from doing any of it. She wouldn't even go camping with us. She enrolled Callum in a music program with the symphony over in Bozeman and got Cadence into a dance school over there."

He blew out a sigh. "That's where she met the guy that she left me for. He's some rich guy from California. Turned out that all the nights she was staying over there in Bozeman – after the kids' classes and performances because it was too late to drive home – she was staying with him. *My kids* were staying at his place. At first, they thought he was Mommy's friend. Then, I guess they just got used to him being around – and me not being.

"I tried. I used to get over there for as much of it as I could. But she hated me being there, and the kids seemed kind of embarrassed by me. I own my part in it all. If I'd done more, tried harder, they might not have wanted to leave me. But when she was ready to divorce me and move to California with him, they were happy to go, and they weren't too worried about not seeing their dad much anymore.

"I got visitation rights. I could have them in the summer and school breaks. I used to go to California in between." He closed his eyes remembering how hard those visits had been – how much they'd hurt. "But the kids weren't interested. I was an inconvenience to them by then, an unwanted obligation. When the summer came that they both told me they didn't want to come – and they didn't want me to go there to be near them either, I gave up. I mean, I didn't lose contact with them. I still called to talk to them – even though they mostly blew me off. I never stopped paying child support and I had a college fund for each of them. But …" he stared out at the mountains, "they didn't want to know me. I guess they were more her kids than mine. They're happy – from what I hear – with their lives in California. I still send cards but that's about it. I gave up."

He realized that he'd been talking for a while and Candy hadn't said a word. He closed his eyes and waited. She'd probably tell him that she needed to go now. She'd hate him. She'd think he was a loser – and she'd be right. What kind of man couldn't keep a relationship going with his own kids after a divorce? Everyone knew that only deadbeats and selfish bastards let their kids go – weren't a part of their lives.

His eyes opened when Candy rested her hand on his arm. "That has to be so hard for you. I'm sorry."

He turned to look at her; her eyes were filled with tears. She wasn't judging him. She felt for him. He hadn't experienced that kind of compassion from a woman before. It made his heart clench in his chest. "I should have tried harder. Should have done more."

She shrugged. "What could you have done? I haven't known you for very long, but I already know that you wouldn't give up easily – that you did everything in your power, everything you could think of. Sadly, sometimes, that isn't enough. Some things just aren't meant to be."

He blew out a big sigh, not knowing why after all these years, her words made him feel better. He felt like he'd confessed his sins and been … understood, if not forgiven.

"Maybe one day something will happen that will bring you closer to them," she said.

"I hope so. I still reach out a couple times a year – Christmas, and birthdays. I let them know that I love them, and that I'm always there for them, and that if ever they want to visit …" He let out a bitter laugh. "I usually say if they have any interest in seeing Montana or seeing Yellowstone. I don't want to put on the pressure or deal with the rejection of asking if they want to see me."

Candy squeezed his arm. "I hope it'll happen someday."

"Yeah. Me too. What about you?" he asked, wanting to change the subject. "You were a foster mom to Spider and Rocket; no kids of your own?"

He didn't miss the flash of pain in her eyes before she masked it. "No."

He shook his head, feeling bad that by trying to avoid talking about a subject that hurt him, he'd steered them into one that hurt her. "How about I go and finish getting dinner ready?"

"Okay. Can I do anything to help?"

He smiled. "You just sit here, enjoy your drink, and the mountains." He jerked his chin toward the west, where the sun was dipping toward the snow-covered peaks. "I won't be long."

~ ~ ~

Candy set her fork down and turned to smile at Deacon. "That was wonderful, thank you. I don't know how to grill, but you'll have to let me cook for you. Sometime," she added quickly. He'd been good company while they ate, but things had changed between them since he'd told her about his kids and asked if she had any. Maybe he wouldn't want to do this again.

He smiled back at her. "Sometime soon, I hope?"

She nodded happily. "I'd like that. I'm a better baker than I am a chef, but I can still feed you well."

"I'll look forward to it."

She sucked in a deep breath. She might do better to keep her mouth shut, but that had never been one of her strengths. She wanted to make him feel better if she could. "I'm sorry that you missed out on your kids, but I don't think any less of you for it."

The look on his face told her that she'd hit the nail on the head. He blew out a sigh. "Thanks, but I doubt that's true. I mean, you fostered kids, you went out of your way to be a parent to kids who weren't yours. And I'm guessing that you would have loved to have kids of your own but for some reason, you couldn't. I must seem like a real asshole to you, that I have kids, but I wasn't a part of their lives – and I'm still not."

"No. It's not that cut and dried. It never is. Whatever her reasons, your wife …"

"The woman I was married to," he interrupted. "Sorry. I don't even call her my ex. She's not *my* anything, just the woman I was married to."

Candy nodded. "I get that. I feel that way about Len. He's just the man I was married to. He didn't even feel like *my* husband when we were married."

Deacon raised his eyebrows, but she didn't want to get into that, she wanted him to hear what she had to say about his relationship with his kids. It was obvious that he beat himself up about it, and she hated that for him.

"Well, whatever her reasons, she didn't want you to be part of your kids' lives. And my guess is that life would have been a lot harder for them if you'd pushed it. If you'd insisted on being there, on making them spend time with you – on what you wanted for yourself, it would have been miserable for all of you. I saw it so often with the kids I fostered. Sometimes, neither parent wanted the kids or was capable of being a parent to them. Sometimes one parent wanted them back and didn't want the other parent to be part of it. The kids who had it the worst – the ones who were the most miserable, were the ones caught between two parents who were both focused on their own interests."

"I guess."

"It's true. I know it must have sucked for you. I imagine that it still does. But don't make out that you're the bad guy. You're not. Any mom who loves her kids wants what's best for them. Maybe she genuinely believed that you not being in their lives was best. But even if she did, she was wrong."

He cocked an eyebrow. But she nodded emphatically. "Any kid would benefit from having you in their life – in any capacity. Mateo proved that today. I feel sorry for yours that they didn't have that relationship with you, but I hope that one day they might."

Deacon sighed. "I doubt that'll ever happen now. I'd love it if it did, but I've learned to accept it."

"Never say never."

"Yeah. Do you mind if I ask …?"

"Why I never had kids?" She knew where he was going, and it was only fair. She'd waded in with her opinion on his life. He had the right to ask about hers.

He nodded. "You can say no. Tell me to mind my own business."

She smiled. "I don't mind telling you. It's what friends do."

He held her gaze for a long moment. She couldn't read the look in his eyes, so she cocked an eyebrow in the same way that he did, hoping that he'd explain.

He smiled. "You're right; it is what friends do. But I have to tell you, Candy … I'm hoping that we're going to get to be more than friends."

A rush of warmth filled her chest, and she smiled. "I hope so, too." Her smile faded as she remembered what she was supposed to be telling him. "I … I couldn't have kids. I was young when I married Len. He got me pregnant, but he said it was too soon, that we needed more time together just the two of us before we had children." She closed her eyes against the tears that even after all these years still threatened to fall whenever she thought about it.

"He wanted me to get an abortion, but I wouldn't. I couldn't do that. I think it's a very personal choice, and that everyone has the right to make that decision for themselves, but it wasn't what I wanted. We fought about it a lot, and I said I'd rather leave him and have the baby by myself. He let up after that, said that we'd be okay – that things would work out.

"The way they worked out was that …" she took a deep steadying breath, "I got mugged on my way home from work. One guy took my purse and the other one beat the crap out of me. I … lost the baby, and never managed to get pregnant again."

Deacon reached for her hand and brushed his thumb back and forth over her knuckles. "I'm sorry."

"Thanks. It broke my heart. I didn't want to give up; I went to see specialists, and fertility doctors, and everyone I could think of. Len even went with me." She sat back and looked Deacon in the eye. "It was only a couple of years ago that I found out that he was the one responsible."

Deacon frowned. "Responsible for what?"

"It turned out that he paid those guys to beat me up. He told them to make sure that they hit me in the stomach as much as they could."

"Damn!"

"Yeah. It's a long time ago now, and I would have gone to my grave thinking that it was just bad luck, you know? Just one of those things. But when Len started getting himself in deeper, the bastards he was working with tried to use me against him. They told me every shitty thing they knew about him to make me hate him. Apparently, one of the men that Len paid to *mug* me had told people about it."

Deacon frowned. "Who are they? And what …?"

Candy shook her head, shocked at herself that she'd given so much away. She'd made a vow to herself that once she moved up here to Montana, she wasn't going to talk about anything that had happened during the last few years of Len's life – or since he died. "It doesn't matter. It's all water under the bridge now." She forced a smile. "I like to find the bright side wherever I can, so I tell myself that if I'd had kids of my own, I might not have been able to help so many foster kids over the years."

Deacon didn't look like he wanted to be put off so easily, but he nodded slowly. "Maybe."

"Anyway, can I help you clear up?"

Deacon looked at the table and then back at her. "You can. I'll let you change the subject, and I'll let you help clear up, but only after you make me a promise."

"What's that?"

"I want you to promise me that if ever Len's trouble comes looking for you, you'll let me help. You don't have to tell me about it if you don't want to. But you do need to know that I have your back if you need me, okay?"

She stared at him for a long few moments, wondering how he'd managed to figure things out. She wanted to brush him off, to tell him that she didn't know what he was talking about, but she wouldn't insult him like that. And she loved that he wanted to help. Even if there was no way that she'd let him. Eventually, she nodded.

"Thanks, Deacon. I'm hoping that it'll all be over soon, and I won't need your help. It'll be finished."

"But you'll let me help if you need me."

She nodded. "Thank you."

He brushed his thumb over her knuckles again. "Thank you. You don't have to face things on your own anymore."

She loved the way that sounded. She might have been married, but she'd faced things on her own for her whole life. She loved the thought of Deacon having her back, but she shouldn't get too carried away. He didn't mean it like that. It was just that people looked out for each other here in the valley.

Chapter Eight

Deacon came awake at the feel of pressure on his chest. A heavy weight made it hard to get a full breath. He smiled. It wasn't the kind of pressure in his chest that a guy his age might dread. No. It was Clawson.

When he opened his eyes, Clawson fixed him with a demanding stare and started kneading at the blanket. Deacon reached up and scratched the cat's ear. "Would you stop making biscuits in my blanket, buddy?"

Clawson meowed loudly and then started to purr as he settled himself down.

Deacon wanted to laugh but he didn't, knowing that the movement would make Clawson leave. It wasn't often that he got snuggly, and if he left now, he'd only demand his breakfast straight away. Deacon was happy to lie here for a few minutes and wake up slowly.

His smile grew when he remembered what had happened yesterday. He'd started out the day feeling off. He hadn't been happy knowing that Luke was taking Candy to the yard sale. He'd been mad at him when he'd seen him with his arm around her shoulders, and even madder when Luke had set him up so that he'd have to take her home.

He wasn't mad anymore though. He was grateful. He was a little surprised at himself but still grateful. He'd thought that he'd passed the stage of life where he'd have any interest in a woman again. He had plenty of reasons to steer clear of them. He'd tried steering clear of Candy, but that was behind him now. Now, instead of finding ways to avoid her, he was eager to find ways to spend time with her.

He'd enjoyed her company last night. She was easy-going and fun. She laughed a lot, and she talked a lot. Two things that usually annoyed him. She didn't annoy him. He enjoyed hearing what she had to say, enjoyed hearing her laugh – especially when he made her laugh. That made him feel good. She was kind, too. She had a good heart. He was still surprised that he'd told her about Willa and the kids, but she'd tried to make him feel better about it. He did feel a bit better after talking to her. He knew that he'd done the best he could in a bad situation, but he still felt like he'd failed as a father – as a man. He hadn't been what Willa wanted, he could live with that; marriages failed all the time. But he hadn't been good enough, in Willa's eyes, to be a good father to their children. No matter what anyone said, that would always weigh heavy on him.

He absently petted Clawson as he remembered the way the evening had ended. Candy had said she had to leave, and he'd been surprised that she wanted to call it a night so early. She'd explained that it was only because she had to be up so early for work. He'd thought that she had Sundays off, but she said that she went in for a few hours first thing to get everything started.

He checked his watch. It'd be a while before she was finished. He was going to take her down to the park this afternoon. He couldn't believe that she hadn't been yet. He knew that she'd started work at the bakery the day after she arrived in Montana, but she'd had days off since. He'd been mad at Rocket and Spider for not doing more to show her around. But she'd explained that they wanted to, she was the one who'd refused to let them.

It was obvious how much she loved those two – and kind of amusing to hear her talk about them like little kids, when he only knew them as a pair of big, scary-looking dudes. She'd explained that she was over the moon happy to see them both settled and enjoying their lives with Janey and Frankie. The last thing she wanted to do was take up too much of their time or intrude on the new lives they were building with their women.

Deacon had wanted to tell her that they probably wanted to make her part of those new lives – that she was family, and that's how it worked. But he'd bit his tongue. Things would work themselves out with time. He'd known Janey and Frankie since they were kids. They might let Candy get away with keeping her distance for a while, but they'd make sure that they included her in whatever their new family looked like.

In the meantime, he was just going to be grateful that he could be the one to show her more of life in the valley. He could take her to the park, take her to Chico – she hadn't even been there yet, except for Janey and Rocket's bachelor party. He didn't know yet whether she'd enjoy camping, or fishing, or horseback riding, but he hoped that he might be the one to introduce her to everything there was to enjoy in the valley.

Clawson meowed and started making biscuits on his chest again. It made Deacon laugh.

"I thought you did that to make yourself a soft spot to lie down on, but you're already lying there. What's it about, big guy?"

Clawson meowed again and narrowed his eyes as he fixed Deacon with a stare.

"What? You want to go out? You want your breakfast?"

At the word breakfast, Clawson jumped down from the bed, and Deacon knew it was time to get up.

~ ~ ~

"Miss Candy!"

She had to laugh at the way Rocket towered over with his hands on his hips. He was trying to look stern, but he wasn't pulling it off. At least, not to her he wasn't. Candy would only ever see him as an overgrown version of the scared little boy who'd first arrived in her home nearly thirty years ago. Although, she could see how he would appear pretty damned intimidating to most folks.

"What's up, my little Rocky?"

He rolled his eyes and chuckled. "What's up is that you said you were only going to stay for a little while. Sunday is supposed to be your day off, but you've come in every Sunday since you've been here. I know we can't bake like you do, but we get by. Folks can eat what we make one day a week. You should sleep in, have a rest."

She shrugged. "I usually take a nap on a Sunday afternoon. It's not as though I stay all day. I just like to get everything started for you, that's all."

"I know. And I appreciate it. Spider does, too. But you've been here for hours already. You should go home, put your feet up."

"I will soon."

Rocket's expression softened. "Want to sit and have a coffee with me before you go? It's quiet out there."

"Aww, I'd love that."

"Okay. You go and sit down then, take a load off, I'll bring our drinks out."

She rolled up on her tiptoes, but Rocket still had to lean a long way down so that she could kiss his cheek. "You're a good boy, Rocket Armstrong. Wait, no – Rocket MacFarland now. Is the paperwork all done?"

Rocket grinned and nodded as he pulled his wallet out of his back pocket. He took his driver's license out and handed it over. "Yeah, it took forever, but everything's changed over now. I got this last week." He laughed. "I used to dread going to the DMV in LA, but it's so different here. There were only two other people there. I was in and out in twenty minutes."

Candy laughed. "That's amazing. I need to go and get mine changed over. You're only supposed to drive on an out-of-state license for sixty days after you move here."

Rocket raised his eyebrows. "You'd better get it taken care of then, huh? We wouldn't want you getting in trouble with the sheriff, would we?"

Candy tried to hide her smile. She was surprised that he hadn't mentioned it yet, but she was sure that he must have heard about Deacon bringing her home from the yard sale yesterday. "I think I'm probably safe there."

"Anything you want to tell me about?"

"Not yet. Maybe soon."

He looked serious as he held her gaze. "Okay, but …"

She laughed. "But what?"

"I dunno. I don't know what to say. But I'll be keeping an eye on him. Keeping an eye out for you."

She waved a hand at him. She loved that he wanted to look out for her, but they both knew that she had nothing to worry about with Deacon. "You go and get us those coffees. I'll go and grab us a table."

She waved at Jim Sheridan as she made her way between the tables to a booth by the back wall. She loved Jim. He must be as old as the hills, but he was full of life. It seemed that everyone in the valley knew and respected him.

He smiled and nodded when she neared the table where he was sitting. "Top of the morning to you, Candy."

"And to you, Jim. How are you?"

"I'm doing great, thanks." He lifted his mug to her. "Enjoying my coffee in peace, and one of the best donuts I've ever had, thanks to you." He chuckled. "And when you think how many years I've been walking this Earth and eating donuts, you'll take that as the compliment it is."

"Aww, thanks, Jim."

He nodded. "Are you making the most of the lull, for your break?"

"I am." She looked around the almost empty bakery. "It always amazes me that Sunday mornings are like this. It's crazy busy early on, and then it goes dead for about an hour and a half. Then all of a sudden it gets crazy again until early afternoon. It's the same every week."

Jim laughed. "And you don't know why?"

"Not a clue."

"Church."

"Oh! That hadn't even occurred to me. It makes sense now you've said it, though. I didn't realize this was such a churchy place."

Jim nodded. "Aye. Most folks will be there whether they want to be or not. Some of 'em believe. Some of 'em go because they're expected to be there, but most all of 'em go."

"Not you, though?" Candy covered her mouth with her hand. "Sorry. That was rude. It's none of my business."

Jim laughed. "Not a problem. When my good lady wife was still here, I used to be one of them who went because he was expected to." He winked. "But my church has always been in the mountains. I can talk easier with my maker when I'm surrounded by his work – under the shining stars or by the running river – than I ever managed to inside a musty old building full of sinners."

Candy smiled and nodded. Church had never been part of her life. She didn't have anything against it, she knew that a lot of people built their lives around it, but it was outside her experience. She could relate to what Jim said, though. If there was a creator, she'd found more to believe in since she'd moved to Montana than she had in any musty old church she'd ever set foot in.

"Go on with you. It looks like your coffee's coming." Jim nodded at Rocket, who had just emerged from the back with their drinks.

"Okay. It's good to see you, Jim. You take care."

"Aye, you too."

Just as Rocket sat down, the front door opened, and he sighed as he got back to his feet. "Every time," he said with a rueful smile. "Hopefully, I'll only be a minute."

Candy turned to see who had come in and smiled when she saw Deacon just inside the door, looking around. He smiled when his gaze landed on her, and she smiled back.

Rocket raised an eyebrow at her. "I might be more than a minute."

"No! You come right back and sit with me." Of course she was pleased to see Deacon, but she'd be spending the whole afternoon with him. She didn't often get the chance to sit down and have Rocket all to herself.

He made a face but didn't say anything as he made his way back to the counter and let himself through to serve Deacon.

Candy watched the two of them with a smile on her face. She loved how well they got along. It said a lot that someone who looked like Rocket respected and admired the sheriff – especially after a lifetime of being judged by his appearance instead of his character. The same was true the other way around. Deacon had obviously taken Rocket as he found him, not at face value. The result was a solid, if unlikely, friendship.

Once he had his coffee, Deacon lingered at the counter and Rocket came back to Candy. He narrowed his eyes at her as he sat back down. "Are you two avoiding each other or something?"

"No!" Candy glanced at Deacon again, panicking for a moment that he might be avoiding her for some reason.

She was reassured when Deacon raised his mug to her with a smile and winked.

"Why?" she asked Rocket.

"Well, you told me not to make myself scarce because he was here, and then he told me not to let him interrupt our conversation – that I should bring my ass back over here and sit back down."

A rush of warmth filled Candy's chest. "You know I love to make the most of any time I can get you to myself. And Deacon knows that. He's just making sure that he doesn't interrupt."

"What about you getting time with him?"

She couldn't hide her smile. "I'll get that later."

Rocket didn't look as surprised as she expected him to. He chuckled. "Deacon told me that he's taking you to the park this afternoon."

"He did?"

"Does that bother you? That he told me?"

"No. It surprises me, but it doesn't bother me."

Rocket smiled. "It shouldn't surprise you, Miss Candy. In fact, I'd guess that you'll need to get used to it. He wanted to make sure that I wasn't going to worry about you."

"I'm not some package that you need to shunt around between you menfolk, you know!" She wasn't sure how she felt about that.

Rocket laughed. "And we all know it. It's not like that. Deacon knows that Spider and I are protective of you and that we feel responsible for you. I'd say that he feels the same way. Telling me that he's taking you to the park is his way of letting me know that he's looking out for you too, and that he understands how I feel about you."

"Oh."

Rocket laughed again. "Is that okay with you?"

"I think so."

"Well, if you haven't decided whether it is or not, can I suggest that you be okay with it?"

She met his gaze. "Why?"

"Because Deacon's a good guy. I know that you're doing your best not to impose on me and Janey or Spider and Frankie. I appreciate it, even though I'm not thrilled about it. But if you're not spending time with us, then I want you to get to know people, and Deacon's one of the best people I've ever known."

Candy nodded. She knew that Rocket liked Deacon, but she hadn't realized that he felt that strongly about him. "Okay."

They both sipped their coffee in silence for a few minutes before Rocket said, "And Luke's smarter than any of us were giving him credit for."

She had to smile when it hit her why Luke had asked her to go to the yard sale with him. She couldn't be mad at him.

She looked over to where Deacon was sitting at the counter, drinking his coffee and flipping through the newspaper. As if he felt her gaze on him, he looked up and smiled. And in that moment, she had a feeling that she would be forever grateful to Luke.

Chapter Nine

It was getting late by the time they got back from the park. Deacon felt bad that Candy looked tired, but she'd insisted that she wanted to see Old Faithful before they headed home. He'd loved seeing the park through her eyes. To him, it was nothing spectacular; it wasn't much different from the valley where he'd grown up and spent most of his life.

Sure, there were the geysers and all the spots that the tourists made such fuss over, but he'd never seen what the big deal was. Not until today. As they'd trailed around the boardwalks with hundreds of other people, Candy's gasps, huge eyes, and awed whispers had made him see it differently. She'd told him how she'd grown up in LA. The beach wasn't far away, but it was always crowded with people. She could see the mountains sometimes – when she got out from between the buildings, but she hadn't spent any time in the open countryside.

She'd asked Deacon about the first time that he'd seen the ocean, and that had helped put it in perspective for him. He'd gotten used to the ocean over the years, even grown to love it. But that first time he'd seen it, after growing up here surrounded by mountains, it had taken his breath away.

He brought the truck to a stop in the driveway and turned to look at her. "You look beat."

"Sorry."

"No!" He reached across and stroked his fingers down her cheek. "There's nothing to say sorry for. That came out wrong. You still look beautiful. It's just that I can tell you're tired and I feel bad."

"Why?"

"Because I knew that you were up early, and I know that you have to be up early again tomorrow, but I still kept you out all afternoon and into the evening."

She smiled and pressed her cheek into his hand. "I am tired, but it was so worth it. I loved every minute of this afternoon. I had no idea that Yellowstone was so amazing." She chuckled. "And you might say that you kept me out, but I seem to remember insisting that I wanted to see more. And think about it – isn't this better than how disappointed I would have been if you made me come back early?"

He laughed with her. "Yeah. I did think about it a few times, but I couldn't bring myself to end your fun."

"There's so much to see. It's so big. I had no idea."

"Yeah. It'd take days just to see all the big tourist attractions. It'd take weeks if you wanted to see the real park."

"You mentioned that. The backcountry, right?"

He nodded.

"I'd like to see that – to go where there aren't hundreds of other people."

"I'll take you if you want?"

"I'd love that. Thank you."

"I wasn't sure if you'd be happy off the beaten track. Didn't know if you'd be scared about the bears and the wolves."

She smiled. "I won't be scared of anything if you're there."

Deacon couldn't help smiling back. Her words made him feel like he was ten feet tall. "I'll take care of you." He blew out a sigh. "Right now, I think that taking care of you means getting you inside and off to bed."

Her smile faded.

"What's up?"

She shrugged. "You're right. It's been a long day."

"And you're tired." He didn't want to pack her off up to the apartment yet, but it had seemed like the right thing to do. However, if she wanted to hang out with him a while longer, he'd be more than happy. "But if you're not too tired, do you want to come in for a drink before we call it a night?"

She nodded happily. "I won't stay for long. I just … It's probably silly, but I don't like the idea of you dropping me off at my door like this was a date. I mean, it kind of was one, but it's more important to me that we're friends, too. And friends hang out together when they get home. They don't just say thank you and goodnight."

Deacon chuckled. "Yeah. I know exactly what you mean. Wait there. I'll be around."

He smiled as he jogged around the back of his truck to get her door. He was glad that she was thinking of this afternoon as a date – and even happier that she wanted them to be friends as well.

~ ~ ~

Candy blew out a big sigh of contentment as she settled back on Deacon's sofa with her soda. He'd offered something stronger, but she didn't need it, and more importantly, she was better off without it. He'd been right; she was tired. But it had been such a great day that she didn't want it to end. She'd have to say goodnight to him soon and take herself upstairs to bed.

She'd be dragging when she got up for work in the morning, but it was worth it.

She smiled when Clawson jumped up beside her and headbutted her arm. She scratched his ears, and he climbed onto her lap before curling up and starting to purr. She'd never had a cat; Len didn't like them. He hadn't wanted animals in the house, and he'd mostly gotten his way. She smiled to herself – mostly.

Deacon came and sat down beside her. "What's so funny?"

She laughed. "I was just enjoying Clawson's company and thinking about how we almost never had animals in the house."

"Almost?"

She nodded happily. "You might have noticed that Rocket has a way with animals."

"Yeah." Deacon smiled. "Clawson loves him, and … well, I was going to say that's unusual. Clawson's not the friendliest cat usually. He can be a vicious little bugger. But he took to Rocket, and now it seems that he's taken to you, too."

Candy chuckled as Clawson's purr grew louder and louder.

"Did Rocket have a cat when he lived with you, then?"

"No. Len wouldn't have animals in the house. But Rocket found a baby raccoon. I don't know what had happened to it; it had a broken leg, and it was so sick when he brought it home, I didn't think it'd make it. I don't know where he found it. He hid it in his bedroom because he knew there were no pets allowed. He thought I didn't know at first, but I helped him with it. He's always had a soft heart, that boy. He cried his eyes out after he set it free when it was all better. It broke his heart to let it go, but he knew it was the right thing to do."

"He's a good man."

"He is. Thank you for letting him rent the apartment when he first came here. I know he doesn't look like the kind of man you'd want around."

Deacon held her gaze for a moment. "I'd like to say that I knew – that I could see he was a good person. But I won't lie to you. I rented the apartment to him because I wanted him right under my nose where I could keep an eye on him."

Candy laughed. "I wouldn't expect anything else. I bet it didn't take you long to see that you could trust him though, did it?"

"No. And Clawson here knew before I did. Like I said, he's not the friendliest cat, but he took to Rocket straight away. He was always sneaking off upstairs to visit with him."

"He's a good judge of character."

Deacon made a face. "I kind of agree, but not completely. He could see Rocket was good people, and there's no question that he took to you right away. But there are lots of folks who – if he were a good judge of character – he should like, but he doesn't. He scratches the hell out of Luke any chance he gets. He's not thrilled when Ace comes over. He doesn't like Emmett much, either."

"Emmett's the vet, though, isn't he?"

Deacon laughed. "He is, but he's not Clawson's vet. Janey is. And he loves her to pieces."

Candy shrugged. "I guess you just like who you like, don't you, Clawson?"

The cat purred loudly in response.

"So, what does the week ahead hold for you?" asked Deacon.

"Not much. I'm at work every morning. That only really leaves me with the time and the energy to come home, eat dinner, and get to bed early so that I can do it all again the next day. I'm not complaining," she added hurriedly when she saw the frown on his face. "It'll be better when I'm more used to it. And when I'm more used to living here. I could go up into town after work if I really wanted to, but I haven't gotten used to that drive yet. It probably seems silly to you; I know you go up there every day. But I lived my life in a five-square-mile radius before. Driving thirty miles used to be something of a road trip. Now, I have to do it just to get to the grocery store."

Deacon slung his arm around her shoulders. The way he smiled took her breath away. It was such a different look on him than the frown that she'd been used to seeing on his face.

He'd opened his mouth to say something but stopped and cocked an eyebrow when he saw her sharp intake of breath. He started to pull his arm back, but she grabbed his hand and held him there.

"It wasn't because I didn't like it."

"What then?"

She shrugged. "It just … oh, what the hell, I don't care how it sounds, I'm going to say it. You smiling like that took my breath away."

He held her gaze as a big smile spread across his face. She had to laugh. "Yes, that. It suits you; you should smile more."

"I have a feeling that I'm going to; now that you're around."

"Aww. Aren't you a sweetheart?"

Deacon laughed. "Nope. I've never been accused of that before." He pressed a quick kiss to her lips then pulled back and narrowed his eyes at her. "Grumpy the sheriff? Yeah. That's a fair description, but a sweetheart? Don't kid yourself, darlin'."

She rested her head against his shoulder, loving that she felt so at ease with him – and that he seemed to feel the same way. "I'm not kidding myself. You're a sweetheart."

"Whatever you say. Anyway, what I was going to say is, do you want me to ride up to the grocery store with you one day?

I'm working the early shift next week, so I'll be home by three most days. I can ride up there with you if you want."

"Aww. And you say you're not a sweetheart? It's lovely of you to offer, but I don't want you to do that. For one thing, it'd mean you driving all the way home and then going back up there again when you don't need to – that'd be over a hundred miles in a day. That's crazy. And for another thing, I really need to get used to driving myself."

He tightened his arm around her. "It's no problem to go back up there again; there's many a day when I have to go back and forth to town three or four times. I don't even think about it. It might seem a long way to you, but it's just the way of things when you've grown up here. After you've been here for a while, you won't think anything of it either. And I wasn't offering to drive you. I agree that you need to get used to driving yourself. I just thought it might help if you had some company on the ride for the first few times."

"You really are a sweetheart. I wouldn't have thought that would even occur to you, but you're right; it would help to have some company."

"Just tell me which day you want to go then."

"And you wouldn't mind riding in my little car? I thought a big tough guy like you would have to drive himself. And that you'd only travel in trucks. I mean, even when you're not driving your big sheriff truck you have your own. I certainly wouldn't have thought you'd want to be a passenger in a little car like mine."

He smiled through pursed lips. "I don't make a habit of riding shotgun unless I have to. And I'm not thrilled about your car. But I don't mind riding in it – for you."

She didn't have any words for that, she just smiled at him.

He chuckled. "I should warn you, though; I am going to try to talk you into trading in that little car for something else.

Maybe not a truck, but something with four-wheel drive and preferably an SUV."

"Hmm. I don't know about that. That Nissan's bigger than my old car, and I'm struggling to get used to that."

"You're kidding me, right? That Nissan's tiny."

She laughed. "I kid you not. My little Chevy was way smaller."

"Chevy doesn't make toy cars!"

She shook her head at him. "You're such a guy! Chevy might make all your big, manly trucks, but they make a lot of other cars too – including my teeny, little Spark. I love that car. I told you, I never used to go very far. I only needed something small so that I could get myself and my groceries around. It's always a hassle to find parking at home so, the smaller the car, the more chance I had."

She noticed that he wasn't smiling anymore. "What?"

"You said home. Are you still thinking of LA as home? Do you plan to go back?"

She blew out a sigh. She'd been trying not to think about that. She didn't want to go back. She'd promised Spider and Rocket that she'd stay for as long as she could to help them, and she wanted to make her home here. But there were still some things she had to sort out.

"I don't want to go back. I called it home out of habit – I lived there all my life."

Deacon's smile was back. "Are you saying that I might be able to persuade you to stay, then?"

She smiled back at him. "I hope so. I still have some things, some … legal things I need to go back and deal with but …"

"Mind if I ask you something?"

"What?"

"The other week, that first time you came over and we sat out back, you got a phone call."

Shoot. She knew that she'd messed up by talking to Saunders while Deacon was listening. She nodded, wondering what he was going to say.

"You said that you knew that they could subpoena you."

She nodded again.

"Want to tell me what that was all about?"

She sighed. "The honest answer is, no, I don't. I'm not in any trouble," she added hurriedly.

"I didn't think you were."

She let out a short laugh. "I'd be pretty dumb to start seeing the sheriff if I were, right?"

"Yeah."

"It's a long story, and maybe one day I'll tell you the whole thing. The short version is that Len had gotten himself into some trouble – a lot of trouble – before he died. He owned a pawn shop, and he was selling stolen goods for some bad people. He … he was also helping drug dealers make their money look clean – launder it."

The scowl on Deacon's face made her hesitate. "I didn't know about any of it until after he died."

Deacon touched her cheek. "I didn't think you did. It seems like you can read my every expression, but I wasn't angry at you. I was angry at Len and whatever he dragged you into."

She felt herself relax a little at that. He must have felt it too; he tightened his arm around her as he said, "Sorry, go on."

She shrugged. "After he died, I started going into the shop. I thought that maybe I'd be able to take it over, keep it going. But there were all kinds of people coming in – scary people. And the things they expected me to do – things that they said were part of their deal with Len. I was scared, but no way was I going to help criminals. I was scared to go to the police as well, though. I knew Len's friends wouldn't be happy with me if they found out. So, I talked to a guy I used to know growing up. He was a police officer until he had to retire – after he got shot. He put me in touch with a detective and I met with him a few times to tell him what was going on."

Deacon's frown was back.

"What?" she asked.

"Please tell me they didn't put you in the middle of it?"

She shrugged. "I was already in the middle of it. I owned the shop after Len died, and they knew me and expected me to keep things going the same way he had."

"So, the detective used you? You were his informant?"

She shrugged again. "I wasn't very good at it. I couldn't stand those assholes. I couldn't keep my mouth shut. The things they brought into the shop were things that they'd stolen from good, hardworking people – and the drug money? I spent my life trying to keep kids away from drugs. I couldn't pretend to be okay with the men who supply them!"

"What happened then?"

"I think Saunders – the detective – was happy when I said I couldn't do it anymore. I was more likely to blow it than to help gather enough evidence so that they'd be able to arrest them all. I told him that he could have the shop. I'm better off without that in my life anyway. He brought in an undercover guy who we said was my nephew. Everyone was so relieved not to have to deal with me anymore that they just accepted him at face value. They'd had too many disruptions; Len died, his wife was a pain in the ass to deal with and not the pushover they'd been expecting. So, when Tony – my supposed nephew – took over, they were relieved that they had someone new they could blackmail into doing what they wanted."

"They just took over your pawn shop – the LAPD did?"

"Well, it's not quite that straightforward. I said that I'd rather just walk away free from the whole thing. I couldn't just gift them the shop, but they're using it as part of their whole deal. I imagine that when it's all done. When, hopefully, they've arrested the whole gang of them, I'll see what I need to do about shutting it down or selling it or whatever. But I don't care. I've never had much money. I earn as much as I need. And it's not like I'd make much if I sold the place, anyway. If it can help take burglars and drug dealers off the street, then I'm happy to give the whole thing away and call it good."

Deacon held her gaze for a long moment. She stared back at him, not knowing what he was thinking. If he was going to get mad at her, try to tell her that she'd done wrong somehow, then she was going to get mad right back at him. She'd done what she felt to be the best – what she felt was right, and she wasn't going to apologize for that to anyone – not even him.

"What?" she asked when she couldn't take the silence any longer.

He gave her a wry smile. "You're something else."

"What does that mean?"

His eyes shone as he leaned closer and rested his forehead against hers. "It means that I think you're quite a lady, Candy."

She didn't have time to figure out what he might mean before his lips brushed against hers. When his fingers came up around the nape of her neck, she lost track of all coherent thoughts. Shivers chased each other down her spine, and goosebumps rose up on her arms.

Clawson jumped down from her lap when Deacon reached for her and drew her closer. She slid both arms up around his neck and clung on as he kissed her like she'd never been kissed before.

Chapter Ten

Deacon sat in his truck for a few moments when he pulled into a space outside the bakery on Monday morning. He wanted to try and wipe the stupid grin off his face before he went in there – people would know there was something going on with him if they saw that.

He couldn't help it though. He'd been smiling ever since he woke up. And it was all because of Candy. He'd enjoyed this weekend more than he'd enjoyed himself in a long time – probably years. There was just something about the woman that made him smile. She was smart, and funny, and she had no problem speaking her mind.

His smile faded at that; the thought of her speaking her mind to the kind of criminals her dead husband had been involved with was no smiling matter. He wanted to know more about that whole situation. He was going to have to get her to tell him more. He knew that she'd rather just forget about it. That had been apparent when he'd overheard her phone call the other week. But it wasn't going to be that simple – especially if the detective down there, Saunders, she'd said his name was, was talking about her being subpoenaed. That must mean that they were getting close to making a move. Deacon was going to see what he could find out about Saunders, too. He could do it in an official capacity. He wanted to know that nothing was going to follow Candy up here to Montana.

He shook his head and got out of the truck. There'd be time to get to all of it. Right now, it was time for him to get his ass to work, and he needed his coffee and his scone for the ride. More than that, he wanted to see Candy. She wasn't always out front when he came in in the morning, but he was hoping that she would be today.

He pushed the door open with a rueful smile. He had it bad. He was like a kid, hoping to see his girl before he had to start his day. It was still early, but there were a few folks seated at the tables, and a couple more sitting at the counter.

Ford MacFarland turned and greeted him with a puzzled smile. "Morning, Deacon. What are you smiling about?"

Shit. So, he hadn't managed to wipe the smile off his face. He shrugged. "Hoping it's going to be a good day. How are things with you?"

Ford nodded. "All right."

Spider set a to-go cup in front of him, and Ford smiled. "Looking up now that I've got my coffee. Have a good 'un."

"Yeah. Thanks. You too."

"What can I get you?" Spider asked as Ford walked away. "The usual?"

Deacon nodded. "Black coffee and –"

"Wait! Is that Deacon?"

His smile was back in full force when he heard Candy call from the back. It grew even wider when she appeared in the doorway from the kitchen.

Spider looked as though he was trying to hide a smile of his own when he said, "I'll get you that coffee."

He moved away when Candy came straight to Deacon with a brown paper bag in her hand and set it on the counter in front of him.

He cocked an eyebrow at the bag as he murmured, "Morning, darlin'."

She grinned. "Good morning to you, too. *That,"* she pointed at the bag, "is something new."

He reached for it and peered inside. "Looks like a scone to me."

She chuckled. "It is. But it's a banana-nut scone. I know you can't eat muffins on your way to work, but I was thinking about it, and I don't know why banana-nut scones aren't a thing. So, now, they are."

Deacon had to laugh. "Thank you. That's …" He shook his head. He didn't know what to say.

She shrugged. "I hope you'll like it."

"I know I will."

Spider came back and set his coffee down on the counter. "There you go."

"Thanks." Deacon reached for his wallet, but Spider waved him away. "It's on the house."

Deacon frowned, but Candy laughed. "You're not going to get anywhere by scowling at anyone; we know better than to be fooled by that. So, just say thank you and get yourself off to work."

He grinned. "Okay. Thank you."

"You're welcome."

"I'll see you later?" He didn't want to say too much with so many people around – half of whom he just knew were straining their ears.

Candy seemed to know what he meant. They hadn't arranged to do anything tonight, but Deacon couldn't imagine not spending some time with her. She nodded happily. "See you later."

~ ~ ~

As she left the bakery on Thursday afternoon, Candy had no idea where the week had gone. She still hadn't made it up to the grocery store – even though Deacon had offered to go with her every afternoon. She kept saying that she didn't need to go just yet, but that wasn't entirely true. It was just that she preferred spending the time with him doing more fun things.

On Monday, he'd driven her out to Dailey Lake, and they walked around. It was a gorgeous spot, and she couldn't believe that there wasn't another soul there. He was right that, although the park was beautiful, it wasn't the only place worth seeing. When they'd walked around Old Faithful and Mammoth Hot Springs, it was amazing, but she could have been in any national park. At Dailey Lake, the solitude enhanced the beauty of the place, and she knew without a doubt that she was in Montana.

On Tuesday, they'd gone for an early dinner at a little restaurant called The Riverside. She loved it; it wasn't anything fancy, just a burger joint. But sitting out back eating at one of the picnic benches, surrounded by the majestic mountains, had felt special. Last night, Deacon had made her dinner, and they'd sat out in the backyard, keeping an eye on Clawson while he prowled.

She rummaged through her purse for her phone when it rang just before she reached her car. She hoped it might be Deacon. They hadn't arranged to do anything tonight, but she really should take him up on his offer to ride up to town with her. Maybe he'd let her buy him dinner while they were there. She knew there were some nice restaurants, and she wouldn't mind going for a stroll, getting to know the town better.

She frowned when she saw that it wasn't his name on the display. It was an LA number, but she didn't recognize it.

"Hello."

"You're going to pay, bitch."

"Excuse me? Who is this?"

"You don't need to know who I am. You only need to know that you screwed up, and you're going to pay."

Her heart raced in her chest. She might not know exactly who he was, but she'd put money on the fact that he was one of the men who came into the pawn shop.

"I don't know what you're talking about."

"Sure, you do. You might think that you're safe in Montana, but you're not."

That made her heart leap into her mouth. She looked around wildly, suddenly convinced that someone was watching her – maybe even the man on the phone.

"What do you want?" she asked in a shaky voice.

The man laughed. "Nothing yet. You screwed with me, so I'm going to screw with you. All I want for now is for you to be looking over your shoulder every day – the same way I have to. There's a big difference though. One day, when you look over your shoulder, shit's going to catch up with you. It's not catching up with me. You want to be careful, Candy. You never know which day it might be. Could be today."

She heard him laughing before the call cut off. She knew he was only trying to mess with her. Whatever he was talking about wouldn't happen today – would it? She hurried into her car and locked the doors for the short drive back to the house. Her heart was still pounding when she pulled up in the driveway.

When she'd first arrived in Montana, she'd been constantly looking over her shoulder. She'd been convinced that those men knew what she'd done – knew that she'd gone to the police about them, and that Tony wasn't her nephew. She'd been skittish for a while, always thinking that someone could have followed her here – and would want to make her pay.

The feeling had worn off, though. She'd been relaxed for the last few weeks, especially this last week, with Deacon. She swallowed and looked around before she got out of the car. She was going to have to tell him. She didn't want to. She didn't want to worry him. But she lived in his house. If someone was going to come after her, there was a chance that Deacon might get hurt. That chance would be much greater if he didn't know what was going on. As she unlocked the front door, it crossed her mind that she should perhaps find somewhere else to live. She scowled at the thought. That'd be stupid. For one thing, she didn't want to, and for another, no matter how much she didn't want to put him out, or put him in danger, Deacon was the freaking sheriff! She'd be crazy to move away from him.

"Hey!"

She startled so badly that she dropped her purse and her keys.

Deacon hurried to her and picked them up. "Sorry." He gave her a rueful smile. "I didn't mean to scare you. I just wanted to catch you as soon as you got back. Would I be right if I guess that you need to go up to town this afternoon?"

"What?" She was still too shaken to focus on what he was saying.

"You need groceries, right?" He gave her a puzzled look. "What's wrong, darlin'?" Without giving her the chance to answer, he put his arm around her shoulders and led her into his place. He steered her to the sofa and once she was sitting, he sat on the edge of the coffee table, facing her. He rested his elbows on his knees and leaned toward her, looking worried.

"What is it?"

She gave a shaky laugh. "You don't miss a thing, do you?"

"It'd be hard to miss how badly I frightened you when you arrived, and you're – you look like you're in shock. What happened?"

She blew out a big sigh. "I'm okay. Nothing happened. Well, I got a phone call, but nothing actually happened." She couldn't help thinking *yet.* But deliberately didn't say that part.

"What was the phone call?"

"Someone from LA."

"About the pawn shop?"

She nodded.

"What did they say?"

"That I screwed them over, so they're going to screw me over. I don't know which one of them it was, but …" She shrugged. "He said that I might think I'm safe in Montana, but I'm not."

Deacon scowled. "Who knows that you're here?"

"I didn't tell anyone where I was going, but it wouldn't be hard to find out."

"Did you call this Saunders, let him know what's going on?"

"I will. Whoever it was only called a few minutes ago, just as I was leaving the bakery. As soon as he hung up, I came straight home."

"And you were going to tell me, right?"

Candy was glad that she'd already decided that she'd have to tell him. She wouldn't be able to lie about it and she could tell that he'd be pissed if she wanted to hide it from him.

"I was." She nodded emphatically when he looked doubtful. "Honestly! I can't say that I wanted to tell you, but I knew that I had to. I'd be stupid not to. I live in your house; I could bring trouble to your door. There's no way that I wouldn't tell you."

His scowl only intensified. "I'm not worried about me, Candy. And you shouldn't be either. I'm worried about you. The more information I have, the more I can do to keep you safe."

"I appreciate that; I'm not thrilled about it – I don't want to be some damsel in distress that you need to look out for. But don't tell me not to worry about you – I will, no matter what you say. I know you're the big tough sheriff and everything, but I hate thinking that they might go after you just because I'm staying at your place."

Deacon leaned farther forward and rested his hands on her knees as he looked into her eyes. "You're not some damsel in distress or *some* anything. You're my woman. They're not coming after me – I'm going after them. And …" the look in his eyes was intense "… you're not just staying at my place. You live here. And I might as well tell you now that if things between us keep going the way they have been, I'll be asking if you want to live *with* me."

Her eyes widened as she leaned back to get a better look at him. Had she heard that right? Apparently, she had.

He smiled. "I know it's too soon to be talking like that, but what can I tell you? I'm not trying to rush you into anything; not trying to rush myself either. But saying goodnight to you and watching you walk back up those stairs to your room while I go to bed alone is already getting old, darlin'."

It was hardly the time – she should be focusing on the possible danger she was in, but Candy couldn't help smiling and nodding. "I'm not that thrilled about it either."

Deacon winked at her. "Good to know. And we'll come back around to that but first things first. Do you need to go to the grocery store?"

"I do."

"Okay, then let's go. And what do you think; I know what we said about you getting used to driving, but do you want me to?"

She blew out a sigh of relief. "Please. I …"

"You've got enough on your mind. I'll drive and you can tell me everything you can remember about that phone call on the way. And when we get back, how would you feel about letting me download an app on your phone?"

"What kind of app?"

He met her gaze and held it. "One that will allow you to record any more calls you get." He pursed his lips. "I'd also like to get you one of those tracker apps, so that I know where you are." He shrugged. "I'm not trying to be controlling or …"

She laughed. "Wow, it wouldn't have occurred to me that you were; it's just a police thing, right?"

He shook his head slowly. "No. It's not a police thing, it's a Deacon thing. I'm going to be worrying myself sick about you. I'd like to be able to check and see where you are, to put my mind at ease. And if, God forbid, anything should happen, it'll be useful to know where you are."

She looked back into his eyes. She knew that some people would be freaked out at the thought of a man they hadn't known for very long wanting to be able to track their every move, but she didn't mind. In fact, she liked the idea. No one had cared that much about her before – Len certainly hadn't. And Deacon wasn't some controlling boyfriend – he was the sheriff.

That night, Deacon lay in bed thinking about everything that Candy had told him and everything he needed to do. He'd put in a call to Saunders but had only reached his voicemail. He'd be calling him again first thing in the morning – and he'd be calling as the sheriff, not as … what else did he want to call himself? Candy's man – that was what he wanted to be. It had come at him out of the blue, but he wasn't going to deny that was how he felt.

He stared up at the ceiling in the darkness. He knew that he shouldn't have said anything about wanting her to live with him. It was way too soon for that kind of talk. It was hard to believe that he felt that way. He would have said that wasn't who he was, and he'd have been right – until Candy.

He hadn't had a relationship in years. He didn't trust women, didn't particularly like many of them. He'd thought after Willa that he'd be a bachelor for life. He'd been with a few women; he wasn't exactly celibate. But since he'd had no interest in a relationship, it hadn't been easy. Everyone in the county knew him. It wouldn't be right for the sheriff to be going around picking up women for the night, so his opportunities had been few and far between – and he'd been okay with that.

He wasn't okay with it any longer. Just the short time he'd spent with Candy had opened his eyes to how different – how much better – life could be if he got to share it. Share it with her. He wasn't under any illusions that she'd merely opened his eyes to what might be possible with a woman by his side. No. It was all about her. Who she was. He admired her as a person. He was attracted to her as a woman. She was turning out to be his perfect match when he'd thought such a thing didn't exist – and that he wouldn't have wanted it if it did.

He'd never been happier to be proved wrong. Their conversation had moved right on from the point when he'd told her that he was going to want her to live with him. But they'd circle back around to it when the time was right. He could wait. Hell, he'd waited fifty-two years for her. He'd wait however much longer it took for the time to be right. But he was glad that he'd planted the seed – that she knew where he wanted this thing between them to go.

Clawson jumped up onto the bed and meowed before settling down on Deacon's chest. Deacon petted him absently as he continued to run through the mental list he was preparing. He needed to call Brad first thing and get him to come out to the house to see about installing an alarm system. It might seem strange in a place where most folks never locked their doors. He'd joked with Brad many a time that if it wasn't for the transplants from California, there'd be no call for alarm systems in the valley at all – probably not in the whole state of Montana. He couldn't help smiling to himself as he realized that he'd finally met a California transplant whom he hoped would never go back to where she came from.

He was going to have to talk to Rocket and Spider as well. He wanted to hear whatever they knew about the pawn shop and Len. Of course, he'd like to hear what they knew about Saunders and the assholes he was building a case against, but he had the feeling that they didn't know – that Candy hadn't told them anything.

He closed his eyes, hoping that Clawson's loud purring might lull him to sleep. It was going to be a busy day tomorrow, and he needed to be up early.

Chapter Eleven

Frankie patted the space beside her and winked at Candy. "You may as well just smile and roll with it, Miss Candy."

She rolled her eyes and blew out a sigh as she settled into the booth. "I still haven't decided whether I should be angry or flattered."

She'd been about ready to go home after cleaning up the kitchen and leaving everything ready for the boys for what was left of the afternoon. Spider had come into the kitchen and told her that Frankie, Janey, and Sierra were out front and had asked if she wanted to join them for a coffee and a catch-up.

It was only when she was hanging her apron up, and Rocket had said that she should stay and chat with the girls until Deacon got back from work that she understood what was going on. They were all keeping an eye on her – making sure that she wasn't left alone.

"Flattered, definitely flattered," Janey said. She was sitting across the table from Candy and Frankie with Sierra by her side.

Sierra smiled. "I know that you're used to dealing with everything by yourself, but I have to tell you, it feels pretty amazing when all these guys decide that you're one of them and step up to take care of you."

"I know. You're right. But …" Candy shook her head. "I just hate that everyone's going out of their way because of me. I came here to be a help, not to be a burden on anyone."

"You're not a burden," said Janey. "If you think about it, it's better that you're here. If you were still in LA, Rocket and Spider would want to come down there to help you – they'd have to leave the bakery."

Candy made a face; she didn't want to spell out that if she were still in LA, the boys wouldn't know anything about what was going on, so they wouldn't be worried about her.

Frankie gave her a shrewd look. "I can guess what you're thinking. But can you imagine how bad they'd feel if something happened to you, and they hadn't known anything about it?"

"I know, I know." She was just having trouble processing everything that had happened since she'd gotten that phone call yesterday – everything that Deacon had done.

He'd come upstairs while she was getting ready for work this morning and informed her that he'd be going with her.

Janey grinned. "I've never seen Deacon this way. I know it's scary what's going on, but it is kind of awesome seeing the way he is with you."

Frankie laughed. "I love it! I love Deacon. He might come off a bit … I dunno, he's more … stern than the rest of them. Is that the right word – stern?" she asked Janey.

Janey laughed. "Kind of. Maybe it's just because he's the sheriff, so we see him that way, and he has to be more … professional."

She smiled at Candy. "I know you met most of those guys at our wedding – the whole big group of them. My eldest brother Cash, and Frankie's brother Mav, and Ace, Emmett, Travis, and Trip."

Candy nodded.

"There's Blane and a few more of them, too. Frankie calls them the big brother brigade."

Frankie laughed. "Because they are. Blane is Brooke's big brother – you've met Brooke, right?"

"I have." Candy liked Brooke; she seemed to pop up all over the place. She worked at the gas station up in town, and she watched Emmet's girls sometimes, she'd even started doing her own delivery service for folks who wanted to order from the bakery but couldn't come by to collect.

"They're all great guys," said Janey. "And they're all big personalities. Emmett's the responsible one because of his daughters. Ace is the one all the women chase. Trip, he's the doctor, and the one who married us, remember? He's an all-around good guy."

"He's rich, too," added Frankie.

"Yeah," said Janey. "And Travis is the joker. Mav is …" she looked at Frankie. "How would you describe Mav?"

Frankie laughed. "He's a bossy badass."

Janey laughed with her. "Yeah, that. And my brother Cash. He's … well, he's just Cash."

Sierra sighed and fluttered her eyelashes. "Cash is dreamy!"

Candy had to laugh with the other girls at that. Cash was a good-looking guy, no question about it. She'd met him at Janey and Rocket's wedding. He was a larger-than-life personality. He'd planned the whole wedding in a week – and it had been amazing. Since she was the mother of the groom, kind of, and

Cash was the one to give Janey away, Candy had chatted with him quite a bit and done the official dance with him after Janey and Rocket had their first dance. He was quite a character, and she knew that Sierra wasn't the only one who thought he was dreamy. But she was still waiting for the girls to get to Deacon. She could see why they said that he was the stern one, but she was hoping that they were going to come up with a better word than that before they were done.

Janey shook her head with a smile. "Cash is just Cash. But what I was trying to do is figure out how to describe Deacon."

"Deacon's grumpy."

They all turned to see Luke standing there.

"What?" he asked with a grin before sliding into the booth next to Candy. "We're describing the brothers, right? Deacon's the grumpy one. He's also the conscientious one, the protective one, and the responsible one." He turned to Candy and winked. "You're not going to deny that he's the grumpy one, are you?"

Candy felt the heat in her cheeks. He knew that she'd called Deacon Grumpy the sheriff, she could tell he did. And that could only mean that Deacon had told him.

He laughed. "Don't worry; he liked it. And I think we have you to thank for him not being so grumpy lately."

She shrugged.

Frankie winked at her. "I think we do, too. But what are you doing down here?" she asked Luke. "I thought you'd be up in town, ready for a Friday night out."

He shrugged. "I came down to see you lovely ladies."

Candy pursed her lips. "Did Deacon send you?"

"No. He didn't send me. He told me what's going on and I volunteered to come down and hang out with you until he gets home."

She shook her head. "That's sweet of you, Luke. And I appreciate it, I do. But this has to stop. Deacon was up at four-thirty this morning and came in here with me until Spider and Rocky arrived. Now, they've got all you girls hanging out with me, even though I've finished for the day. And you," she looked at Luke, "have driven all the way down here when you don't need to. It's too much. You kids should be getting on with your own lives, not worrying about me. I'm fine. And I'll be fine. I appreciate that you all want to keep me safe, but I'm not stupid. I can go to my apartment and lock myself in; I'll be safe there."

"You don't get it, Miss Candy." Rocket had come over to the booth and stood beside Luke with his hands on his hips. Spider came and stood beside him.

"What don't I get?"

Rocket smiled. "You said that we should be getting on with our lives – what you don't get is that we are. You're part of our lives, a very important part. We all want to do whatever we can to make sure that you're safe. We'd all rather be right here, hanging out with you than doing anything else. Not because you might be in some kind of danger and we feel that we need to babysit you, but because we enjoy spending time with you."

She had to blink away the tears that pricked behind her eyes.

Spider nodded. "You've kept saying that you don't want to intrude on our lives since you got here. Kept saying that we need our time with our girls – and we do. But we also want – and need – our time with you. We've missed you all these years. We wanted you to come up here to be part of our lives, not just part of the bakery."

Luke smiled at her and wrapped his arm around her shoulders as she sucked in a deep breath and tried not to cry. "And the rest of us, who didn't know you before, can see what an awesome lady you are, and we want to spend time with you and get to know you better, too." He held her gaze for a moment. "We all want you to be part of our lives – to become family."

She looked around at their eager, smiling faces. She loved them all. If they wanted to go out of their way for her, how could she tell them no? She'd gone out of her way for people her whole life. She'd done her best to be like family to Spider and Rocket. Why would she push them away when they were trying to do the same thing for her? Especially now that she was the one who might need help.

"I love you guys."

They all smiled and nodded and a chorus of *love you toos* washed over her and made her heart happy.

~ ~ ~

Deacon scowled at the phone on his desk when it rang. He wanted to get out of the office and go home. He was seriously considering taking some time off, especially after his conversation with Saunders this afternoon. He'd been inclined to dislike the man until he finally managed to speak to him, but now he was glad that he was the one handling the case involving Candy and what was going on with her pawn shop.

He blew out a sigh and picked up his phone.

"Sheriff Wallis speaking."

"Hey, Deacon, it's Trip. What's up, Chief?"

Deacon shook his head. "Is this official business?"

"No, why?"

"Can you call me back on my cell phone then?"

"Sure. Everything okay?"

"Everything's fine. I'm just trying to get out of the office. I'd rather talk to you on the drive home than hang around here any longer."

Trip laughed. "I get it. I'll give you five minutes and call you on your cell. I know how it goes; if you stick around to take a personal call, you'll probably end up getting roped into something else just because you're still there."

"Yeah. Talk to you in a few."

Deacon hung up. As much as he wanted to hightail it out to his truck and back down the valley to the bakery, he took the time to check in with the undersheriff and the deputies who were on the late shift before he left.

He was just pulling out of the parking lot when his cell phone rang.

He hit the button on the steering wheel and said, "Talk to me, Trip. What's up?"

Trip laughed. "Nothing's up. I haven't caught up with you in a while. I wanted to check in and see how things are going."

"Everything's good in my world. How about you? Staying busy?"

"You know it. Between the clinic and the hospital, there's never a dull moment. Have you got a busy weekend? Want to get together for a beer or three? I was thinking about calling Ace as well. I might even try Emmett. He keeps saying that it's about time he came out with us. He says he feels okay about it, now that the girls are used to Brooke coming over to hang out with them."

Deacon laughed. "He's been saying that for years. He talks a good story, but when it comes down to it, he can't bring himself to go out and leave the girls at home, whether it's with Brooke or Janey or anyone else."

"You're right. I think he's getting closer, but he might not be ready yet. But you're up for it?"

Deacon pursed his lips as he waited at the red light. He hadn't caught up with his friends in a while. They tried to get together at least once a month, but it had been more like two since the last time they'd all gone out for a beer. He wanted to do it, but he didn't want to leave Candy by herself. It wasn't just because he wanted someone with her at all times either; no, it was because he wanted to be with her.

"You still there?"

"Yeah."

"You can bring her if you like."

"Who?"

Trip laughed. "Who do you think? That little lady who's living in your upstairs apartment: Candy."

Deacon didn't know what to say. He shouldn't be surprised that Trip knew there was something going on. There was no way to keep anything secret in the valley. He frowned. It wasn't that he wanted to keep her a secret anyway. He didn't like that idea. He had nothing to hide. More importantly, he'd hate for Candy to feel that he didn't want people to know what was going on between them – even if he didn't know exactly what it was himself yet.

"Say something!" said Trip. "If you're pissed at me, you can tell me to butt out, and you know I will. But the fact that you haven't bitten my head off yet says that you're not mad at me. You're …"

Deacon smiled to himself. Trip had a habit of doing that. Maybe it was his way to elicit information from patients. Deacon used the tactic himself when he was trying to gather information. It was human nature to finish a sentence for someone just to fill what would otherwise be an uncomfortable silence. He normally wouldn't fall for it. But what the hell. "You're right. I'm not mad at you. I'm …" He wasn't sure that he knew how to explain it.

"Out of your element?" suggested Trip.

"Yeah. That. I … I've been spending some time with her."

"So I hear."

Deacon didn't even want to ask where he'd heard. He probably didn't want to know just how far the gossip about his personal life had already spread. "Yeah. She's … she's a lot of fun."

"It's more than fun, though, isn't it?"

Deacon blew out a sigh. "Yeah."

There was no point in denying it. Not to Trip. Trip was one of his oldest friends. They'd grown up together. They'd been friends all the way through grade school and high school – even though Deacon's dad was the town drunk, and Trip's dad was a retired Hollywood actor who'd bought one of the biggest ranches in the valley. It hadn't mattered that Deacon had lived in a rundown rancher in town while Trip lived in a full-blown mansion on the bank of the Yellowstone River surrounded by several thousand acres of land. They'd had no secrets from each other in kindergarten, nor in high school, nor when they'd served together in the military.

It wasn't that he wanted to keep anything secret from his friend now. It was just that he didn't know what to say.

"Listen," said Trip. "I've got another call coming in. I'm going to have to go. But if you want to bring her out, you know we'll make her welcome. For what it's worth, I like her. I know you don't need my opinion, but I'm going to give it to you anyway. I think she'd be good for you. From what I've seen, she's down-to-earth, she's good fun, and her heart's in the right place. She's everything that Willa wasn't. Maybe it's time to move past what Willa did to you. Move on. Be happy."

"I moved on years ago," Deacon said indignantly.

"Did you really?" Trip laughed. "I'm not looking for an answer. I've got to go. But maybe you want to think about the question. Call me if you want to go out. In fact, call me either way. Even if it's only to chew me out for overstepping. See ya."

The call ended and Deacon fixed his gaze on the highway ahead of him. He didn't know what Trip was getting at, but he had half an hour's drive ahead to think about it.

Before he did, though, he wanted to make another call.

"What's up?" Luke answered.

"Are you at the bakery? Is Candy still there?"

Luke laughed. "Yeah. She's fine. I came down here because I didn't want her to be by herself till you got back, but she's got plenty of company."

Deacon's heart rate picked up at that. "What do you mean? Who's with her? You're not or you wouldn't be talking about her like that."

"Jesus, Deacon, keep your hat on! I just went to the bathroom. And Candy's surrounded by the girls. Frankie, Janey, and Sierra have been with her since she finished work. And Libby arrived a little while ago. I should have thought about it before. Libby must be around the same age as Candy.

The girls all love her, but it might be nice for her to have someone older to talk to. She can't help it; she joins in the fun, but she's like a mom to all of them."

Deacon had to smile. He'd noticed that about Candy. She was just a natural nurturer. He didn't know if Luke realized it, but she did it with him, too.

"Do me a favor?"

"What?"

"If Libby looks like she's going to leave before I get there, either ask her to hang on or tell her I'll give her a call?"

"Sure. It's good to see her out. I hate that she's not one of the gang anymore, not like she used to be."

"Yeah." Deacon did, too. Libby was another one he'd known all his life. She and Frankie's brother, Maverick, had started going out in their sophomore year of high school and they'd been together – mostly – since then. They'd gotten married young, but they'd been on again and off again for years. It looked like they were finally off for good now. They'd gotten divorced a few years ago. Maverick had only set foot in the valley a handful of times since then. And Libby had withdrawn from their group of friends, which none of them was happy about.

If becoming friends with Candy might mean that Libby started hanging out with everyone again, then Deacon was all about it. He'd love to see both women happy.

"I'll be there in about twenty minutes."

"Okay, see you then."

Chapter Twelve

Candy looked over at Deacon as his truck bumped its way down a long gravel road. He was gorgeous! Ever since she'd admitted that to herself – when he'd answered his door with no shirt on – it seemed like he got more attractive every day. Right now, he looked relaxed as he drove. He was dressed in jeans and a light blue button-down shirt. She loved the way he looked in his uniform, but she was definitely enjoying the more casual look on him, too.

He chuckled. "What? If you have something to say, you can just say it, you know."

She laughed when she realized that she'd been ogling him, and he'd caught her. "I was just enjoying the view." She loved the hint of pink that appeared on his neck. He wasn't exactly the shy, retiring type. He was more confident and commanding. It surprised her that he'd get embarrassed. It surprised her, but she liked it, too; liked knowing that she could affect him that way.

He rolled his eyes and mumbled something about her eyesight; she just laughed.

"Are you sure you're okay with this?" he asked. "We won't stay late. I just …"

"Of course not. I'm looking forward to it. I feel bad, though."

He shot a puzzled look at her. "Bad? Why?"

"Well, from what I've gathered, this is your night out with the boys. I'm kind of crashing it because you want to keep an eye on me." She'd told him several times that she really didn't think there was much reason for concern. She wasn't going to take any silly risks, and she'd be fine locked in her apartment.

He reached across the console and took hold of her hand, lacing his fingers through hers. "You're not crashing it. I want you here. I didn't ask you to come so that I can keep an eye on you."

She tried not to laugh and ended up making a very unladylike snort instead.

Deacon laughed. "Okay, so we both know that I do want to keep an eye on you. But that's not why I asked you to come tonight. I want you to get to know the guys. They want to get to know you, too. I …" He squeezed her hand before letting it go and taking hold of the steering wheel again.

"I've told you how I feel about you. I haven't dated anyone since my divorce. I haven't brought a woman out with my friends since Willa." He sucked in a deep breath and blew it out slowly. "I asked you to come because I want you to be here – with me. Not because I don't want you to be home alone."

Candy reached across and rested her hand on his arm. "Thank you."

He smiled. "Thank you. Thanks for coming and thanks for understanding what I mean. No pressure or anything, but this is a big deal to me."

She struggled to sit up in her seat and leaned across to land a kiss on his cheek. "It's a big deal to me, too. I love that you're looking after me, but I love even more that you want me around."

"I want you around."

Candy settled back in her seat with a big smile on her face. She could see herself wanting to be around Deacon for a long time to come.

"Are you ready for this?" Deacon asked as the road followed the creek through an avenue of cottonwood trees. "When we come around the bend in a minute, you're going to see Trip's place." He made a face. "You might decide that you'd be better off with him than me when you do."

Candy slapped his arm. "Don't you dare say stupid stuff like that. I don't know whether to be mad at you for thinking that I'd like some other guy more than I like you or mad at you because you think I'm the kind of woman who cares about money and big houses. Either way, I'm mad at you."

He shot her a shamefaced smile. "Sorry. It wasn't about you. I know you're not like that. It was about me … I …"

She smiled at him, wanting to reassure him. He might have surprised her with what he said, but she understood. "It's not even about you, is it? It's about Willa."

He frowned and nodded. "Yeah. I guess it is. I've been nervous about bringing you out here. Trip's a great guy. He comes from a great family. He's loaded. He's a doctor. Willa made no secret of the fact that she wished I was more like him. I think she was okay with me until I brought her to live here.

In the Navy, I was one of a group of equals. Out here, everyone knows my background."

Candy raised her eyebrows. "I don't."

"Yeah, you do. I was the town drunk's kid. The one who dragged himself and his little brother up because no woman would stick around to raise us. I suppose you don't know that the Wallis name has been as good as mud in this town for generations."

"But you're … you're Deacon!" Candy didn't know how to put what she meant into words.

"Yeah. I'm the sheriff now, and people have learned that I'm worthy of their respect, but …"

"No! I mean, yes, of course, you're the sheriff and everything that comes with that. But people can see who you are – Deacon the man, not just the sheriff, the position, the badge, but the living breathing man who wears it." Candy hated that he could think of himself as being any less than his friend – or anyone, for that matter.

He shot her a quick smile. "You mean that, don't you?"

She nodded emphatically. "I do."

"Thank you. But anyway." He pointed through the windshield. "There it is."

Candy had forgotten to look for the house when they'd emerged from the trees. Deacon hadn't been joking – it was beautiful. It looked more like a ski lodge than a house to her. It was so big. She shuddered.

"What's up?"

She laughed. "Just in case you don't believe me from everything else we just talked about it. I'd hate it if you lived in a place like that."

"Why?"

She laughed again. "I'm a practical soul. My first thought was how much work it must be to clean it, and my second was that I bet the heating bills are horrendous."

Deacon laughed with her. "Sounds like we're a pair together, then, you and me. I could buy another place if I wanted, something bigger, fancier. But I don't need it. My place suits me. I've always liked having the apartment and being able to help people by letting them rent it when they're new in town, or when they're making a change in their lives." He shot her a quick smile. "It's handy, too. I don't want to live up in town. But I like being right there by the highway – and by the bakery. I've always been happy about that, but I'm even happier about it lately."

She smiled back at him. "I'm very happy about it, too. I was scared to death when I first arrived here. I thought I was going to have to drive for miles and miles in the dark to get to work every morning. Your place is perfect. But the fact that it's close to work isn't what I like best about it."

"No?" Deacon cocked an eyebrow, and she could see a little smile playing on his lips as he asked, "What is then?"

"It's the fact that you live there."

He brought the truck to a stop next to a couple more that were already parked behind the house. He unfastened his seatbelt and leaned toward her, beckoning with his finger for her to come closer.

She couldn't help smiling as she rested her arms on the console and met his gaze. His eyes were twinkling, and she really needed to get him to wear that smile more often.

"I like a lot of things about that house, but I have to agree with you. What I like best about it is that you live there, too."

He tucked his fingers under her chin and planted a soft, sweet kiss on her lips that made Candy's heart feel as though it was melting in her chest.

He leaned back and smiled, but she followed him and planted a peck on his lips. "You, Deacon Wallis, are amazing."

He chuckled. "I'm glad you think so because I'm going to do my best to make you never want to leave that house of mine."

She nodded happily. She already knew that she'd stay forever if he wanted her.

~ ~ ~

Deacon got up from his seat and started gathering plates. Dinner had been great – good food and even better company. Emmett hadn't made it, but Libby had surprised him and texted him back to say that she'd be here.

As he followed Trip through the patio door into the kitchen, he looked back over his shoulder. Seeing Candy and Libby sitting there chatting with Ace made him feel good. It felt like he was seeing his past and his future come together. He'd known Ace and Libby nearly his whole life and seeing Candy sitting there with them on Trip's deck, the majestic mountains glowing under the setting sun behind them made him feel as though he was entering a new chapter.

Trip took the plates from his hands with a grin when he reached the kitchen. "You good, Chief?"

Deacon nodded.

"I'm glad you came, and even more glad that you brought her."

"Me too." He wasn't sure that he was up for talking about what was going on between Candy and him, but he was glad that Trip liked her. He already knew that Ace liked her. He glanced back out through the door. Ace had the two women laughing. He'd always been the ladies' man of their group.

"I'm glad you managed to talk Libby into coming as well. I feel bad that we don't get to see much of her anymore."

"Yeah. It's her choice, though. We've all tried asking her. She usually says that she's too busy. I hate that she kind of chose sides for us after the divorce – and she put us on Mav's side."

"I don't think she sees it that way. She just doesn't want to put us in a difficult position."

"How would it be difficult?" Deacon asked. "Mav's never here anymore. He came back for Frankie's engagement – because Spider asked him to be there when he proposed. Before that, he came when those two first met."

Trip laughed. "Because he was ready to run Spider out of town rather than let him anywhere near his little sister."

"True. But do you remember the last time he was here in the valley before that? I don't. He has Ace running the ranch for him. He has no need to come back, and we both know that he stays away because he doesn't want to run into Lib. So, it wouldn't be difficult or awkward for her to hang out with us – because he's not here."

Trip blew out a sigh. "You're right. Let's just hope that tonight's a turning point, and she'll be around more in the future. I don't think she's had much of a life these last couple of years. She has her riding program, teaches the kids, but other than that, I don't know what she does with herself. I know she's living in that little apartment in town – and that has to suck after living on the ranch."

"Yeah." Deacon looked out through the door again. Ace was getting up from the table and heading toward them.

Trip chuckled by Deacon's side. "Whatever you're worried about, you don't need to."

"Huh?" Deacon gave him a puzzled look.

"We've been in here for less than five minutes, and you've looked out to check on her at least three times. You can bet your ass that she's not going to come to any harm out on my deck – even if someone has followed her here from LA, this isn't the time or place they'd make a move to hurt her. She and Libby have been getting along great – I'd guess that they're going to become good friends before you know it. The only other thing I can think that you might be worried about is Ace making a move on her." Trip laughed. "Yes, I'm joking. We both know he never would. But even if he did, he'd be out of luck. He might be the one the ladies usually go for, but Candy only has eyes for you. She is one smitten kitten."

Out of everything he'd just said, Deacon could only laugh at that last part. "Smitten kitten? Do people even say that?"

Trip shrugged and grinned at Ace as he came through the door from the deck.

"Did the party end up in here?" Ace asked.

"I was just taking our friend aside for a moment of truth," Trip said with a smile.

Ace turned to Deacon. "You need a pep talk?"

"No. I'm good."

Ace laughed. "I hope you are. Candy's awesome. If you're having any doubts, you'd better spill 'em right now, and we'll help you work past 'em. You don't want to let that one get away."

Deacon had to smile. Conversation between the three of them was usually wide-ranging, covering anything from sports to cattle to state politics. He couldn't remember the last time they'd talked about women. Definitely not about a woman one of them was involved with. For that matter, he couldn't remember the last time any of them had been in a relationship. Sure, there had been times over the years when one of them had been seeing someone, but rarely for more than a couple of weeks. "You're right, I don't want to let her get away."

His friends grinned at him.

"Then let's get back out there and set up a time when we can do this again," said Ace. "Candy's a bit more outgoing than you are. We can help you set up a social life for her."

Deacon gave him a rueful smile. Ace might have a point, but he was also the one who was always eager to get out and do more.

~ ~ ~

Candy hugged Libby one more time. "You be sure and call me, okay?"

"I will. And I'll make sure that I stop into the bakery on my way up or down the valley this week, too."

"Good." Candy really liked her. The two of them had hit it off straight away, and she was looking forward to getting to know Libby better.

She watched as Deacon hugged her next. When he stepped back, he put his hands on Libby's shoulders and looked into her eyes. "I'm glad you came, Lib."

Libby nodded. "Me too. Thanks again for asking me."

Ace stepped forward and slid his arm around Libby's shoulders. "Can we call tonight a new beginning? We've missed you."

Candy had been surprised at first by how close Ace and Libby were. But when the men had gone inside, Libby had explained that when she was married to Maverick and lived down on his ranch, she'd been around Ace every day since he lived there, too. She'd said that she missed all the guys since she and Maverick had divorced.

Libby rested her head against Ace's shoulder and nodded. "Yeah. I'd like that."

"Okay. I'll play social secretary, then," said Ace.

"How about we go for something once a week for the rest of the summer at least?" asked Trip.

Libby looked hesitant, but Ace took hold of her chin and nodded it up and down, saying, "Yep, we're both up for that."

Candy laughed and looked up at Deacon.

He cocked an eyebrow at her. "I'm waiting for you to say if it's okay with us."

That sent a rush of warmth through her. She liked the idea of them being an *us*. She liked it a lot.

She laughed. "You might wish that you hadn't left it up to me if I rope us into more than you want to do."

Trip winked at Deacon. "She knows you well, my friend." He turned to Candy, "How about we make the arrangements, and if he whines about it, you come and tell me."

Deacon scowled, but she could see the twinkle in his eyes as he said, "I don't whine!"

Trip just laughed. "You might start if we line you up with a hopping social life when all you want to do is stay home with your lady."

Candy felt the heat in her cheeks at that. The thought of staying home with Deacon instead of going out conjured up ideas of what they might want to stay in for.

Deacon tightened his arm around her shoulders and narrowed his eyes at his friend.

"Just let me know what you come up with," said Libby. "I need to get going."

Ace nodded. "Me too."

Once they were back in Deacon's truck and bouncing their way back along the gravel road, Deacon reached for her hand and linked his fingers through hers.

"Did you enjoy tonight?"

"I loved it! Thank you so much for bringing me. I already knew that I liked Ace from the times that I've seen him in the bakery. I like Trip, too, but I've only met him a couple of times before tonight. And Libby's lovely. I can see us becoming good friends."

Deacon smiled happily. "I was hoping you might say that. Libby's great. I'm not trying to orchestrate your life for you, but I think it'll be good for you to have her as a friend, and I think it'll be good for her, too."

"It sounds like it," said Candy. "She didn't get into it too much, but it sounds like life hasn't been easy for her since her divorce."

Deacon shot her a quick look. "Not easy how? What did she say?"

"Nothing in detail. And I wouldn't repeat it to you if she had. I'm just reading between the lines. She said that she used to live on Maverick's ranch, and from the way she talked, I couldn't miss that she loved it there. Now, she's in an apartment in town, and that's not really who she is, is it?"

Deacon blew out a sigh. "No. It's not. She could have stayed on the ranch. Mav would never have asked her to leave."

Candy held her hand up. "You don't need to defend him to me. Libby didn't complain about him or say anything bad. She said that he was more than generous in their divorce. If I had to guess, I'd say that she's still in love with him."

"Yeah." Deacon let go of her hand and gripped the steering wheel again. "There's no need to guess. We all know it. She's still in love with Mav, and he's still in love with her. But sometimes, I guess even love isn't enough."

"That's sad."

Candy stared out the window for a long while, lost in her thoughts. When Deacon finally brought the truck to a stop before turning out onto the highway, she looked up at the big arch that marked the gravel road they'd been on. "Wow! This is the entrance to Trip's place? I thought he just lived at the end of a very long dirt road."

Deacon laughed. "That dirt road is Trip's driveway."

She shook her head. "I can't even imagine." She couldn't imagine owning a property with a driveway that had to be a couple of miles long. And she couldn't imagine what it must be like to be in love with your husband and yet have so many problems that you felt the need to divorce each other.

"Penny for them?" Deacon asked after they'd been on the highway for a few miles.

"I was thinking about Libby and Maverick. It's so sad to me. Most of us never seem to find someone we're truly in love with. I know I never felt even half as strongly about Len as Libby still does about Maverick. Not even when we were young, and I thought I was in love with him. If those two can't make it, what hope is there for the rest of us?"

She couldn't wipe the smile off her face when Deacon reached for her hand again. She loved the feel of his long, strong fingers wrapped around hers. And she loved it even more when he said, "There's hope."

~ ~ ~

Clawson greeted them with his scratchy meow when Deacon let them into his place. It had struck a chord with him after they got home from their visit to the park and Candy had said that friends hung out together when they got home – and that she didn't want to go straight upstairs to the apartment. He'd made sure ever since that he brought her back to his place and let her decide when it was time to go.

It was getting late now, especially since she had to be up for work in the morning – which meant that he did too; no way was he letting her go to the bakery by herself at four-thirty in the morning when he didn't know how much of a threat the assholes from California posed. But no matter how late it was, he wasn't ready to say goodnight to her yet.

She bent down to greet Clawson, and he had to remind himself not to stare at her ass. She smiled at him when she straightened up. "Thanks again for tonight."

"Thanks for coming with me. I enjoyed it." He went to her and closed his arms around her, loving the way she fit so perfectly against him. "I know I shouldn't keep you, but …"

She smiled up at him. "I know. I should go up and try to get some sleep. But I'm kind of wired anyway. I had such a good time. And maybe a little too much wine."

He chuckled. "Do you want a glass of water – try to dilute it?"

"Please."

When he came back from the kitchen, she was settled on the sofa with Clawson in her lap. The sight hit him right in his chest. She looked right sitting there. It felt right having her here. He handed her the glass and sat down beside her.

After she'd had a drink, she set the glass down and then leaned against him, her head resting on his shoulder, her eyes shining up at him. "I think I'm more comfortable here with you than I ever was in any of the places that Len and I lived."

He curled his arm around her and held her closer. "I like having you here. This place feels more like home than it ever did before – with you in it."

She blew out a happy sigh. "I know I should go, but what do you think, do you want to watch TV for a while?"

Deacon reached for the remote. The last thing he wanted to do was watch TV, but if it meant that he got to sit here and hold her for a while longer, he was in.

When the TV was on, he gave her the remote. "Find whatever you like."

She flicked through the channels and settled on some reality show with a bunch of guys all dating the same woman. Deacon wasn't sure he liked or understood what was happening on the TV, but he loved watching Candy enjoy it. She laughed and tutted, and talked at the people, giving advice that made him laugh.

After a while, he realized that she'd gone quiet and when he looked down, he saw that she was fast asleep. He knew that he should wake her up and pack her off upstairs, but he didn't want to; not just yet.

He managed to lie them down on the sofa, his arm wrapped around her, her back to his chest. He rested his chin on top of her head and smiled. He'd just enjoy this for a little while.

It was after midnight when he opened his eyes again. Shit. He really should have let her go to bed. She was going to be tired tomorrow and it'd be all his fault.

He moved to sit up and she smiled at him through bleary eyes. "Sorry. I must have fallen asleep. I should go. What time is it?"

"It's my fault. It's after midnight." He got to his feet and took both of her hands to help her up.

She wrapped her arms around his waist and pressed her cheek against his chest. "I wish I didn't have to go."

"Then don't."

She leaned back to look up at him, and he smiled. "All I'm saying is that my bed's closer than yours. We'll both have to get up in a couple of hours. Do you want to just stay? I only mean to sleep. I'm not …"

She smiled big and nodded happily. "It felt so good sleeping with you on the sofa. I'd love to sleep with you … I mean, you know, *sleep* with you." She let out a low, sexy chuckle. "Don't worry, I'm too tired to ravage you. I'll keep my hands to myself."

Deacon laughed with her. "Damn! Maybe next time."

She held his gaze for a moment and nodded. "Definitely next time."

He swallowed and led her to the bedroom.

When he came out of the bathroom, she was already snuggled under the covers. He had no idea what she was wearing – but he was hoping for as little as possible. He only planned to hold her all night, but he couldn't wait to feel her skin against his. He'd dug out a pair of pajama bottoms from the dresser out of respect, but no way did he plan to wear a shirt.

She smiled up at him. "I hope you don't mind that I got undressed?"

He shook his head, not knowing if his voice would work.

She eyed his pajamas. "Do you always wear those?"

He shook his head again, and she laughed. "Don't let me put you out then."

He had to laugh as he pushed the pajamas down and off. "Thanks." He slid under the covers and curled his arm around her, drawing her to him.

He had to bite down on his bottom lip when her naked breasts pressed against his chest, and he couldn't hold back a moan when she slid her leg between his. "I know we're only sleeping," she said with a big smile, "but I still want to make the most of this."

He cleared his throat and nodded.

She laughed and pressed a kiss to his lips. "You're just too sweet. Would you rather I went over to the other side and kept a respectable distance?"

He couldn't help it; he closed his hand around her ass and held her against his aching cock. The way she gasped and writhed against him made him feel like he was ten feet tall. "Not only no, but hell no."

She chuckled. "Okay. I'll be right here then."

He pressed a kiss to her lips. "I think you'd maybe better turn over or I won't be getting any sleep."

She pecked his lips then pulled back. "And that's as much of a kiss goodnight as you can have – or you definitely won't be getting any sleep."

She turned over, and he wrapped his arm around her, holding her back to his chest. He couldn't resist running his fingers up and down her arm, before flattening his hand against her stomach.

She turned and looked up over her shoulder at him. "If you keep that up, all bets are off."

He chuckled and nuzzled his lips into her hair. "Okay. I'll behave – for now. But what do you think, should we get to bed earlier tomorrow night?"

Her eyes shone as they looked up into his, and she nodded. "Yes. We definitely should."

His already aching cock twitched at her answer. He pressed one last kiss to her lips. "Okay then. We will. But for now. Get some sleep."

She faced forward again and pressed her ass back against him. "Goodnight, Deacon."

He closed his eyes and held her tighter. "Goodnight Candy. I've set the alarm." He was hoping that knowing they had to be up at four-thirty might help him to focus on getting some sleep instead of on the woman in his arms. But he knew it was a forlorn hope – it was going to be a long night.

Chapter Thirteen

Candy checked her watch again. She was ready to go home. She'd loved staying with Deacon last night, but she hadn't slept very well. She'd drifted in light sleep, wanting to enjoy every minute of lying there with his arms around her.

She was paying for it today, though. He'd come over here to the bakery with her at four-thirty to open up. He'd hung around drinking coffee while she got everything set up for the day and the first batches of bread and pastries into the oven. He'd offered to help, but she didn't know how to let him. She had a system to get everything done, and it was easier to stick with it.

He'd left when Rocket showed up at six. The poor man still had to go home and get ready then drive up the valley to work. He'd said that he was going to try and finish early so that he could come back and take her home. He didn't want her going by herself. She didn't mind that, but the longer she had to wait, the more she was starting to think that it was a silly idea. That man on the phone had just wanted to scare her. He was hardly likely to come all the way up here after her.

"What time's Deacon coming?" asked Spider.

She shrugged. "Soon, hopefully. He said he'd call and let me know."

"We can figure something else out if you like. I don't imagine it's easy for him to get away, not with his job."

"I know! I keep telling him that I can just go home by myself."

Spider shook his head. "Not an option. If you want to go, Rocket or I can go with you."

"*That's* not an option."

"It's fine. The time you finish is the quietest part of the day anyway."

"I know, but it's also when you do cleanup out front. You both need to be here for that."

"One of us can handle it just fine. And if not, we can always flip the sign to *Closed*."

"Paul Webster! No way am I going to start costing you money, young man. You stay open to catch the stragglers."

Spider laughed. "Okay, Miss Candy. Don't get mad at me. All I'm saying is that you're more important. And you don't need to worry about costing me any money. This place is doing great. We could close every day at two if we wanted to and do just fine."

"Wow!" Candy was surprised at that. "I knew you were doing well, but … No, you couldn't do that. The whole valley comes in here on Friday afternoons, and from what I hear they always have – for years. You'd have a riot on your hands if you said you weren't going to be open."

Spider laughed. "I didn't mean Fridays. Just the rest of the week. Or maybe even the first half of the week. It's just an idea I've been kicking around. I …" He stopped and smiled when her phone rang.

"I bet that's Deacon. Come out front when you're done. We can either sit and have a break while you wait for him, or I'll take you home."

"Okay." She wasn't thrilled about the idea, but she was tired enough today that if Deacon wasn't going to be back soon, she might just let Spider go back to the apartment with her. She felt bad about it – but she wasn't the one who insisted that she couldn't be by herself.

"Hi, Deacon."

"Hey, darlin'. How are you holding up?"

She had to smile. She loved the sound of his voice – especially when he called her *darlin'*. "I'm okay. Tired, if I'm honest."

"I knew you would be. I'm sorry."

"I'm not."

He chuckled. She loved the way that sounded, too. "Listen, I hate this, but I'm not going to be able to get away for a while yet. Something's come up at work."

"That's fine, I can …"

He sighed. "Please don't say you can go by yourself."

"Aww."

"Aww, what? I thought you were going to be mad at me for bossing you around."

She laughed. "You're not bossing me, and if I thought you were, I would be mad. You're just trying to do what you think you need to. And I appreciate it, even if I don't totally agree that it's necessary. But just like you're looking out for me, I'm looking out for you, too. I had a feeling that you might not be able to get back early. And I hate that you think you need to. You don't. But since I know that it bothers you, I was just talking with Spider and he's happy to go with me. On a normal day, I'd just hang around here a while longer, but I really am tired."

"I know, and I'm sorry …"

"Don't be. I'm not."

She could hear the smile in his voice when he spoke again. "I know we talked about going to bed early tonight, and I still want to do that. But what do you think, should we just sleep again?"

"Yeah." She had to smile. She'd love to go to bed with him to do more than sleep. But that time would come. In her mind, it was more important that they were comfortable enough with each other to want to share a bed. The rest would come – she had no doubt about it. Her cheeks flushed as she remembered the way his hard cock had pressed against her ass for much of the night.

"I'd like that." She looked over her shoulder before she added, "I'll look forward to the rest, too, but we'll get there when the time's right."

"We will – and I should warn you that I don't think I'll be able to wait too long."

"Good. I don't want to."

"And you're sure Spider's okay to go with you? I was going to call Ace and ask him."

"Honestly, we were just talking about it when you called. I promise you that I wouldn't lie to you. If I was going to go by myself, I'd tell you."

"Thanks. I'd come back right now if you were."

She laughed. "I know. That's the only reason I'm letting Spider go with me. You need to know that I'm okay, but you have to work. I get it."

"Yeah. And speaking of work, I need to go."

"Okay. I'll see you later. Oh, do you want me to let Clawson out?"

"If you don't mind. There's a key on top of my door frame. I left it there for Brad."

She had to laugh. "Do you remember how short I am?"

"Shit." He chuckled. "But Spider's with you, right? He can reach it."

"True. I'll see you later then."

He was quiet for a long moment.

"What's up?" she asked eventually.

"Nothing's up, darlin'. I just … I guess I was waiting for you to ask what time I'll be there, and what I'm doing that I can't come right now and …"

Candy sighed. "You'll be here when you get here, and if you want to tell me about it, you'll tell me when you get home. If I keep you on the phone any longer, I'm only holding you up from whatever it is that you need to do, right?"

"Right."

She chuckled. "It's all okay, Deacon. It's good. We're good. I'm happy."

"Good. That's all I want."

"Okay. I'll see you later then."

"Yeah. See you later." She heard him suck in a deep breath before he said, "Candy?"

"Yes?"

"I …"

Her heart started to race. She didn't know why, but it felt like he was about to say something important. She held her breath as she waited to hear what it was.

"I'll see you later. Bye."

She didn't get the chance to finish her "Bye" before the call ended. Whatever it was he was going to say, it seemed he'd changed his mind. Bless him.

Deacon shook his head as he set his phone back down. He'd chickened out. He'd wanted to tell her … what? What exactly had he been planning to say? He didn't even know. He just wanted her to understand how much she meant to him.

He'd been dreading calling to let her know that he was stuck at work. He'd expected a barrage of questions. He'd expected to hear at least disappointment, if not resentment, in her tone. Instead, she'd been her usual sweet, straightforward self.

Every time he braced himself for her to react badly to something he said or did, every time he was ready to defend himself and appease her, she showed him that he didn't need to worry.

Maybe Trip had a point, and he needed to move on from everything Willa had done. He'd thought he had moved on. It was a long time ago now, and he'd thought that it was all behind him. But he was starting to see that his reactions and expectations when it came to women – in particular when it came to being in a relationship with a woman – were born of his relationship with Willa.

Candy was nothing like her. She was a sweetheart. And not just with him, but with everyone. It was who she was. He was being unfair to Candy every time he waited for her to react in the way that Willa would have done. And now that he understood that it didn't sit well with him.

He blew out a sigh and pushed to his feet. The sooner he got back to work, the sooner he could go home. As he reached for his hat, he couldn't help thinking that Candy would laugh with him later when he told her the reason that he was late home. The assistant director at the old folks' home had asked him to come in and reassure some of the residents that the government was not about to take their vegetable garden through eminent domain. He didn't know how that rumor had gotten started, but he'd guess that Leland Pryor, a former lawyer, and current Sunnyside resident with dementia, might have something to do with it.

After he quelled the uprising – apparently Mrs. Connelly was trying to organize the other residents to defend the vegetable garden – he was going to have a chat with Leland. It was tough to see him as he was now. Deacon remembered him as a brilliant attorney, who argued and won many a case at state. He didn't know whether he'd get to talk to Leland the attorney, or Leland the rabble-rouser today. But either way, Deacon was fairly certain that he'd be able to talk him down – and avert a revolution.

Luke caught him in the hallway as soon as he came out of his office.

"Where are you off to? Are you headed home?"

"Not yet. I've got to stop at Sunnyside first."

Luke frowned. "Is everything okay?"

"It will be. I just need to reassure some of the old folks."

Luke checked his watch. "What about Candy?"

Deacon couldn't hide his smile. They hadn't talked about it, but at some point, he was going to have to thank Luke for setting him up to drive Candy home from the yard sale the other week. Deacon didn't know how long it would have taken him to wake up to his feelings for Candy otherwise. Or if he would have. That thought didn't sit well.

"What?" Luke gave him a puzzled look. "What are you smiling at me like that for?"

Deacon laughed. "I like that you're looking out for her. That's all. And …" He cleared his throat. No time like the present. "And I'm grateful that you were looking out for me, too."

Luke grinned. "No need to thank me. I'm just happy that you got your head out of your ass. I could see what was going on. I knew it was a risk to push you, but it worked out okay, right?"

"More than okay."

"I know. I'm hoping for big things for you and Candy."

Deacon pursed his lips. He wasn't going to ask what kind of things.

"Do you want me to ride down there and take her home? I heard you guys were over at Trip's last night. I don't imagine that she'll want to hang out at work after her shift. I'd offer to go to Sunnyside for you so that you can go, but you're the only one those guys will listen to."

"It's okay, thanks. I already called her. Spider's going to go home with her and stay till I get there."

"Okay. How real do you think the threat is? Has she heard anything else?"

"No. Nothing since that phone call. I'm inclined to think that whoever called was just messing with her. But at the same time, it's not a risk that I'm prepared to take."

"I agree. She might think it's a pain in the ass to always have one of us around, but she's better off being irritated than having something happen to her."

"Yeah. And she's … she's not that irritated. She gets it." Deacon smiled. "She says that she doesn't necessarily agree, but she understands that I have to do what I think I have to do, so she's okay with it."

Luke grinned at him. "I like her."

"Yeah."

"Go on, admit it. You like her?"

Deacon laughed. "What are we – kids on a playground? I think it's kind of obvious that I like her."

"And things between the two of you are going somewhere?"

"Yeah."

Luke grasped his shoulder and nodded. "Awesome. I want to see you happy, and I think Candy's the one who can make you happy."

Deacon held his gaze. He didn't want to spoil the moment, but he had to say it. "I could say the same thing to you, little brother."

Luke's smile faded, and Deacon thought he'd blown it. He was relieved when Luke said, "If you did, you'd probably be right. But it's a lot more complicated for me." He chuckled. "And besides, you're the one who's getting old. It's more pressing for you to sort your shit out."

Deacon had to laugh with him. "I'll let you get away with that since I have to go, but I'm not that old, and you can't keep making excuses."

"I know. I'm thinking that next time she comes home …"

Deacon waited, but Luke just shook his head.

"Next time she comes home, maybe I won't be such a coward."

"I hope you won't."

"Anyway, don't you need to get your ass to Sunnyside?"

"Yeah. I do. But don't think I'm letting you off the hook. Next time she's home, I'm going to remind you about this conversation."

Luke had already turned away and simply waved over his shoulder as he headed for the breakroom.

~ ~ ~

Later that night, Candy snuggled into Deacon's side as they sat on the sofa. She was having trouble keeping her eyes open, but it was early, and she didn't want the evening to end. She'd decided that as much as she loved sitting out in the yard, looking at the mountains, sitting with Deacon on the sofa like this was her new favorite place.

He tightened his arm around her shoulders and kissed the top of her head.

"Time for bed?"

She turned to look up at him. "I don't want to go."

"I don't want you to, either. I thought you were going to stay again."

"I am. If you want me to. But once we go to bed, then we'll go to sleep, and then today will be over."

He cupped her face between his hands and pressed three quick kisses to her lips before leaning back so that he could look into her eyes.

"But then tomorrow will be here, and we'll get to do it all again. That's how I want this to go, darlin'. I want to wake up with you every morning and go to sleep with you in my arms every night."

"I want that, too, Deacon."

She loved the way his eyes shone when he smiled like that. "Then you've got it. I'm not great with words or mushy stuff, but you mean a lot to me already. Every day that passes you mean more to me. You become an even bigger, more important part of my life." His smile faded. "I hope you're okay with that?"

She nodded happily. "I am. And I hope you understand that I feel the same way about you. You're … you're something special, Deacon. I feel … close to you. Closer than I think I've ever felt to anyone before."

He pressed another kiss to her lips. "I'm the same with you. Come on, I want to get you into bed and hold you close all night."

She took his hand and let him pull her to her feet. Then she planted her face in his chest and wrapped her arms tightly around his waist. "I'm looking forward to the day that we get to go to bed and do more than sleep."

A rush of heat coursed through her veins when he slid his hands down to cup her ass and held her against him.

"That day's coming real soon, darlin'."

His breath in her hair as he spoke sent shivers down her spine, and she wanted to persuade him that day – or night – was already here. But she was tired, and she knew he was. It was better to wait. And besides, sleeping wrapped up in his arms was almost as good.

He held her tighter, and the feel of his hard body pressed against hers made her smile to herself. Sleeping together might be *almost* as good, but she knew without a doubt that *almost* wouldn't come anywhere close to everything else they'd share.

Chapter Fourteen

Deacon checked the clock on the wall. It had been a long week, and he was ready to go home. He was going straight to the bakery to collect Candy, and their plan was to sit out back, have a few drinks and a quiet dinner, and then watch TV. It made him laugh. The TV had been on more since he'd known her than it had for years before. He didn't mind, though. She enjoyed watching it, and he enjoyed watching her – and listening to her. She liked to talk to the people on the box and she usually made him laugh. Sometimes, she made him stop and think with what to her were throwaway comments but to him were a whole new way to look at things.

He blew out a sigh when his phone rang, and he saw the name on the display. Mostly, he loved his job. Not everything that he did was enjoyable, far from it. But with most of his duties, he felt like he was doing good – like he was contributing to his community, making it a better place.

Whenever Sharon Anderson called, though, he knew that he was going to be called upon to do something that he didn't enjoy – and that he didn't feel was doing much good. He wouldn't deny that her fundraisers contributed to the community. She'd raised a lot of money for the school, and the animal shelter, and a few other good causes. What he didn't get was why she always wanted him to be there. He didn't mind giving money. He didn't mind showing his face when he knew it made sense. There were plenty of events where that was true. But when it was just a case of the wealthier members of the community getting together to slap each other on the back …

He reached for his phone. He should just get it over with.

"Sheriff Wallis."

"Deacon, darling. It's Sharon."

He couldn't stop the shudder that ran down his spine. He knew that group of women all called each other darling – usually while they were kissing the air somewhere near each other's cheeks. But he wished for the hundredth time that she'd just call him Sheriff.

"Sharon. What can I do for you?"

She laughed. He really had to get over it. Even her laughter grated on his nerves.

"Always so obliging."

He was, but only because he felt he had to be.

"I'm calling to let you know about the next fundraiser dinner. It's for the fire department. They have a shortfall on their budget this year, as I'm sure you know."

Deacon pursed his lips. He knew all about the budgets of the various county departments – because he had to draw up his own and then sit through endless meetings with the county treasurer and everyone else who was vying for funds.

Of course, county budgets were a matter of public record, but Sharon's recent and budding *friendship* with Scott Lopez, the new fire chief, was a matter of public record, too. Deacon wasn't sure that her putting her fundraising power behind his department would be well received by some folks.

"Most departments fell short this year," was the most non-committal, non-judgmental reply he could come up with.

"Yes. And the committee plans to help everywhere we can. We're starting with the fire department since it's mostly volunteers."

"Yeah." Deacon wouldn't begrudge her that.

"Anyway. We're organizing a dinner on the seventeenth. I wanted to give you as much notice as possible. I've seated you at the head table." She let out a coy little laugh. "And of course, it'll just be you. Won't it?"

Damn! She was digging! He should have expected it, but she'd caught him off guard. It wasn't often that someone suckered him, but she'd managed it. Deacon smiled through pursed lips. He knew Candy was okay with people knowing that they were together. And he knew that she'd probably enjoy herself. In fact, he'd probably enjoy it too, if she was with him.

"As a matter of fact …" He almost laughed when he heard Sharon inhale sharply – she was probably thrilled that she was getting the official scoop on some gossip. "I'm going to need two tickets, and two seats together."

"I see." Deacon could just picture her rubbing her hands together. "Do you mind if I ask …?"

He couldn't help chuckling. "Come on, Sharon. Be real with me for once. Do you really need to ask?"

She laughed. "I don't know. I'm hoping that you're planning to bring the lovely Candy from the bakery."

"I am, too."

"Oh, Deacon!"

He was surprised at the emotion in her voice.

"What?"

"Just … I know you think I'm just a nosey old bat – that we're just a group of gossipy women with nothing better to do with our time, and you might be right. But we care about you. You're a good man. You deserve to be happy. And Candy's a sweetheart. We've all been hoping to get to know her outside of the bakery. If we can get to know her as your lady, that will be even better."

Deacon swallowed. He didn't know what to say to that.

Sharon laughed. "Sorry. I know I just over-stepped. I'll go now, but please, don't go thinking that we're a bunch of vultures looking to tear you apart and get the lowdown on your life. We'll all look forward to welcoming Candy into the community – and to seeing you happy. And now I'll stop talking. Bye."

"Sharon?"

"Yes?"

"I … err … thanks."

"There's no need, Deacon. Thank *you*."

Deacon shook his head as he hung up. Who knew? It seemed more and more lately that he'd been judging people and situations from a very cynical perspective. He still wasn't a hundred percent convinced that Candy would be safe with Sharon and her gaggle of friends. But he knew that she was more than capable of holding her own. And he'd have her back.

Candy maneuvered the car into a spot between two huge pickup trucks and breathed a sigh of relief when she cut the engine. Getting used to driving out here was more of a challenge than she'd bargained for.

Libby turned in the passenger seat and smiled at her. "Relax. You did it."

"Yes, but only because you were with me. I would have freaked out before I even made it up to town if I was by myself. And the interstate?" She shook her head. "I drove from the airport when I first arrived, but other than that this is the first time I've been on I-90. It's …" She shook her head again.

"It's all new and different, that's all. You'll get used to it."

Candy wasn't sure that she would. "Sorry, I'll stop being a wuss. You must think I'm pathetic. You drive up and down the valley every day from town to the ranch. All I did was get on the interstate and make it to Bozeman."

"It's different," said Libby. "You can't compare because for me, driving up and down the valley is my comfort zone. For you, everything that you've done since you moved out here has been outside your comfort zone. I don't think you're pathetic, far from it. I think you're awesome. If you took me to LA, I'm sure I'd be scared to death of things that you just take in your stride."

"Hmm. I didn't think about it that way." She wasn't about to tell Libby about some of the things she'd had to take in stride since Len had died; things like drug dealers, thieves, and criminals. But putting it that way did make her feel a bit better.

"You should. Give yourself some credit. You're doing great."

"Thanks. But now that we're here, you have to lead the way. I don't know where anything is or where to start."

Libby grinned at her. "I am happy to introduce you to the delights of shopping in Bozeman. There are some over-the-top super expensive places, but they're just traps for tourists and displaced Cali … Shit! Sorry."

Candy laughed at Libby's shame-faced expression. "No need. I understand. You weren't having a dig at me. I'm hardly one of the stereotypical Californians who moved out here and wants to throw my money around and turn the place into New California."

"I know. But I shouldn't talk like that, no matter what. It's not fair. It's like you said, that's only a stereotype. Some of the people you meet who moved here from there don't live up to it."

"Only some?"

Libby chuckled. "Stereotypes exist for a reason. But come on, you didn't drive all the way over the pass for us to sit here talking in your car. Let's hit the stores and see what we can find you to wear."

"I'm glad we did sit here for a few minutes. I think my legs have finally stopped shaking."

Libby put a hand on her arm. "I'll drive back if you like?"

"Hell no! I mean, thanks but no thanks. It might scare me silly, but I'll get the hang of it. The more I do it, the sooner I'll get used to it, right?"

Libby grinned at her. "Right. If you want, we can do this once a week – or however often you can fit it in. It'll get you used to driving, and it'll do me good, too."

Candy locked the car and they walked down Main Street arm in arm. "How will it do you good?" she asked after a little while.

Libby squeezed her arm. "I've kind of closed myself off from life these last few years. You know since … since Mav. I need to get myself a life again."

Candy nodded. "Well, I'd like to be your friend if you want one."

"Thanks. I think we're going to be good friends, you and me."

"I think you're right. I've never had a close female friend." She let out a short laugh. "I don't think I've had any friends really since high school."

"Aww, that's sad."

Candy shrugged. "Maybe. It's just how life worked out. How about you? You must have loads of friends. You've lived here your whole life, right?"

"I have but … I mean, sure. I know a lot of people. I have friends. But they're friends because we know each other by being around each other – when you go to a small school in a small town and you grow up with all the same people, you call them friends – whether they really are or not. God, sorry! That sounds wrong. There are lots of good people. I just, I don't have anyone I trust. Anyone who knows me inside out, who I can turn to. Well, I did. Mav was my best friend, even in school. And all those guys. Cash, Deacon, Travis, Trip, Ace, and Emmett. They were my friends."

Candy turned to look at her. "Did something happen? Something after your divorce – with the other guys?"

"What do you mean?"

"I mean, why don't you still consider them to be your friends?"

Libby shrugged. "I do but they were Mav's friends first. And … they're guys. I didn't want … don't want to make things difficult for anyone. So, I just closed myself off."

"Mind if I say something?"

"Go ahead."

"I think maybe you're not giving them enough credit. I think they still want to be your friend. Still want to be close with you. You know it yourself from the other night at Trip's house."

Libby nodded. "I know. You're right. And I'm … trying. At least, I'm going to give it a test run. See how things go. I've missed the guys and I'd love to have them back in my life, but the second Mav comes back again, I'm out."

"How likely is that?"

Libby shrugged again. "Frankie and Spider are talking about their wedding, aren't they?"

"Oh! Of course."

Libby smiled. "I don't think Frankie was too worried about how long they waited before they got married. But then Janey went and stole her thunder. I'd guess that Frankie won't want to wait much longer."

"Right, but Mav would only come back for a weekend, wouldn't he?"

Libby chuckled. "Frankie's not the only one who doesn't like to be outdone. Cash arranged Janey's wedding. Mav will probably want to do the same for Frankie – the same or better."

"Wow! I wouldn't have had two big, strapping cowboys like them down as wedding planners."

"They're not. They're just fierce, capable men who would do anything for the people they love."

Candy felt bad when she saw the tears shining in Libby's eyes. "Crap! I'm so sorry. I shouldn't …"

Libby held her hand up and sniffed. "Don't worry. It's nice to be able to talk about him – to think about the good side of him." She let out a short laugh. "To remember that he has one. Anyway. Here we go." She stopped outside a storefront and pointed at the window. "I do believe this is going to be the place where we find our fancy frocks for this fundraiser."

Candy laughed. "I don't think I've ever done a fancy frock or even a fundraiser before."

"Don't worry. It's nowhere near as snooty as it sounds. We'll have fun." Libby smiled. "And Deacon will. You have to know that by making him happy, you're making a lot of other people happy, too."

"Aww. He's a good man."

"He is, and he needs a good woman. I wasn't sure that he'd ever find one strong enough to break down his walls, not after Willa. But you're perfect for him."

Candy couldn't wipe the smile off her face at that. She wanted to be perfect for Deacon. She already knew that he was perfect for her.

"Here you go, gorgeous."

Deacon scowled at Tanner as he set Candy's drink on the bar in front of her.

Tanner just grinned at him. "Is there a problem, Sheriff?"

Janey laughed from her seat on the other side of Candy. "I'd say that the problem is that you're being a little too familiar with the sheriff's lady."

Deacon nodded and narrowed his eyes at Tanner.

Tanner just grinned at Candy. "Damn. Can't a guy pay a beautiful lady a compliment anymore? I'm just happy to see you here. Happy to see you smiling. And until *he* turned all grumpy on me, I would have said happy to see you out with this guy."

He leaned across the bar and beckoned Candy to come closer. She laughed and leaned toward him.

"If he gives you any trouble, you come tell me, okay?"

Deacon had to laugh. He'd spoken those exact words to more than one girl Tanner had been trying to charm into bed when he was a teenager. He was a good kid; well, he wasn't a kid anymore. He was in his mid-thirties, but he was a little younger than Luke. So, to Deacon, he'd probably always be a kid.

Candy nodded at Tanner and then sat back and leaned against Deacon. "Thanks, Tan. But I don't think he'll give me any trouble that I can't handle."

Deacon wrapped his arm around her shoulders with a smile. "You're right there, darlin'."

He hadn't been sure about this idea at first. When he'd stopped to pick Candy up from the bakery on his way home from work, Rocket had suggested that they all come over to Chico for a drink. It was still early. There were only a few tables occupied in the saloon. But this felt good.

Janey and Frankie had both shown up a little while after they arrived. Luke had called to say that since he was coming out to Chico tonight anyway, he'd just come early so that he could hang out with them for a while before they went home.

"What do you think?" asked Janey. "Should we go and get a table?"

"Aww." Tanner gave her big, sad puppy dog eyes. "Stay at the bar with me? I can hang with you here till it gets busy, but if you go and sit down I can't."

Deacon raised an eyebrow at Candy. He wasn't sure how she'd feel about perching at the bar.

He needn't have worried. She nodded happily and said, "I like it here. I haven't sat at a bar in years."

Tanner grinned at her. "You stick with me."

Deacon scowled at him again, but it was only for show. He loved the way Tanner made Candy smile.

"Hey, family!"

Deacon turned to see Luke making his way to the bar with a big grin on his face.

"Greetings, little brother."

Luke nodded at him then leaned in to kiss Candy's cheek.

Deacon had to hide a smile. The looks on Spider and Rocket's faces said that he wasn't the only one who felt protective toward her.

Luke laughed when he saw the way they were both looking at him. "Jesus, guys! Come on. Didn't you hear what I said?"

Rocket frowned. "What?"

"I said, *hey, family*. Because when you think about it, this is like a … a …" He looked puzzled for a moment and then laughed. "It's a family pre-union."

"*Pre*-union?" asked Spider.

"I don't get it," said Frankie.

Luke grinned, unperturbed. "If you think about it, this is like our first family gathering, and we're not even a family yet," he explained.

Deacon raised an eyebrow at his brother. He knew that family was a big thing for Luke. They'd never really had anyone but each other. Luke had grown up running wild with the MacFarland boys and wanted to belong in the way that they did with each other. Of course, he'd wanted to become a part of their family, too. But that was a whole different story.

Luke grinned at him. "Candy is Spider and Rocket's mom. Which makes Frankie and Janey sisters-in-law – even if you girls weren't already cousins," he added. "Tanner's Janey's brother, so he's already Rocket's brother-in-law and Spider's some kind of cousin-in-law or removed or something."

"Right," said Frankie. "But you …?"

Deacon's heart started to pound when Luke put his arm around Candy's shoulders, just below where his own lay. He looked Deacon in the eye over the top of Candy's head and told Frankie, "If Candy's your mother-in-law, and my sister-in-law then I don't know what the name is, but we're related somehow."

Deacon held his breath. The only way Candy would be Luke's sister-in-law was if she were his wife. He waited for the panic and horror to set in, but it didn't. He'd said that no way in hell would he ever get married again. But when Candy's head snapped back and her panicked gaze met his, he … loved the idea. He loved it so much that he smiled and nodded at her.

He didn't know what had come over him, but he didn't even care that all the kids were staring at him when he winked and dropped a kiss on her lips before he said, "He's right, darlin'."

Chapter Fifteen

It was still early when they got back to the house, but Candy felt like she'd had the best night out in years. She loved seeing Spider and Rocket with Frankie and Janey. Not only were they both happier with their girls than she'd ever dreamed for them, but the girls were close, too. The four of them were creating their own version of family.

That thought sent a shiver down her spine. Family. It was something she'd always wanted yet hadn't quite managed to create. She'd provided a home for the kids she'd fostered, but it had only ever been a temporary one. She'd wanted to adopt Spider and Rocket, but that just hadn't been possible – not with Len. She'd always felt that she was supposed to be a mom and gather a big loving family around her, people she could care for – and who'd care about her, too.

She'd thought she'd lost any possibility of that a long time ago. Since she'd moved up here, she was starting to believe that you could have a family like that made up of the people that you chose, even if they weren't 'family' in the traditional sense. But what Luke said? About if she were his sister-in-law?

She glanced across at Deacon when he brought the truck to a stop in the driveway. He cocked an eyebrow at her and gave her a sexy half smile.

"What's up, darlin'?"

She shook her head. "Nothing's up at all. I'm great. Happy. I really enjoyed that. Did you?" She wanted to hear what else he might have to say about Luke's take on how they were all becoming family. She'd panicked at first, thinking that he might be horrified. But his reaction had taken her breath away – in the best way. When he'd said that Luke was right, he wasn't just confirming a fact, he'd looked … happy about it.

Then again, maybe she was just getting carried away. She hadn't thought that she'd want to get married again; she doubted that he would either.

Clawson greeted them at the door, and Candy went to let him out the back door while Deacon got his bowl ready. She felt bad that the cat had been on his own all day. She'd gotten into the habit of coming to take him upstairs with her on the days when Deacon couldn't get back early, and Rocket or Spider came with her instead.

She leaned in Deacon's kitchen doorway and watched Clawson prowl around his usual spots before sharpening his claws on the fir tree. Then he ran up the fence and stalked his way along the top, looking for all the world as though he was surveying his property.

A flash of movement on the other side of the fence caught her attention and wiped the smile off her face. She'd pretty much forgotten about the phone call – about the man who'd told her that she wasn't safe here. It was hard to feel anything but safe with Deacon around.

She relaxed when he came to stand behind her and slid his arms around her waist. She leaned back against him and folded her arms over the top of his.

"In case I forget to tell you later, I had a wonderful time tonight. Thank you."

He chuckled and the feel of it rumbled through his chest and into her back, sending shivers chasing each other down her spine. They'd shared his bed every night since that first time, but all they'd done was sleep.

She loved the feel of him, of his arms, and of his bare skin against hers. But she was ready for more. Every time he touched her or held her, her skin heated, and an ache that had long ago become unfamiliar throbbed between her legs.

He rested his chin on top of her head and held her tighter. "I had a great time, too. But tonight isn't over yet."

There was something different about his tone, his voice was lower than usual, a little huskier. She turned within the circle of his arms and when she looked up into his eyes, she could see that he was feeling it too.

She slid her hands down to cup his firm ass and pulled him closer. "Are you saying what I hope you're saying?"

He chuckled again and the way his erection pressed into her belly gave her his answer even before he spoke.

"I wasn't sure if I should say it yet. But if you're hoping …"

She nodded happily. "I'm hoping. We're not kids. We both know what we're doing, and we both know what we want."

He nodded, his gray eyes stormy and intense as they held her gaze. "I know what I want, darlin'. I want you and I have for a while. I can wait until whenever you're ready, but it's getting harder."

She laughed and reached between them to cup the bulge in the front of his pants. "I noticed."

He smiled through pursed lips. "You're playing with fire, Candy."

"Ooh. I like the sound of that. Are you going to burn me up?"

He waggled his eyebrows. "I'll do my best." He looked over his shoulder. "Just as soon as we get that damn cat back in the house. "Clawson? Come on, buddy. Time to go in."

Candy inhaled deeply. This was it; the time was finally here. It'd been years since she'd had sex, but she wasn't nervous. She was eager – excited. She had a feeling that tonight would change things for them, change them for the better, and solidify what they already shared. She was more than ready.

~ ~ ~

As soon as Clawson came through the kitchen door, Deacon closed it behind him. He'd wanted this for a long while now. He loved having Candy sleeping in his bed, but every night it had gotten harder. He smiled through pursed lips – in every sense.

After he locked the door, he turned to Candy, wondering how to play this. It'd been a long time since he'd been with a woman. And even then, it hadn't meant much. This? This meant everything. He hadn't been able to shake Luke's words about Candy being his sister-in-law. Far from making him want to cool things with her or run, the thought of making her his wife made him want her more.

If he was ever going to open himself up – open his home, his life, his heart – to a woman, Candy was the one. When he met her gaze, all hesitation, all thoughts of maybe sitting on the sofa, talking for a while, doing anything other than what he now desperately needed, left his head.

Her eyes were shining; she didn't look nervous, she looked eager. He closed the distance between them in one long stride. When he reached her, he put his hands on her hips and drew her to him.

She opened her mouth to speak, but he lowered his head and claimed her lips in a kiss that declared his intentions. He'd kissed her a lot over the last several weeks. But this kiss was different. It wasn't about getting to know each other. It wasn't an exploration, or even an end in itself. No, as he tangled his fingers in her hair and pulled her head back to give him better access, this kiss was a claiming. As her hands came up to grasp his shoulders, he swept his tongue inside her mouth, letting her know what to expect. She was opening herself up to him, and he was about to make her his.

Keeping his hands on her hips, he started walking her back toward the bedroom. This wasn't the time for words. That time had passed. His heart swelled in his chest, and his dick swelled in his pants when her hands came down and started to unbutton his shirt. She felt it, too.

Without breaking the kiss, he fumbled with the buttons on her blouse, and had it open just as he backed her into the bedroom. His hands came up and closed around her full, heavy breasts.

The way she moaned into his mouth spurred him on. He reached around and unclasped her bra, then finally lifted his head so that he could stand back and get rid of his shirt. She let the bra fall to the floor, and he moved back in. He dropped his head needing to taste her skin. That vanilla smell of hers had driven him crazy for weeks. His bed smelled of her, he'd spent many of his night-time hours lying with his nose against pressed into her neck while she slept. Now, he finally got to taste.

Her hands came up and gripped his hair as he teased first one taut peak and then the other with his lips and tongue. He filled his hands, pinching and squeezing, loving the needy little noises she made.

Then her hands were on his belt, freeing him, pushing at his pants. He sucked harder on her nipple when his cock sprang free, and she closed her warm little hand around him. He stood back and pushed his pants and boxers down, kicking out of them and his shoes and socks in as much of a hurry as he could. He was glad that Candy was getting rid of her jeans and didn't notice that he was hopping around like a fool.

Then they were both naked. He put his hands on her shoulders and let his gaze travel over her. He bit his bottom lip, wanting to get back to worshiping her breasts again. But he wanted to drink in the rest of her gorgeous naked body first. She was round in all the right places. He loved that wherever he touched her, she filled his hands. This wasn't the time to be thinking about Willa, but she'd been slender; she prided herself on it, but there was no softness to her.

Candy looked up into his eyes and smiled. "I'm not going to make any excuses. I've never been skinny." She chuckled. "I'm built for fun."

He chuckled with her, loving that she wasn't ashamed of her body. He cupped his hand around the back of her neck and pressed a kiss to her forehead. "You're gorgeous. Perfect." He leaned back so he could look down into her eyes. "You're built for me."

Her expression softened and she put her hands on his chest as she rolled up onto the balls of her feet and pressed a kiss to his lips. "I like the sound of that." Her eyes sparkled with fun, then she glanced over her shoulder at the bed. "What do you think? Should we get in there and find out if you're built for me, too?"

He cocked an eyebrow, not understanding. He'd seen the way she looked him over. He was hoping that she might say he was built for her, too.

He saw the first sign of hesitation when she lowered her eyelashes and dropped her gaze.

He tucked his fingers under her chin and made her look back up at him. He didn't want to ask. It'd kill him if she wanted to change her mind. But he had to know. "You think I might not be?"

She pressed her lips together, and her cheeks flushed a deep red. "I … it's been a long time for me, Deacon. Years and years – so many that I've lost count. And …" she dropped her gaze again, and this time he realized that she was looking at his cock, which was standing proud, impatient for the talking to be over.

"… you're …" She rolled her eyes. "I knew you were packing a decent-sized weapon down there, but … damn! You might be built for a bigger woman than me."

A rush of emotions hit him at once. Of course, he liked hearing that she thought he was big. But he hated that it made her nervous. And even more than that, he hated that she could think of him with any other woman.

He cupped her face between his hands and looked deep into her eyes. "We're going to fit together just perfect, darlin'. You'll see. We won't even try until you're good and ready for me. And I'll tell you now – I'm built for you. No other woman. Ever. I'm yours. And after this …" He jerked his head toward the bed, not knowing what words to use. "After this, you're mine. All mine. Is that good with you? Because if it isn't …"

She nodded rapidly. "It's more than good, Deacon. It's … you're …" She smiled through pursed lips. "We're good. You might need to go slowly to start with. But you being mine? Me being yours? That's what I want. More than anything."

He held her gaze for a long moment and then nodded before he dropped his head to kiss her again. They'd said what they needed to. He was tempted to say one more thing. But he'd show her with his body before he told her with his words what his heart already knew.

~ ~ ~

Candy scrambled onto the bed and held her arms up to Deacon. Her heart was pounding as he lay down beside her and curled one arm around her, drawing her closer.

"I keep thinking that we're all done with words, but there's one more thing we need to talk about."

Candy's breath caught in her chest. She'd thought they were done talking, too. "What is it?"

"Like you said, we're not kids. But we still need to talk about …"

"Oh! Contraception? I didn't even think about that. I told you, I can't have kids."

The lines around his eyes crinkled deeper, and he pressed a kiss to her lips. "I didn't forget that, darlin'."

Of course, he wouldn't have forgotten that. She'd shared the biggest, darkest secret of her life with him, and he cared.

"I told you it's been a long time for me, but I've haven't been a monk. I get tested every year with my physical."

"Oh!" Candy felt dumb. He wasn't talking about contraception; he was talking about diseases. She made a face. "I got tested, too. After Len died. We hadn't had sex for years, but I freaked out when I found out about all the things he was into – the kind of man he really was. He could have been sleeping with other women our whole marriage and I wouldn't have known. I think getting tested was part of making sure that he hadn't left anything else hanging over my head that I didn't know about yet."

Deacon nodded.

"So, yeah." She wanted to bring him back to the moment, distract him from whatever he was thinking about Len – that had to be the cause of the thunderous look on his face.

She smiled. "If we want to find the bright side – and you know I always try to – he did me a favor. He made me feel the need to get tested. So, I know that I'm clean and we're good."

She pushed two fingers into his chest, wanting to see him smile again. "You should be happy about that. It'd suck if I'd never been tested and was only panicking right now about if he'd left me with one final issue to deal with."

She slid her hand down over his stomach and curled her fingers around him. The fact that she couldn't even close her fingers made her heart beat faster. But she was still trying to get him to smile.

She stroked her hand up and down his length. "I think we'd both be disappointed if we had to call time out right now."

He closed his eyes briefly, and when he opened them again, he smiled. "You're right. I'm glad we're good. Now. Are we finally done talking?"

She chuckled. "Umm, I think so. Unless you want to talk about …"

She didn't get the chance to finish the sentence as he put his hand to her shoulder and rolled her onto her back. Then he was there above her, his eyes smiling down into hers. "I don't."

He kissed her deep and hard, and she loved the weight of his body over her. She writhed underneath him, rocking her hips.

He lifted his head and made a tutting noise. "Don't be in too much of a hurry, darlin'."

"A hurry? I've been dying for this to happen for weeks!"

He pressed his face into her neck and when he chuckled there, it sent shivers racing over her skin.

"We're here now. Now, I get to touch you, and taste you, and learn every inch of this beautiful body of yours."

"Deacon." His name came out on a whisper as he nibbled her neck. One hand closed around her breast, his thumb circling her nipple.

He kissed his way over her collarbone and then down between her breasts, turning to nip and suck each one before he moved lower.

Her hands came up and gripped his hair tight when he dipped his tongue into her belly button. "Oh my God!'

He chuckled against her stomach and did it again. "You like that, huh?"

"I … Deacon!" This time he held her hips with both hands and kissed her deeply, right there in a place that had never occurred to her might be sexy before.

All she could do was hang on to his head until he lifted it. When he did, he gave her the sexiest smile. "I ever told you that you taste even better than your pastries?"

She swallowed and shook her head. She couldn't form words. She was soaked and aching for him after what he'd just done. And she knew what was coming next.

He proved her right when he kept moving down with that smug, sexy smile on his face. "I was hooked on the smell of you before I knew it. It's the vanilla."

Candy had to close her eyes when he pressed his nose against her skin – just above the place he was undoubtedly headed. He breathed in deeply.

"Yep, even down here. Vanilla. The smell of you has made me hard for months. And the thought of tasting you?" His hand slid up her inner thigh and she gasped as he traced his fingertips over her entrance. "Here?"

He gave her a wicked smile. "But sorry. You wanted to be done with the talking, right?" He used both hands to spread her thighs wider. "I'll be quiet now."

Candy's heart felt like it might beat right out of her chest. He held her gaze as he lowered his head. His fingers were still caressing her, and when he traced his tongue over her, she felt like she might have died and gone to heaven.

He lifted his head again and grinned. "Fucking vanilla! I knew it."

All she could do was lie back and hang onto his head as he worked her with his tongue and his fingers. He pinched her clit between his finger and thumb, and when her hips surged up in response, he sank his tongue inside her.

"Deacon!"

His only reply was to switch it up. His lips latched onto her clit, and he lashed her with his tongue.

She tensed when his finger breached her, but he moved slowly, pressing deeper but not too hard, not at first. Soon she was rocking her hips, desperately begging for more.

When he added a second finger, she switched her grasp to the sheet beneath her, afraid she might pull all his hair out if he kept this up.

She could feel the tension building low in her belly. Part of her wanted to make it stop. It was beyond her control. She was at his mercy. He was commanding her body to give him what he wanted and … and nothing had ever felt this good.

She gasped when he scissored his fingers inside her. He was stretching her, and a rush of heat coursed through her veins when she understood why.

He was getting her ready for … him. Then he added a third finger, slowly pushing his way inside her. She tensed at first, but when he started to move faster, she had no choice but to go with him. Her hips rocked in time with him as he pumped in and out of her.

When he closed his lips around her clit again and started to suck, she screamed. She hadn't felt anything like it before. Her orgasm hit her like a huge wave cresting over her. It was so powerful she felt she might drown. But Deacon was there, carrying her through it, driving her through wave after wave, until she was a gasping, shuddering wreck.

He eased her down, and then slowly, gently withdrew his hand. He didn't speak, but his smile said it all as he crawled back up over her body and wrapped her up in his arms.

She lay against him, boneless, incapable of words or even movement.

He pressed a kiss into her hair. "That was amazing."

"Huh? It was amazing for me! But how can you say that?"

The smile he gave her might have been his best one yet. He looked like the cat who got the cream. "Darlin', I got to drive the woman I love wild. I got to see you trust me – with your body, yeah – but more than that, with yourself. You gave yourself to me. You let me take you where you weren't even sure you wanted to go."

How did he even know that?

He pressed a kiss to her lips. "You let yourself go. You're even more beautiful when you come." That wicked smile was back, and he winked. "You ready to come again?"

She swallowed. She doubted that she could after that.

"I want to go with you this time."

Oh, well in that case. It was only fair if … He curled his arm around her, drawing her under him. Then he opened her legs wider with his knees. The feel of his hard cock pressing against her sent new shocks of excitement zinging through her veins. Maybe she could come again?

He propped himself up on his elbows with a more serious look in his eyes. "Do you want this? Do you want me?"

"I want this, I want you, more than I've ever wanted anything in my life, Deacon."

His smile melted her heart. "Okay then. Hang on for the ride."

She wasn't sure what he meant, but she took him at his word and closed her hands around his ass. If she was going to hang on, why not?

She closed her eyes when his hot, hard head pressed against her entrance.

"Look at me, darlin'."

His eyes were right there, inches from her own. The connection between them there was just as intense as the connection they made as he slowly pressed inside her. He was big, and so hard. She could feel the heat of him, feel him throbbing as he stretched her. She'd never had sex like this before.

She brought her legs up and curled them around his as he kept pushing deeper. Then he stopped. If that was all, it wasn't going to be so bad.

"Are you okay?" she asked when he closed his eyes with a pained look.

He grunted. "You feel so damned good. Hot. Wet. I'm trying to take it easy on you, darlin'."

"I think I'm good; we should go for it." The way the veins were pulsing in his temples told her how much restraint he was using. She wanted this to be good for him too.

"You sure?" He ground the words out.

"I am."

She grasped his ass harder and urged him on. Then all the air rushed out of her lungs when he thrust deep and hard, burying himself inside her. She'd thought he was done, but he hadn't even begun!

He stretched her, filled her, it felt like he became a part of her. And then he started to move. She'd told him to go for it. And he did. They moved together in a pounding rhythm that felt like it might just drive her out of her mind.

With every thrust, the base of his cock hit her just right. Despite her doubts, he was quickly driving her to another orgasm. She clung to him desperately, afraid that she might not recover from this one.

He held her gaze as he drove deeper and harder.

"Deacon!" she gasped.

"Come for me."

"I … I … Oh God!" He drove her over the edge again, pushing her higher and higher until she felt she might dissolve around him. Then she felt him tense, and grow impossibly harder. He pushed up on his hands and arched his back as he thrust deep and held hard.

She could feel it, feel him letting go inside her. It carried her higher still, made her feel powerful. Powerful and … loved.

As he throbbed inside her and she pulsated around him, his words hit her. He'd said *I got to drive the woman I love wild.* The woman he *loved*?

She wrapped her arms and legs around him as tightly as she could and breathed, "I love you, too, Deacon."

His gaze locked with hers and he gave her a small nod and a big smile as he lowered himself onto her. "I thought you missed that."

"I did. But I caught up."

"Good. I knew I loved you before. But now that we've made love …"

"What?"

He chuckled. "After that? There's no going back after that, darlin'. I love you. I want you. You're mine."

He looked so pleased with himself, that she had to laugh with him. "Well, it works out then, because I feel the same way. I love you. I want you. You're mine."

He pressed a kiss to her lips. "I am."

Chapter Sixteen

Deacon didn't even attempt to wipe the smile off his face when he went into the bakery on Monday morning. It'd be pointless to try. He hadn't stopped smiling since Friday night. He felt like Luke had set the tone for the rest of his life at that little meet-up at Chico.

Deacon loved the idea of becoming a family with Rocket and Janey, and Spider and Frankie, having Candy by his side. His smile faded a little. The day was coming when he was going to have to kick Luke's ass for him. He'd wasted enough years. But when – if – he finally figured it out, he'd be part of that family group in more ways than one.

His heart sank and sat heavy in his chest. Of course, he already had a family. He had two kids. But they didn't want to know him. He'd never give up, but he wasn't going to hold his breath either.

"Deacon!" Ace greeted him with a grin as he approached the counter. "I thought you'd be here early with Candy."

"No. Spider and Rocket decided that they were going to start coming in at the same time she does a couple of days a week. I told them they don't need to but …" He shrugged.

Ace waggled his eyebrows. "They don't need to because you go to bed just as early as Candy does – and you like getting up when she does?"

Deacon shook his head but couldn't hide his smile. "So? You got a problem with that?"

"Hell no! I think it's great. And you're going to bring her to the fundraiser dinner on Saturday, right?"

"I am." Deacon narrowed his eyes. "Who are you going with?"

Ace laughed. "Don't worry. Not one of Sharon's cronies."

"Who then? I thought they were the only women who went to these things."

"Yeah, mostly. But there's a woman who's been staying in one of the cabins on the ranch. She hasn't left the property since she arrived. She says she just wants some rest and peace and quiet. But … when Sharon offered me two tickets, I said I was bringing someone – just to stop her from setting me up. Then, I figured I'd ask Stella, give her the chance to do something other than sit in the cabin and watch the river flow by the whole time she's here."

Deacon cocked an eyebrow. "Anything else you want to tell me about this Stella?"

Ace laughed. "I know, you'd think, knowing me … but, nope. I've hung out with her a few times and chatted, but I'm not interested, and neither is she. She's good people, but I like her as a friend. Nothing else. She just got through an acrimonious divorce. Sounds like she was kind of beaten down in her marriage – not physically, but mentally and emotionally. It took a lot out of her to stand up to him and divorce him. He threatened her life. Threatened her business."

Deacon scowled.

"I know, right? So, she's here, hiding out, taking some time to decide her next moves. I reckon it'd do her good to get out of her own head for a while. Have a few drinks, talk to some strangers."

"Have you told Candy?"

Ace gave him a puzzled look.

"I'm sure she'll want to take her under her wing."

Candy appeared in the doorway from the kitchen and smiled at him. Deacon felt himself smile back. She was so damned beautiful. He loved the way her eyes shone when she looked at him, and they seemed to shine even more these last few days – ever since he'd told her that he loved her – and she'd told him that she felt the same way about him. He pressed his lips together to keep in a chuckle. All the sex might have something to with it, too. He knew it had put a twinkle in his own eye.

He loved that she came out from behind the counter and straight to him. He didn't even hesitate to close his arms around her and drop a kiss on her lips.

"Hey, darlin'."

"Hi. I've got your scone ready."

"Thanks."

"And don't worry about getting back early today, remember. Libby's going to pick me up from here, and we're going for a drive."

"A drive? I thought she was going to hang out here with you."

"No. She volunteered to ride around with me while I get used to driving."

Deacon nodded slowly. She'd more than likely be safe on the road. He couldn't help remembering what had happened to

Sierra, but lightning rarely ever struck twice. He didn't want to seem like he was being bossy or controlling either, but he wasn't thrilled at the idea.

"Are you okay with that?"

She was so sweet; she wouldn't let him tell her what to do but she did try to consider him.

"Yeah. Just be careful, okay? And keep your phone with you."

"I will."

Spider came and set a to-go cup and a brown paper bag on the counter with a smile. "There you go."

Deacon checked his watch. He needed to get a move on.

Candy rolled up onto her tiptoes and he bent to peck her lips.

"Go on, I don't want to make you late."

"Okay. I'll call you later."

"I'll be fine."

Ace winked at him. "Don't worry, we're all keeping an eye out for your lady."

Deacon loved that Candy didn't even blush anymore when people called her that. Instead, she smiled a little bit bigger.

He gave her one last quick peck. He wanted more, but he knew he was making a spectacle of himself as it was. More than a few heads had turned in their direction since Candy came out from the back.

She laughed and patted his ass. "Go on! I'll see you later."

He was still chuckling when he got back into his truck. He could imagine what people would have to say about that!

~ ~ ~

"Have you met Stella?" Candy didn't dare look across at Libby while she was driving, but she was starting to feel confident enough to chat.

"I haven't. Ace had told me about her. But I don't like to hang around at the ranch. When I get done with my classes, I leave."

Candy hated the sadness in her new friend's voice. "It must be hard."

"It is. But let's talk about something else, can we?"

"Sorry."

"Don't feel bad. I just don't want to drag you down when you're obviously so happy. That's all."

"Okay. Well, I was thinking – since we're heading down that way, that we could go and check on her. But if you don't like being there ..."

"No. I think that's a great idea. She might not want to see us, but we'll know pretty quickly if she doesn't and we can just say hi and bye."

"And you really don't mind?"

"No. It's … she's staying in one of the cabins by the river. We can just go straight there. I don't like hanging around at the house. It's just … sad. That place used to be so full of life when we lived there, and Frankie was there whenever she was home, and Ace was around most of the time. These days, that house is like a ghost. It reminds me of myself – empty and full of memories. Oh, shit. Don't listen to me!"

Candy risked a quick glance at her, but Libby just rolled her eyes. "I'm fine. Honestly. Jeez. I'm on the ranch almost every day. It's no big deal."

"Okay. If you're sure."

"I'm sure. Maybe one day in the not-too-distant future, I'll be brave enough to follow through on my plans. Once I do, I'll never set foot on the ranch again – not even for you."

"What plans?"

Libby sighed. "They're more like dreams for now. If I get around to making them real, I'll tell you."

"Okay. Can I ask one question?"

"What?"

"You don't mean you're going to leave the valley, do you? It might be selfish of me, but you're my first real adult friend. I'd hate to lose you."

"No. Sometimes I think about that – about just getting in my truck one day and leaving – but I doubt I'll ever do it. I don't need to leave the valley. I just need to make the final break with the ranch."

"Because it's your final tie to Mav?"

"Yeah. But look, see that mile marker coming up? You're going to turn right a little way after that."

"Okay, thanks." Candy still had more questions, but she needed to pay attention to the road. And Libby was probably grateful for the reprieve anyway.

As her little car bumped its way over another long gravel road, Candy shot a glance at Libby. "Is this the driveway?"

"It is. Don't worry, I'd tell you if you were going the wrong way."

"It's not that. It's just that I'm getting the hang of just how big some people's places are out here. It was the same with Trip. I thought he lived at the end of a very long road. I didn't realize that road was just his driveway."

Libby sighed. "Yeah. Some folks own thousands of acres. While others live in little boxes in town."

Candy knew that she was thinking about her life with Maverick and her life without him, but she didn't know what to say that might help.

Libby pointed to where the road split. "Take the left-hand fork. Although surely, you've been out here before – to see Spider and Frankie?"

Candy chuckled. "I came once not long after I first arrived. But at that point, everywhere looked the same to me. It was all just long gravel roads and beautiful mountains and rivers. I wouldn't be able to tell this place apart from anywhere else."

Libby nodded. "I get it. I'd feel the same way in the city. I wouldn't be able to tell one street full of high-rises from another. In case you don't remember, Frankie and Spider are staying in the cabin over there." She pointed toward where the river glistened in the afternoon sun. "Although why they won't finally move into the house is beyond me."

Candy shrugged. She wasn't about to tell her new friend what Spider had confided in her about him wanting to get a place closer to the bakery, and Frankie still living in hope that Libby and Mav would one day get back together – and live in the ranch house again.

Instead, she bravely lifted her hand from the wheel and pointed through the windshield. "Is Stella staying in one of those cabins?"

"Yeah. The one on the right."

Candy parked the car a few minutes later and smiled to herself when she realized that she was getting more relaxed about driving. She'd been more concerned about Libby, Spider and Frankie, and even Stella and how she might feel about this unannounced visit than she had been about maintaining a death grip on the steering wheel.

She smiled and waved when a woman came out onto the front porch with a wary expression on her face.

Libby climbed out of the passenger side at the same time as Candy scrambled out the driver's door and they both called, 'Hi,' at the same time.

They looked at each other and laughed before Candy turned back to Stella. "Hi, Stella. It's lovely to meet you. I'm Candy and this is Libby. Sorry to drop in on you unannounced but …"

The woman visibly relaxed and smiled at them. "Oh, I forgot. Ace did tell me that the two of you might stop by. What can I do for you?"

"Not a damn thing," Candy said as she made her way up the steps and onto the porch. "We just wanted to let you know that we're around if you want us, and if there's anything we can do for you, you just let us know."

Stella smiled as she shook hands with her and then turned to shake with Libby, too. "Well, thank you. I appreciate it. I don't think I need anything. But it's kind of you to offer. I've just been … I'm …" Her eyes welled with tears, and she swiped at them. "Jeez. I thought I was over that. I'm just hanging around here, trying to piece my life back together." She shrugged. "I think I'm figuring out though that sitting here in the middle of nowhere isn't going to help me build a new life. I need to go back and start doing things, instead of sitting here and thinking about what I could do."

Candy reached out and touched her arm. "Sometimes, we just need a bit of time and space before doing anything even feels possible."

Stella gave her a small smile. "Let me guess, you're divorced, too?"

"No. My husband died eighteen months ago."

"Oh, God! I'm sorry. I …"

Candy waved a hand at her. "It's okay. I should have divorced him years ago. I mean, it's sad that he died, but he'd created a life that wasn't worth living anyway – for either of us."

Stella nodded. "Can I offer you a drink? I don't mean a drink; I mean lemonade or something."

"That's totally up to you," said Libby. "We wanted to stop by and let you know that you have us if you want us, but we don't need to impose if you don't want us."

Stella checked her watch. "Well, if we're being honest with each other, I appreciate the visit and the intention behind it, and if you want to leave me your number, I can call you sometime. But I'm supposed to be talking to my lawyer soon and I was planning to spend the next little while psyching myself up ready for whatever she has to tell me now."

"Okay, I'm glad we are being that honest," Libby said with a smile. "How about you take both our numbers and if you want you can give us yours."

Stella pulled a notebook and pen out of her back pocket and handed them over with a rueful smile. "I plan to sit out here when I talk to Ari and make notes of whatever she says. I find it hard to focus when I'm on the phone with her."

"Ari's your lawyer?" Candy couldn't help asking.

"She is. And she's a ballbuster. I don't think I would've survived this divorce without her, in any sense."

Candy wrote her number below Libby's and handed the notebook back. She was pleased when Stella took a new sheet and wrote her own number on it before handing it over.

"Well, we won't keep you," said Libby.

"Good luck with your lawyer," said Candy.

Stella nodded. "Thanks. I feel like I'm going to need it. The divorce is final now, but he keeps hitting me with more. I don't know what she's going to tell me today but …" she shrugged.

"Well, if you want to vent after you're done with her, you have two new sounding boards you can call," Candy told her.

"Thanks. And you two are going to this fundraiser dinner? If nothing else, I'll see you there?"

"We are," said Libby. "And if you don't feel like calling or talking before then, don't worry about it."

"Thanks."

They all turned at the sound of a vehicle approaching. Stella frowned and checked her watch again. Candy recognized Ace's truck just before he brought it to a stop and climbed out.

She was used to seeing Ace with a smile on his face, so his frown took her by surprise. He was, in theory, the good-looking one out of their group of friends. But to Candy he didn't have a patch on Deacon – and he sure didn't wear a frown even half as sexily.

"What's up?" asked Libby before he'd even reached the porch steps.

Ace shot her and Candy a brief smile before turning to Stella. "I just heard from your lawyer. Ariana?"

Stella gave him a puzzled look. "That's her. But why did she call you? I'm waiting for her to call me."

"She said she's been trying but can't get through and she needs to talk to you."

"Shit." Stella pulled her phone out of her back pocket and scowled at it. "I have no bars again."

"That's what I figured," said Ace. "If you want, I can take you up to the house so that you can use the landline. She called there hoping to get hold of you. Luckily, I was in the house."

"Please." Stella gave Candy and Libby an apologetic look. "I'm afraid I have to go."

"No problem," said Candy.

Ace gave them a grim smile. "Sorry to break this up, ladies."

"It's fine," said Libby. "We were just leaving anyway."

Ace held her gaze as he nodded. "It's good to see you out here."

Libby made a face at him. "Yeah. If I don't see you before, I'll see you at the dinner on Saturday night."

"Okay."

Candy let Ace pull away in his truck with Stella sitting beside him before she backed out of the spot she'd parked in.

"Don't you see Ace here every day when you teach your riding classes?"

Libby blew out a sigh. "Usually, yes. But he's been trying to make me relax about being out here. Telling him that I'd see him Saturday was my way of telling him not to make too much of the fact that I'm on the ranch of my own accord – and that he shouldn't try to encourage me to spend more time here."

"I see."

Libby shot her a look and then laughed. "Well, I'm glad you do. Because I don't. I don't know what the hell I'm playing at. I should be fine. None of it should matter anymore."

Candy glanced over at her. "But it does."

"Yeah, it matters. It still hurts. And I'm not sure that will ever change. I need to move on, but I don't know how."

"I wish I had some words of wisdom for you, but I don't, I'm sorry."

Libby laughed again. "Don't be. At least you're honest – and you're not telling me what I should do or how I should feel."

"I don't think there are any shoulds. We all just do what we can with what we've got and hope it works out for the best."

Libby sighed. "And if it works out for the worst, we just do what we can with what we've got again."

Candy had to focus on keeping the car on the gravel road as it followed the river around a sharp bend, but Libby's words struck a chord with her. Things had certainly worked out for the worst with her and Len. But she'd kept doing what she could with what she had – and now she was hoping that her life might work out better than she'd ever dared to hope.

Chapter Seventeen

Deacon frowned at his phone before he picked it up, willing Saunders to answer this time when he called. It was getting late, and he was in a hurry to head back down the valley and pick Candy up from the bakery. She'd said that she was fine to hang out there after work today, but she'd finished work a few hours ago now, and he hated to make her wait.

However, before he left the office he really wanted to talk to Saunders. The guy had been good about returning his calls at first, but he'd been quiet for the last few days. The last time that they'd spoken, Saunders had said that he was trying to find out which of the gang of assholes had called and threatened Candy. Deacon understood how it went; Saunders would have many other cases he was working, and there were no doubt others that he saw as a higher priority. But for Deacon, Candy and her safety were his number one priority.

He picked up the phone and punched in the number, scowling to himself as he listened to it ring.

"This is Saunders."

"Saunders, this is Sheriff Wallis from Park County, Montana." Deacon would rather speak to him man-to-man but referring to himself as the sheriff tended to put some weight behind his requests.

"Yeah, Wallis. I've been meaning to get back to you."

"Why? Do you have anything new?"

"Not exactly. It turned out that we were getting in the way of a federal investigation. I just got the call this morning. I'm not shitting you, I did plan to let you know this afternoon."

Deacon pressed the ball of his hand to his forehead. He knew how complicated things could get whenever the feds were involved. "So, where do things stand now?"

"As you know, this means it's out of my hands. From what they told me, they plan to make a move within the next day or two. There are some bigger players involved further up the chain than I was aware of. The FBI guys have what they need to move on the ringleaders. The group that has been using Candy's store are of secondary importance but will hopefully get swept up in the cleanup operation."

Deacon banged his fist on the desk. "Hopefully? That's the best you can give me?"

"Sorry, Deacon, I know that's not what you want to hear. But you know how it goes. My hands are tied. They were the minute the feds walked through my door."

Deacon leaned back in his chair and ran his hands through his hair. This wasn't the kind of news that he'd been hoping for. However, he knew that what Saunders said was true; it was out of his hands.

"Will you at least get a write up of who they detained when it's over?"

"I've already put the request in. I'd like to think that they'll get them all and there will be no danger of any of them still being on the street and free to come after Candy. But we both know that what we would like to think might happen rarely does. As soon as I have a list of who they have in custody, I'll be able to let you know who might still be a threat."

Deacon knew that was the best he could hope for at this point. "Thanks."

"Sure. I wish I could do more."

"Yeah, I do too."

Saunders laughed. "If you think of anything else you want me to do, I'll be happy to. You have my number."

"Thanks. I don't know what yet, but I have a feeling that we haven't seen the last of each other."

"You're probably right about that. Once this is all wrapped up, Candy's going to have to decide what she wants to do about the pawn shop."

"Shit!" Deacon had gotten so used to having Candy around, to thinking of her as part of his life here, even to thinking about any possible threat to her as something that would happen here in Montana, he'd somehow managed to dismiss the fact that she still had remainders of her life in LA.

Saunders chuckled. "Tell me if I'm wrong, but this is personal for you, right?"

Deacon wasn't going to deny it. "It's personal, all right. It's as personal as it gets."

"I thought as much. You know, she's going to have to come back here. At this point, I doubt whether she'll be called as a witness. Turns out the guys in her store were bit players, but it's still a possibility that the feds might call her. But even if not, she's going to have to come back and sell the store or shut it down or whatever she decides to do with it. I'm guessing that when that happens, you'll be with her."

"Too damn right I will." They hadn't talked about it, but no way was Deacon going to let her travel back to LA alone. He pursed his lips, at least, he hoped not.

"Give me a call when you're in town. I'll buy you a beer."

"Thanks. And the same goes, if ever you get up around this neck of the woods, you give me a shout."

Saunders chuckled. "I'll keep that in mind. I get the feeling that's not an invitation you make too often."

Deacon had to smile. "You're right about that. I'm sure you can imagine that the sheriff of the county that's home to the northern entrance of Yellowstone National Park could make himself far too many fake friends if he went around making offers like that to anyone and everyone."

"That's what I thought. I have to go. I wish I had better news for you. I wish I could do more. But you have my word that I'll keep you up to date on everything I learn and if there's anything more I can do to help, I'm on it."

"Thanks. We'll talk soon, I'm sure."

Deacon hung up and shook his head. It wasn't the best news but at least it was some news. He should know within the next day or two whether any of those assholes were still walking free. The best outcome would be that they were all locked up awaiting federal trial, but he wasn't going to hold his breath on that one.

He sucked in a deep breath and blew it out slowly. There was nothing he could do to affect whatever might happen in LA, but Candy wasn't in LA. She was right here in the valley, and it was time he got his ass home to her.

~ ~ ~

Candy covered her face with her hands, even as she laughed. She could feel the heat in her cheeks as she peeked out between her fingers at Trip.

He wasn't exactly a regular in the bakery, but she'd noticed that he was coming in more often recently — since she and Deacon had gone over to his place for dinner. This afternoon, he'd shown up with Ace. They claimed that Deacon hadn't sent them to keep an eye on her, but she wasn't totally convinced about that.

"Go on," said Ace with a grin. "Admit it."

"Okay, okay. That's exactly what I called him. How the hell was I supposed to know that he was standing there listening to me? I thought Clawson and I were the only ones out there."

Trip was still chuckling. "Grumpy the sheriff! It's perfect. You had his number right from the get-go, didn't you?"

Candy shrugged. "I'd like to say that yes, I did, but to be honest I really didn't. I think, in the beginning, I just kept annoying him without knowing how."

Ace winked at her, then turned to Trip. "I think we know why, don't we?"

Trip nodded. "Yes, I think we do. You see …" he smiled at Candy, "our Deacon has worked hard for years to build up walls around himself. My guess is that he knew from the get-go that you would be able to break those walls down if he let you get too close."

Candy held his gaze for a moment. She didn't want to admit it, but it seemed to her that Trip's assessment was spot on.

Rocket came to their table and set down a plate of pastries. Candy made a face at him. "I don't need to be eating this stuff."

Rocket chuckled. "You don't need to be not eating it either, Miss Candy."

Ace grinned as he reached for a Danish. "You won't get any complaints from me. Thanks, Rocket."

"Nor from me," added Trip as he grabbed a mini cherry pie.

Candy just rolled her eyes at them. It seemed that no matter how old they were, men behaved like starving schoolboys whenever a plate of pastries appeared.

Rocket met her gaze. "If you want the truth, I brought the plate over as a distraction tactic. These guys are hanging around for you, and I was wondering if you'd rather go home." He smiled at the guys. "I figured that if I distract them with goodies, I can sneak you out of here if you want to go."

Candy had to laugh at the looks on the guys' faces.

Ace shrugged. "I don't want to keep you if you don't want to be here, but I wasn't sure how you'd feel if I offered to take you home."

They all looked up when Deacon appeared beside Rocket with what looked like a very real scowl on his face. He put his hands on his hips as he towered over Ace.

"Tell me that I didn't just hear you offer to take my lady home."

Candy's heart pounded in her chest. He sounded pissed. She didn't want to believe that he would get mad at his friend for offering to help her. He couldn't believe that Ace would …

Relief washed over her when Ace rolled his eyes, and Deacon cracked. He burst out laughing.

"Come on," said Ace. "You don't think you could fool me with that shit, do you?"

Deacon shrugged. "I wasn't sure. I thought I'd try it and see."

"Well, you sure fooled me!" said Candy.

Deacon cocked an eyebrow as he met her gaze. "Shit, I'm sorry, darlin'. I didn't think. But you've got nothing to worry about. I might be a bit bossy but I'd never …"

Trip cut him off with a laugh. "A bit bossy? That's putting it mildly, isn't it?"

Deacon made a face at him, but Candy reached for his hand. She didn't want him to have to explain himself. She knew what he meant. He *was* a little bossy, but at the same time he respected her, and she knew it.

He smiled as he linked his fingers through hers and squeezed before looking back at Trip. "I don't need to explain myself to you. My lady knows what I mean, and that's all that matters."

Candy smiled at him and noticed that the guys were grinning too.

She got to her feet. "I do know what you mean. I'm not worried. But I would like to go home now."

Deacon wrapped his arm around her shoulders and dropped a quick kiss on her lips. "We're out of here then, darlin'."

Rocket grinned at Candy as Deacon steered her toward the door. She had to laugh at the way Ace and Trip grinned and waved at them as they went.

Deacon simply waved at them over his shoulder with his free hand.

Once they were out in the parking lot, Deacon led her straight to his truck. When they reached it, he leaned in and gave her the kind of kiss she'd been waiting for all day. When he finally lifted his head, she tightened her arms around his waist and looked up into his eyes.

"I'm glad you're here, glad you're in a hurry to get home." She chuckled. "But my car is right over there."

Deacon rolled his eyes. "Well, shit! You're right. I am in a hurry to get you home. I know you could have gone hours ago if it wasn't for me."

She ran her hand up his arm. "Don't go blaming yourself. If I really wanted to go, I would have gone. Spider or Rocket would have gone with me."

Deacon pressed a kiss to her forehead. "True. But now that I've got you, I want to keep you. We can either walk over and get your car later or I'll bring you in the morning."

Candy pressed her cheek into his chest and hugged tighter. "I like that idea. Now that I've got you, I want to keep you, too."

Deacon tucked his fingers under her chin and made her look up into his eyes. "Forever?"

Candy's heart leaped into her mouth. She nodded rapidly without even having to think about it. She was shocked, but happily so, that Deacon was the one bringing up forever. But she couldn't deny that the possibility of a forever with him was something that she'd started to hope for.

~ ~ ~

Deacon opened the door for her to go into his place. He liked knowing that there was no question for either of them about whether she would go upstairs to her apartment instead. He was a little surprised himself that he'd asked her about forever, but he couldn't be happier with her response.

Clawson rubbed around his legs before going to greet Candy in the same manner. Then he meowed at them, making Deacon laugh. He went to get the food bowl while Candy went to open the back door in what had already become a familiar routine.

After he set Clawson's dinner down, Deacon went to where Candy stood in the open doorway and slid his arms around her waist. He rested his chin on top of her head and held her back against him. He knew he had to talk to her about his conversation with Saunders, but he wanted to enjoy this moment first. And he really did enjoy these moments — the shared domesticity. It wasn't something that he'd thought he was missing out on, or that he even wanted. But now, now that Candy was part of his life, he cherished these moments and tried to make the most of every one of them.

She rested her head back against him and looked up into his eyes. "Hi."

He chuckled and pressed a kiss to her lips. "Hey, darlin'."

"How was your day? Did you have to go back over to Sunnyside?"

Deacon laughed. "Not today, but I'm pretty sure I'll be back over there before the end of the week. Apparently, I settled them all down last time and Leland was satisfied after our little talk. But of course, he's forgotten all about it again, and so the cycle repeats."

"You're a good man, Deacon."

His heart swelled in his chest hearing her say that. He did what he could; tried to do the right thing. He'd spent his whole life striving to be a good man, to prove to the world that the Wallis name was better than the man who'd borne it before him. But hearing Candy call him a good man meant more than that, so much more.

He dropped another kiss on the top of her head and held her a little tighter. "How was your day?"

She nodded. "It was good, business as usual; lots of bread, lots of pastries, lots of gossip. Before I came here, I thought that it would be a whole new world, that everything and everyone would be so different from what I've known before." She chuckled. "Turns out that people are the same no matter where you go. It doesn't matter if they live in the big city or out here in the middle of nowhere. They care about each other. They bitch about each other. And when it comes down to it, they're mostly willing to help each other out."

Deacon had to smile at that. He knew that his own take on life, and on people, and their motivations was somewhat cynical. How could it not be in his position? But he loved that despite everything she'd lived through, Candy still chose to see the best in folks.

His smile faded when she asked, "I don't suppose you've heard from Saunders, have you?"

He pursed his lips, wishing that they could just enjoy the moment for a little while longer, but knowing that he couldn't put her off.

"Yeah. I talked to him this afternoon."

She looked up into his eyes. "Go on, lay it on me. I can tell by your tone that whatever he said wasn't good news."

He took her by the hand and led her back inside, heading straight for the sofa, where he sat down and wrapped her up in his arms.

"Saunders isn't in charge of the investigation anymore. The feds have taken over. Apparently, the guys in your store work for some bigger players. The federal investigation is going after the big fish."

Candy blew out a sigh. "So, the minnows in the pawn shop will be left to swim free?"

"Saunders is still hoping that they will be caught up in the net. But yeah, there's a possibility that they won't be. I don't want you to worry though, I need you to know that I'll take care of you. Nothing's going to happen to you."

A rush of warmth filled his chest when she smiled at him. "I'm not worried, Deacon. I feel safe with you. I know that I'm safe with you. What I am is pissed that they might get away with everything that they've already done. They've stolen from decent families, broken into homes, not to mention the whole drug thing and the young lives they're ruining that way."

Deacon nodded. He felt the same way; he dedicated his life to stopping criminals from doing the kinds of things that were going on in Candy's pawn shop. But at the moment, he was more concerned about her. Yes, they deserved to be taken down, but more importantly he needed to ensure that they never got anywhere near her.

She rested her head against his shoulder. "If I have to go back there, do you think you might be able to go with me?"

He kissed the top of her head and chuckled.

She looked up at him, her eyes wide. "Is it such a ridiculous request that you think it's funny?"

He shook his head and narrowed his eyes at her before pressing three quick kisses to her lips. "Tell me you're messing with me. Tell me that you know that there's no way I want to let you go back there without me."

He relaxed when she laughed, and her eyes twinkled. "Of course, I know. I can just imagine your face if I told you I was going back there, and that I didn't want you to come."

He closed his eyes, not knowing what he would do in that situation. He didn't want to be the controlling asshole type, but he already knew that he wasn't the type who could let his woman walk into a possibly dangerous situation without him by her side.

If it were up to him, she wouldn't go at all. He'd go for her, or take care of things some other way.

She wrapped her arm around his waist and snuggled into his side. "I know that we're going to have to face all that. And we will. But we don't have to do it tonight."

He tightened his arms around her. "You're right, we don't. So, how about you tell me what you want for dinner instead and I'll make it."

She burrowed deeper into his side, and he bit down on his bottom lip when she ran her hand up and down his inner thigh. "I'm not hungry yet. Well, I am. I'm hungry for you."

Her words sent a jolt of heat through his veins, and he rose from the sofa, scooping her up in his arms and heading for the bedroom.

Candy laughed as they went. "I love you, Deacon."

He chuckled as he tossed her down onto the bed and crawled up over her. "I love you, too, darlin'. Let me show you how much."

Chapter Eighteen

Candy smiled when her phone rang, and she saw Libby's name flash up on the display. They might not have known each other for very long, but they were becoming fast friends.

"Hey, Libby," she answered.

"Hey, Candy. I don't want to disturb you; are you still at work?"

Candy laughed. "Nope. I'm home already. Spider and Rocket chased me out of there early today. The way they kept saying that I need time to get ready for tonight almost makes me wonder how bad I usually look." She laughed again. "As though I might need a few hours to transform myself into someone who looks respectable enough to go to this dinner with Deacon."

Libby groaned. "Don't you dare … You don't really think that, do you? You're gorgeous. You could go to this dinner looking the same as you do every day in the bakery, and you'd still be gorgeous enough for the occasion. As far as being respectable enough to go with Deacon, the whole valley is already thrilled for him that you guys are together. And even apart from all that, you know damn well that Spider and Rocket don't think that you need the time to make yourself beautiful; they just love you and want to make sure that you have time for yourself. You work your ass off in that bakery for them. They know it, they appreciate it, and if you ask me — and I know you didn't — they wish that you could get the hang of taking it a bit easier. Sure, they need you, but they don't need you to bust your ass in there all day every day."

Candy couldn't help laughing. "Wow! Well, I guess that's me told."

"Shit! Sorry! I'm not trying to tell you how to live your life. I just want you to be happy. It seems to me that you might want to stop and take a breath and realize just how awesome you are and how many people love you."

"Aww." Candy put her hand over her heart, and tears pricked behind her eyes. "Thanks, Libby."

"You don't need to thank me, I'm just glad you're not mad at me. I always seem to mess up when I try to tell someone how much I care about them."

Candy guessed that Libby was talking about Maverick, but she decided not to push her about it. Instead, she reassured her new friend. "You didn't mess up. I love that you're trying to make me stop and think. And I know you have a point."

"Good. Anyway, moving swiftly on … I just wanted to check in with you about tonight. What time do you guys plan to get there?"

"Deacon said that we need to leave here at about ten till seven. We're supposed to be there at seven-thirty, so that should get us there with ten minutes to spare."

Libby laughed. "And you're happy to let Deacon tell you what to do?"

Candy made a face. "I don't see it that way. He's not telling me what to do. He knows what time we need to be there. He knows how long it takes to get there. And he knows much better than I do whether we need to be on time or fashionably late." She chewed on her bottom lip before she asked, "Do you really think that's letting him tell me what to do?"

"Shit! No, sorry. Just ignore me. I might possibly be projecting my own hang-ups onto you. Mav is kind of over-the-top bossy. I think I might have become overly sensitive to it over the years. Deacon's a different animal entirely. He makes things happen, but he doesn't boss people around just for the hell of it. Anyway, all I was really calling for was to check in with you before we get there. Are you looking forward to it?"

"I am. I'm not even nervous. I'm really looking forward to getting to know more people. Of course, I'm looking forward to seeing you and Trip, and Ace and Stella. I have to tell you that I'm looking forward to seeing Deacon in that kind of environment." Candy smiled as a shiver of excitement ran down her spine. "And I won't deny that I'm looking forward to seeing him all dressed up, too."

Libby laughed. "Oh, you're in for a treat. Those guys might look like rough and ready blue-collar types most of the time, but they scrub up well. Each and every one of them."

Candy laughed with her. "I can imagine. And I'm glad that I don't just have to imagine; I get to see them all for myself later."

"Well, not exactly all of them. Of course, the only one that really matters to you is Deacon. Are Trip and Ace the only other ones you've met?"

"No. I met the rest of them at Janey and Rocket's wedding. And Emmett's been into the bakery a few times, too."

"Oh, I forgot about the wedding."

Candy had to think for a minute. She didn't remember seeing Libby there.

"There was no way I was going to miss Janey's wedding," Libby said. "But I managed to stay on the outskirts all day. Of course, Mav came home — Janey is his cousin, but she and Laney may as well be his little sisters just like Frankie. I didn't want to stay away, but I did want to stay out of his way. Ugh, but the only reason I brought it up was that I didn't know if you'd met Blane and Travis yet."

"Only briefly at the wedding. From what Deacon has said, Travis is Trip's best friend, right?"

Libby laughed. "Yes, that's right. Those two were inseparable when we were kids. I'm surprised that Travis has stayed away this long. When Trip came home, we all gave it a couple of months before Travis would follow. He hasn't yet, though. Anyway, forgive me, I didn't call you to chat about the guys. All I really wanted was to check in with you, to make sure that you're looking forward to tonight, and to reassure you if you had any worries."

"Aww. Thanks," said Candy. "That's sweet of you. But I'm fine. I'm not exactly the shy and retiring type, and I haven't had much of a social life for years. I'm really looking forward to this."

"Good, I'm glad to hear it."

"Have you spoken to Stella?" Candy had called the number that Stella had given them a few times over the last few days, but she hadn't managed to get through, and there hadn't been the option to leave a voicemail.

"No," said Libby. "I couldn't get ahold of her, but I did talk to Ace when I was down at the ranch this morning. He said that she's been a bit shaky since the last time she spoke to her lawyer. He thought that she'll still come tonight, but he wasn't a hundred percent convinced."

"I hope she will," said Candy.

"Me too, but I'm more concerned about you. For Stella, being here is a little break away before she figures out the rest of her life. For you, this is the beginning of the rest of your life. I want to do anything I can to make sure that you lay a solid foundation so that you never want to leave. I can guarantee you that Deacon feels the same way, and I want to see you both happy."

"Thanks, Lib."

"There's no need to thank me. I'm being selfish as well; I don't want to lose my new friend now that I've found you. But

I'll let you go; you might not need hours and hours to make yourself look beautiful, but I sure as hell do."

Candy laughed. "Don't give me that crap. You're gorgeous."

"Whatever. See you later."

~ ~ ~

Deacon couldn't wipe the smile off his face as he helped Candy down from his truck. He thought she was a pretty little thing even when he first met her and wasn't thrilled about having her around. The more he'd gotten to know her, the more beautiful she'd become in his eyes. Tonight, she was stunning. And he knew that wasn't just in his eyes.

Dark hair fell around her shoulders in curls that he hadn't seen her wear before but that kept tempting him to wrap his fingers in them. Her hair was shot through with silver but that only added to her beauty. She wasn't a young girl, and he wouldn't want her to be. There was a grace and wisdom in her green eyes that no young girl would ever possess.

He lifted her down from the truck and instead of removing his hands from her hips, he drew her closer and kissed her. He loved that she never hesitated to kiss him back. Right from that very first time when he'd taken her down by the river and pushed her up against his truck, she'd only been focused on him and what was happening between them. He didn't want to give Willa any more brain space, but he couldn't help comparing. No way would the woman he'd been married to have let him kiss her in the parking lot like this. She would have been focused on who might be around, what they might see, and most importantly what they would think. Then again, he hadn't even wanted to kiss her for the last few years of their marriage anyway.

When he stepped back, Candy reached up and ran her knuckles over his cheek. "Are you okay?"

He caught her hand and pressed her fingers to his lips. "I'm more than okay. I'm happy to be here with you, darlin'."

The fine lines around her eyes crinkled a little deeper, and her lips pressed together. "Are you sure? You didn't look very happy for a moment there."

He chuckled. "I swear you're in tune with my thoughts most of the time. But I promise you, I'm happy. Happy to be here with you. If I looked any different, it was only because it hit me how unhappy I used to be." He pecked her lips, then stood back with a smile. "I know how lucky I am to have you, and I ain't wasting another second on what used to be."

As he took her hand and started walking across the parking lot, Candy rested her head against his shoulder. "I get that. I'm the same way. Sometimes, I can't help but compare how good I have it now — with you — to how shitty my life was with Len. My biggest regret is that I didn't meet you sooner. But we can't do anything about that, all we can do is make the most of what we have."

Deacon tugged her hand and pulled her into his side before he wrapped his arm around her shoulders. He waggled his eyebrows at her. "I agree. I have you now, darlin'. I intend to make the most of you."

She laughed and hip-bumped him. "Keep talking, Sheriff. I like where this is going."

They were both still chuckling when they reached the door, and Sharon Anderson greeted them with a big smile.

"Deacon, Candy, I'm so glad you're here."

Deacon reluctantly let go of Candy's hand as Sharon pulled her in for a hug. It looked genuine enough to him, not like the way she usually kissed the air around her friends' cheeks. And Candy didn't look uncomfortable with it. In fact, she looked happy. He might want to protect her in terms of keeping her safe from guys who wanted to hurt her, but he knew that she could navigate social situations for herself. She wasn't some little innocent who was in danger of being taken advantage of.

She could stand on her own two feet, and he admired that about her.

When they finally made it inside, he spotted Trip and Libby standing by the bar. He put his arm around Candy's shoulders and steered her toward them.

Trip greeted him with a grin. "Glad you made it, Chief. I know that we said we were going to do regular meet-ups over the summer, but I didn't expect this to be one of them."

Deacon laughed "Yeah, me neither. But we can make the most of it. And besides …" He smiled at Candy, "… coming out like this tonight will kill a whole bunch of birds with one stone."

Candy gave him a puzzled look. "What do you mean?"

He raised his eyebrows and looked around the already crowded function room. He wasn't surprised to see a good many heads turned in their direction. People had been staring at them since they entered, and there had been plenty of nudging and whispering. Sure, the gossip about Candy and him had been flying around the valley for weeks. But coming out to an official event like this together was finally confirming the rumors.

Candy had followed his gaze, and he smiled at her. "I mean that after tonight, the gossip will start to calm down. The rumors will be confirmed, and we'll become old news. You won't have to endure so many raised eyebrows and whispering behind hands anymore."

She laughed. "I kind of enjoyed that."

"You did?" That surprised him.

She laughed. "I did. I knew that most of those women were jealous that I was the lucky lady who managed to catch the sheriff's attention."

"She's right," said Libby with a smile. "There have been enough women over the years who've tried to catch your attention, and you never even noticed."

That wasn't exactly true. Deacon had been aware of the few women who'd gone out of their way to try to catch his interest – he just hadn't had any. He shrugged and made a face at Trip. He wasn't exactly comfortable with this line of conversation.

Trip wasn't any help; he just laughed. "If I were you, I'd just hang in there until you guys are old news. You know it won't take long. Just as soon as someone else couples up the rumor mill will move on."

Deacon nodded, then his eyes narrowed as he saw Ace appear in the doorway with a woman by his side. He'd heard talk about this Stella before, but he hadn't met her.

He cocked an eyebrow at Trip and jerked his head toward Ace. "Is the rumor mill going to be moving in that direction next?"

Trip chuckled. "It might, but it'll be wrong if it does. There's nothing going on there. I know that's not like Ace, but he's not interested in her. From what he said, he's worried about her."

"Why's that?" asked Candy. "I thought she was fine. I thought that her divorce and the asshole ex were behind her."

"From what Ace told me the other day," said Trip, "the divorce is behind her, but the ex is still trying to make her life hell."

Candy scowled and looked at Libby. "We need to get her talking, see what we can do."

Trip smirked at Deacon. "She's your perfect match, Chief."

Deacon could only smile; it was true, and he couldn't be happier about it.

Candy fanned herself with her hand as she made her way to the ladies' room. Deacon had surprised her tonight. She would never have guessed that he was a dancer. But he'd had her out on the dance floor pretty much the whole time since the dinner and speeches had ended.

She liked to think of herself as a dancer, but she hadn't had many opportunities to dance over the last few years, decades if she was honest. Added to that was the fact that this wasn't just some disco, oh no, these people were serious about their country music.

She didn't think she'd ever danced a two-step in her life before, but she could see that she was going to have to learn in a hurry if she was going to keep up with Deacon.

Libby caught up with her as she let herself into the ladies' room. "I have to hand it to you, Candy. I think I've seen Deacon dance more tonight than ever before."

Candy raised her eyebrows. "Seriously? I assumed that he must be a real twinkle toes. You don't just dance like that if you don't love it."

Libby laughed. "He was always the first one out on the dance floor when we were kids, and when we were younger, Mav used to get mad at him when he asked me to dance. Mav hates it, so Deacon and I were always the ones without a partner. But honestly, I haven't seen him dance in years."

Candy grinned. "Well, it looks like he's ready to make up for lost time, and I'm all about it. I might struggle to keep up with him, but I'll sure as hell have fun trying."

Libby laughed. "It looked like you were holding your own to me. You two are perfect together, and I don't just mean on the dance floor."

A rush of warmth filled Candy's chest. With every day that passed, she was coming to believe more and more that she and Deacon really were perfect for each other.

The bathroom door opened, and Stella came in with a smile on her face. Candy felt bad; she should have stopped to see if Stella wanted to come with them. But then again, they were adults; they weren't teenage girls heading off to the bathroom to compare notes about boys. Even if that was exactly what she and Libby had just been doing.

"Oh my goodness, you and your man, Deacon, are something else. It made me happy just watching you dance together. After all I've been through with the divorce and everything, I'd almost convinced myself that love was just this fairytale. That being happy with a man was just an illusion that we women sell ourselves." Stella shook her head. "Watching you and Deacon convinced me that the fairytale is real. I've just become a little cynical."

Candy went and put her hand on Stella's arm. "You have no idea … Just a few short months ago, I was right there with you, believing that love was a fairytale that the retailers made up in order to sell cards and chocolates on Valentine's Day."

Libby laughed, but Stella gave her a puzzled look. "Are you trying to tell me that things haven't always been that good between Deacon and you?"

Candy laughed. "No. I'm telling you that a few months ago I didn't even know Deacon existed. I spent most of my adult life married to a man who I'm not sure I ever loved, and if he loved me, it wasn't in any way that I understood."

"Wow! I would never have guessed. But yes, you told me that your husband died. I forgot that, and you and Deacon struck me as one of those couples who must've been childhood sweethearts. You know, those lucky ones who figure out who they want to be with early in life?"

Libby made a strangled little sound, and Candy shot her a worried look. She made a face. "I'm fine. This isn't about me. It's about you and Deacon, and you guys are enough to give us all hope."

When they made it back to the head table, Deacon, Trip, and Ace were sitting chatting. Deacon held his hand out to Candy, and when she took hold of it he pulled her down into his lap and closed his arms around her.

She was a little surprised by his open display of affection, but then again it was nothing compared to the way he'd held her on the dance floor earlier.

Sharon Anderson wore a huge smile as she headed in their direction. Candy tensed a little; she liked the woman well enough, but she wouldn't be surprised if there was some meddling or at least mischief behind that smile.

When she reached them, Sharon raised her eyebrows at Deacon. "I have to tell you, Sheriff, that the ladies have all voted you best dancer of the night."

Candy had to laugh. She didn't see any harm in that. There was no denying it was true. She was relieved to see Deacon beam. Apparently, he was proud of his prowess on the dance floor, not embarrassed by it. She should have known; he might be gruff, but he didn't embarrass easily.

Sharon turned her attention to Candy. "Before tonight I would have worried that you'd have to sign him up for lessons before your first dance."

Candy cocked an eyebrow, not understanding. "Our first dance?" She noticed that Libby and the guys were scowling but she didn't understand why. Not until Sharon answered.

"You know, at your wedding."

Candy felt Deacon's arms tighten around her, and she relaxed against him. They hadn't talked about marriage or a wedding, but they had talked about forever. Whatever form that might take was good with her, and she knew that Deacon wouldn't be put out or embarrassed by Sharon's words. Candy didn't even think they were ill-intentioned. The woman just had no boundaries.

Deacon pressed a kiss to Candy's cheek before turning to smile at Sharon. "Thanks for the concern, but as you now know, our first dance will be one to remember for all the right reasons." He turned to Trip. "Do you still have that video camera?"

Trip laughed. "I'm sure I do, in the attic somewhere. But I'll do you better than that, Chief. When you guys get married, I'll hire a professional videographer to film the entire thing."

Candy didn't know what to say, but luckily, she didn't need to; Deacon pressed a kiss to her lips and looked deep into her eyes. "Don't say a word, darlin'. We'll revisit this later."

Candy nodded; she'd be more than happy to.

Chapter Nineteen

Candy looked down at her hand which rested on the console inside Deacon's. His fingers were linked through hers, and when he saw her looking, he gave her hand a squeeze.

"You okay over there, darlin'?"

She smiled and nodded. "I'm great. I had a wonderful time tonight, thank you."

"I'm glad. I did too. I usually dread going to those things, but I was looking forward to this one. Looking forward to going with you, and it turned out even better than I hoped."

Her eyes shone in the dark cab of the truck when she smiled at him. "I more than enjoyed it, I have to tell you; I think that was my best night out ever."

Deacon felt as though he grew taller in his seat. It did weird things to his insides when she said things like that. They weren't kids; he knew that she'd lived a lot of life before he even met her, but he loved the feeling that there were still new things he could introduce her to, firsts that they could share.

"I think it was mine, too."

They rode back down the valley in companionable silence. There was a lot that he wanted to say to her, a lot they needed to talk about — especially after Sharon's comment about their first dance. To his surprise, he wasn't even mad at the woman. He should be, for all she knew she might have put her foot in it big time. But she hadn't and that was what mattered.

In fact, she'd done him a favor. She'd brought up the question of a wedding — of him and Candy getting married. It was a question that hadn't left his mind since Luke had talked about Candy becoming his sister-in-law. He knew that it was what he wanted, and he suspected that it was what Candy wanted too. Seeing the way that she'd reacted to Sharon's words had confirmed for him that not only wasn't she against the idea, but she'd be all for it.

Now, what he wanted to do was find the right way to ask her. She didn't talk about Len much, and whatever she did say made Deacon wish that the man was still alive so that he could hunt him down and punch him. One thing that she told him — when they'd been watching that dating show where all the guys were after the same woman and the final guy had done this huge proposal on a beach with a million flowers — was that she'd always felt like she missed out on a wedding proposal. Len had asked her one day if she wanted to get married, and she told him that she thought she might. The next day he'd come home with the ring and slid it onto her finger. He'd told her that he'd booked them an appointment at the courthouse the following week.

On the one hand, Deacon could understand where the guy was coming from. He'd always thought that weddings were a waste of money; he'd resented all the time and savings that Willa had spent on theirs. But on the other hand, thinking about giving Candy something that she wanted, creating an occasion that she'd enjoy and remember, felt like one of the most important things he could do with his life. And if he was honest, he liked the idea of standing up in front of their friends and family and telling the world that he planned to love and take care of this woman for the rest of his days.

She squeezed his hand as he drove past the bakery without turning off the highway. He turned to her with a smile and cocked an eyebrow. "Problem?"

She gave him a puzzled smile. "I don't know. I hope not. I guess there's only a problem if we were going home."

He shot her a smile before turning his attention back to the road. "And would it be a problem if we weren't going home?"

"Nope. No problem at all. For a second there I thought you might be so lost in your thoughts that you didn't notice we were home. But since that's not the case, and you obviously have something else on your mind, I'll just sit back and relax and see what you have in store."

He loved that about her; he loved that she trusted him. She didn't grill him with a dozen questions about where they were going and why they weren't going straight home. She just accepted that he had something else in mind, and she had enough faith in him to trust that it was something she would enjoy.

He squeezed her hand one more time before turning the truck off the highway. It was late now; the moon was high in the sky. He'd be forever grateful to Spider for insisting that she took tomorrow off. This was the first time since he'd known her that Deacon didn't have to worry about her getting enough sleep before she had to be up again at the crack of sparrow fart.

She didn't complain about the bumpy ride as he followed the rough, gravel road. He thought that she'd figured out where they were going long before they got there, but when he turned the final corner and the lake appeared, shimmering silver under the moon, she let out a gasp of surprise.

"Oh my God, Deacon! It's beautiful! Thank you so much for bringing me here. It's like you read my mind again."

"How?"

"On the drive home, I was thinking how much I enjoyed tonight, you know, being around a bunch of people. That's more the kind of life I've been used to. Not fundraiser dinners, but being in the company of lots of people most of the time. I can't say I've missed that, but I did enjoy it tonight. But at the same time, I was thinking that I couldn't imagine going back to a life where that's all there is. I've already learned to love everything that this life has to offer: the mountains, the solitude, the ability to go just a few miles and be in a place where you wouldn't see another human being for days."

Deacon smiled. "This is one of those places, for sure," he said as he brought the truck to a stop at one of the picnic benches that were dotted around by the water's edge.

He cut the engine and turned to take her hands in his. "I had such a good time with you tonight. I didn't want it to end."

Her smile lit up her face as she leaned across the console toward him. He met her in the middle and brushed his lips over hers.

"I didn't either. I never want this to end."

His heart swelled in his chest. "I never want it to end either, darlin'. I …" He bit down on his bottom lip; he was so tempted to tell her that, if she wanted him, what they had between them would never end. He was as clear as he'd ever been about anything, clear in his mind and in his heart, that he wanted to make her his wife. He wanted to ask her right now but that wouldn't be right. He didn't have a ring. Sure, the setting was spectacular, the lake was beautiful, the moon was an added bonus, but when he asked her, he wanted it to be perfect. He'd take his time and get it right.

He pressed a kiss to her lips. "Wait there, I'll be around."

He climbed out of the truck and jogged around the hood to open her door. He lifted her out and swung her around before setting her down on her feet as she laughed. She made him feel like a kid – the kind of kid he'd never been – carefree and happy.

She put her hands on his shoulders and rolled up on her tiptoes. He lowered his head and claimed her mouth in a deep, sweet kiss that he hoped could tell her just how much she meant to him.

When he lifted his head, he closed his fingers around the nape of her neck, loving the way she shivered at his touch. He might not want to ask her to marry him right here and now, but he did want to make her understand how he felt.

He rested his forehead against hers and looked down into her eyes. "I love you, darlin'."

"Oh, Deacon." Her arms came up around his shoulders and pulled him down closer to her. She kissed him hungrily before finally leaning back and looking into his eyes. "I love you, too."

He kept his arm around her shoulders as they walked down toward the water's edge.

"It's so beautiful," she said.

"Not as beautiful as you are."

She laughed. "I never had you down as a sweet talker."

He rolled his eyes at her. "You know damn well that I'm not. I'm a straight shooter. I'm only telling you the truth, darlin'."

She rolled her eyes back at him, but he could tell that she was pleased with the compliment.

"I liked this place when you brought me in the daytime, but like this, at night? It feels even more special — magical."

Deacon nodded. He wasn't exactly a believer in magic, but he understood what she meant. Her words confirmed in his mind that when he did ask her to marry him, he should do it here.

"It is a special place, and this is a special night." He took hold of both of her hands and tugged her toward him.

The eagerness on her face made him wonder if she was expecting him to ask right now. It wouldn't be out of the blue after what Sharon had said earlier. He hoped he wasn't going to disappoint her, but this really wasn't the time.

"What kind of special?" she asked.

He held her gaze when he spoke. "The most special kind of all. Tonight, if you want it to, marks the beginning of the rest of our lives." His heart hammered in his chest – he knew what he meant, even if she didn't yet.

She smiled and nodded happily. "I want it to. I don't think I've ever wanted anything more than I want to know that you're going to be around for the rest of my life."

He hugged her tight to his chest and rested his chin on the top of her head. "I'm going to be around for the rest of your life, darlin'. At least, I want to be with you for the rest of mine. I know we've been figuring out this thing between us for a while now, but I need you to know that it starts tonight. This is it; from now on, it's you and me, thick and thin, good and bad, all that other stuff, you've got me by your side for all of it. For as long as you want me."

Her arms tightened around his waist. "We already covered that. I want you forever."

~ ~ ~

Candy slid a tray of chocolate croissants into the oven and closed it with a sigh. It felt like it had been a long week already and it was only midafternoon on Tuesday. She wiped her hands on her apron and let out a sigh as she sank down into the armchair that Rocket and Spider had set up in the far corner of the kitchen for her.

She couldn't help smiling; she'd bitched at them about this chair at first. She'd been indignant that they were treating her like an old lady. It had taken Deacon to point out that what they were really doing was trying to take care of her.

And now that she'd gotten used to it, she absolutely loved having the chair in here. She didn't allow herself to sit down for long though. It'd be too easy to settle in and stay a while. She'd thought about bringing her book to work with her, but she knew that if she started to read, she'd lose track of time altogether.

As it was, she felt guilty and sprang to her feet when Spider appeared in the doorway. He just laughed when he saw her.

"I wish you could get used to the idea that seeing you sitting down makes me happy — not mad. Do you honestly think that I'd tell you to get back to work?"

She made a face at him. "No, of course I don't. It's not about you. It's me. It's about what I expect of myself. You know I've never been one to sit around on my ass doing nothing."

Spider came into the kitchen and wrapped her in a hug. "Yeah, I know that. I just wish you could learn. I was coming in to see if you wanted to sit out front with me and have a coffee. It's quiet out there, and I could use a break myself."

"Well, in that case, I'd love to."

"Do you want your latte?"

"Please, do you want me to bring you anything out?"

Spider patted his stomach and gave her a rueful smile. "I don't think so, thanks. I need to start watching myself. It's too easy to eat the good stuff you make, and despite my good intentions, I haven't been making the time to go to the gym up in town."

Candy eyed his muscular frame and chuckled. "It doesn't look like there's a scrap of fat on you to me. But I know what you mean about it being a pain to get up to town. Go on, you get the coffees and I'll bring us a plate out."

Once they were settled in one of the booths, Spider gave her a rueful smile as he picked up a Danish. "I think I need to work on my willpower as much as I need to work on the motivation to get up to town."

Candy laughed. "It works the other way around for me. Because I don't often have the motivation to go to town, I don't need to rely on my willpower so much because I don't have goodies in the house."

Spider fixed her with a look that she didn't understand. It was obvious that he had something to say, but she didn't know what it might be. "Go on, spit it out. Whatever you have to say, say it. We've never had any secrets, you and me."

"It's not so much that I have something to say, more that I have something to ask, and I don't know if I'll be overstepping if I do."

"I don't think you could overstep. Like I said, we've never had any secrets, and I don't plan to start now. So, why don't you just ask your question?"

Spider took a bite of his Danish and looked away as he chewed and swallowed. When he looked back at her, he looked serious. "Do you plan to stay here? And I'm not asking for the sake of the bakery, not even for my own sake — and you know I'm hoping that you will. I'm asking because I like seeing you as happy as you are, and I hope it's going to last. But … and don't get mad at me … Rocket and I did some asking around."

Candy's heart started to pound. The boys didn't know much about what her life with Len had been like the last few years, and she'd rather they never knew.

Spider met her gaze and held it. "We had no idea, Miss Candy. I mean, we knew what you told us – and what Deacon said – about why he's so concerned about your safety. But we didn't know the half of it, did we? Of how things have been for you the last few years. I wish you would have let us know. We could have helped."

She reached across the table and took hold of his hand and gave it a squeeze. "I didn't want you to know. I kept tabs on you; I knew you were both doing well. Well, after Rocket's little bit of trouble there. The last thing that either of you needed was being dragged back into the kind of world I was living in. I can't even say I'm sorry I didn't tell you, because I'm not."

Spider blew out a sigh and nodded. "I get that. I know you were looking out for us." He smiled. "That's what moms do."

Candy had to swallow around a lump in her throat as she nodded, glad that he understood.

"But by the same token, when sons grow up, they look out for their mom, too. Has there been any news on what's happening with the pawn shop? See, Rocket and I were talking, and we could —"

"No!" Candy wagged her finger at him. "The only thing I want the two of you to do about that situation is stay the hell away from it. You hear me?"

Spider smiled through pursed lips. "I hear you, but —"

"No! There are no buts, Paul Webster. You're to stay the hell out of it. By the sounds of it, it should all be taken care of soon anyway."

"I'm not sure I believe that."

Candy shrugged. "If you don't believe me, you can ask Deacon. He's been in touch with the investigator down there, Saunders. From what he said, the whole thing is now part of a federal investigation. Hopefully, all those horrible men will be locked up soon and that'll be an end to it."

"I hope you're right." He looked up when the door opened, and a young couple came in. As he got to his feet to go and serve them, he added, "And I hope you meant it when you said that I can talk to Deacon, because I plan to. We both know that the sheriff won't turn down any extra help when it comes to taking care of you."

Candy couldn't even be mad at him, she just smiled. It was true; she loved the way that Deacon looked out for her — and the way the boys did, too.

She watched him walk over to the counter. As the young couple followed him, the girl, no, she was a young woman, kept glancing over at Candy. Candy gave her a friendly smile and was surprised to see a look of relief wash over the young woman's face.

She watched curiously as the woman caught up with her boyfriend and whispered to him. They engaged in an animated whispered conversation, and both kept glancing over at Candy. It didn't feel uncomfortable. She was more inclined to ask if she could help them with something than to tell them to stop being rude. She figured she'd wait and see if they were going to sit in for a while. She didn't want to be nosy if they were just popping in and out. And, more importantly, if Spider was going to come and sit back down, she'd rather spend the time chatting with him than with strangers.

He chatted with them a little while he fixed their drinks, and then they left. The young woman looked back over her shoulder at Candy one last time on her way out the door. Candy smiled and felt a rush of recognition fill her chest when the young woman gave her a curt nod.

"Are you okay?" asked Spider as he slid back into the booth opposite her.

She nodded slowly as she waited for her heart rate to return to normal. "I think so. What did those two have to say?"

"Not much," said Spider. "They seemed nice enough. It was just strange that right after I was talking about not getting up to the gym in town, that guy asked me if there's a gym around here."

"Did he say why?"

"He did; he's a personal trainer. I told him that if he is looking for work, he'd have to look up in town." Spider chuckled. "Unless he wants to become a private trainer. I told him I'm probably not the only one who would work out more if there were someone local, even someone who would be prepared to do home visits."

Candy raised her eyebrows. "Do people do that?"

"Probably not out here. It's definitely a thing in LA. People don't want to make the time to go to the gym or they want to work out in the privacy of their own homes. I could see it catching on out here, especially with the distances involved."

Candy nodded. She was more curious about the young woman than her boyfriend. But if the woman was who Candy suspected she might be, and the boyfriend was looking for work out here …

No, she was being silly. Just because that young woman had nodded at her in exactly the same way Deacon did, it didn't mean … It couldn't mean … She couldn't be. Then again, maybe she was. And if Deacon's daughter was in town, she should probably prepare him.

Spider gave her a puzzled look. "What's up?"

"You're probably going to think I'm crazy, but do you think that girl looked like Deacon?"

Spider ran his hand over his hair, looking thoughtful. "Damn. I thought she looked familiar, but I had no idea why." His eyes widened. "He has a daughter?"

Candy nodded slowly. "He does, and I have a feeling that was her."

"And I take it he's not expecting a visit from her?"

"No. But not because he wouldn't want to see her, more because he thinks she doesn't want to see him."

She got up and went to the window. She should've gone straight after them, but it was too late now; the parking lot was empty. If that was Deacon's daughter, she would no doubt be back.

Chapter Twenty

Deacon picked up his cell phone and then set it back down on his desk. He got up and paced over to the window. What the hell was wrong with him? He ran his hand through his hair as he looked out at the peaks of the Crazy Mountains in the distance.

He was nervous; that was what was wrong with him. He shook his head with a rueful smile. What was she doing to him? He wasn't the kind of guy who was given to nerves. He wouldn't have survived his childhood, his time in the military, and definitely not his marriage or his role as the sheriff if he was the nervous kind. But there was no denying that going out to buy a ring for Candy had him as nervous as a long-tailed cat in a room full of rocking chairs.

He went back to his desk and picked up his phone again. Ace had told him that he'd be up in town around lunchtime today if he wanted to meet up. Having lunch with his friend was one thing, asking him to come ring shopping was another.

He dialed Ace's number and waited.

"What's up, bud? Are you going to have time to grab some lunch with me? I'm about ten minutes out and I need to hit the feed store, but I can do that after if you're ready to eat now."

Deacon sucked in a deep breath and decided to just go for it. "I'm ready whenever you are; do you want to come straight here?"

"Sure." Ace laughed. "I take it you're hungry?"

Deacon chuckled. "As a matter of fact, I'm not worried if I don't get to eat. I have a much more important errand to run and I kind of want you along for the ride."

Ace was quiet for a long few moments.

"Say something!" Deacon blurted out when he couldn't take the silence any longer.

"This important errand, is it what I think it is?"

"I want to say that I don't know what you think it is, but I have a feeling that I know …" Deacon had to laugh. "Either I know what you're thinking, or you know what I'm thinking."

"If you are thinking what I'm thinking, then that's some serious shit."

Deacon scowled. "Yeah. It's as serious as it gets. You got a problem with it?"

Ace laughed. "Jesus, buddy! Calm down. I don't have a problem. That couldn't be further from the truth. When I said serious shit, I meant monumental, huge. You know? Like a totally big fucking deal. I'm thrilled! I don't mind telling you that I've wondered if it might come to this. But I didn't think … I didn't think you'd want to go there again. I'm glad that you do. I'd say if any woman's worth it, that woman would be Candy."

"I'm glad you think so. So, what do you say? Want to meet me here and go ring shopping with me?"

"Hell yeah, I do. I'd tell you that I'll haul ass, but since it's you I'll just say see you soon."

Deacon was smiling as he hung up. He was kind of surprised at himself that he wanted company on his little shopping expedition, but at the same time, he really wasn't. He and Ace were close.

He went to the door of his office and looked out into the big open area where the deputies sat when they were in the building. Luke wasn't out there. That made the decision not to ask him to come with them easier. He'd love to have his little brother along, especially since he was so close with Candy. But it was probably for the best this way; Deacon couldn't imagine himself not giving Luke a hard time about buying an engagement ring himself if he were there.

When Ace strode into his office less than five minutes later, Deacon tried to scowl at him, but he couldn't help laughing. "Damn, you must've really hauled ass."

"I don't know what you're talking about, Sheriff. You ready to go?"

Deacon grabbed his hat off the hook by the door and nodded. He wiped the palms of his hands on his pants as he followed his friend out to the parking lot. He wasn't nervous about asking Candy, wasn't nervous about what her answer might be — she'd already made that plain. What he was nervous about was finding the right ring. He wanted to find something that she'd love; that kind of went without saying. What surprised him was that he wanted to get her the kind of ring that would tell anyone and everyone who saw it that she was loved by a man who cherished her.

He had to swallow the emotions that clogged his throat as he followed Ace over to his truck.

His friend gave him a puzzled look. "Are you okay? I didn't expect you to meekly follow me."

Deacon gave an embarrassed laugh and shrugged. "Neither did I, but now that we're here, I guess I'm calling shotgun."

Ace tapped out a quick text and then glanced over at him as he pulled out of the parking lot. "Do you even know where we're going? Or am I in charge?"

Deacon shrugged. "There are only two jewelry stores in town. I'd guess we're going to need to hit them both. So, it doesn't really matter which one we go to first. I'm hoping I'll find what I want today, but if not, don't be surprised if I ask you to ride over to Bozeman with me one day soon."

"Yeah. You know I'll go whenever you want me to. I imagine it'll be harder for you to get away than me, considering how you don't like leaving Candy by herself."

"It's not that I don't like leaving her by herself. It's just that I won't take any risks with her safety. We'll both be glad when this whole deal with the guys from her pawn shop is behind us. She's the kind of woman who needs time to herself. She's been good about it, but I know it's driving her nuts to constantly have someone around babysitting her."

Ace shot him a quick grin. "I'm glad you can see it. You're right, she has been a good sport, but even I can see that it's wearing thin."

Deacon blew out a sigh. "It's out of my hands at this point. All we can do is play the waiting game. Either Saunders will call and tell me that the feds have wrapped up their investigation, or …" he scowled at the thought of it "… or someone will show up here and go after her."

Ace nodded grimly. "Even if that happens, she'll be fine. And if those fuckers make it to the valley, I don't like their odds of leaving again — except in a box."

"Yeah." Deacon didn't even want to think about it. He'd do whatever it took to keep Candy safe — even if what it took was putting men in the ground.

"Anyway," said Ace. "This little trip is about you getting the best possible outcome, so why don't we just forget about worst-case scenarios for now?" He pulled his truck into a spot on Main Street half a block down from the jewelry store. He laughed and pointed, and Deacon did a double take.

"And speaking of a little trip …" Ace laughed. "I hope you don't mind but …"

Deacon had to laugh with him. "You told him?"

"Hell yeah, I did! I would've told the others, too, if they were here in town. Even Emmett is over in Billings today, so you'll just have to make do with Trip and me as the two representatives of the gang."

Deacon climbed out of the truck without a word.

Ace gave him a puzzled look as they walked toward where Trip waited outside the jewelry store. "You mad, bro?"

He had to laugh at that. "No. I'm not mad. I'm … I …" He scrubbed his hand over his face.

Trip laughed as he came to greet them. "Leave the man alone, Ace. He's all emotional is what he is."

Deacon rolled his eyes at him and made a dissenting noise that sounded something like a growl. Whatever it was, it was all he was capable of. Because damn him, but Trip was right.

Ace slapped his back and hustled him toward the store. "Come on, let's go do this."

Candy checked her watch and looked out the window. It was the afternoon slump again. She'd love to go home and curl up on the sofa with Clawson and her book. She didn't even collect Clawson and take him up to her apartment when she got back anymore. She didn't collect him because she went straight to him. Deacon had given her a key to his place, and she was going upstairs less and less often. They pretty much lived together now, and she loved it.

Unfortunately, he still didn't think it was safe for her to go home by herself after work. She'd been hoping that he might relent once the alarm system was operational, but his friend Brad had had some delay on the parts he needed, and it didn't look like he'd be finished anytime soon. It was wearing thin – not Deacon looking out for her, but the fact that she never got any time to herself — or even any time alone with her book and Clawson.

She pulled herself together. In the grand scheme of things, she really had nothing to complain about. She was living in this beautiful place, with her wonderful man, surrounded by lovely friends who really were becoming family.

This afternoon, Janey, Frankie, and Sierra were coming in to hang out. And Libby had said that she would be here as soon as she could get here, too. She was down on the ranch giving a private riding lesson this afternoon. That made Candy smile. Libby didn't do many private lessons, at least, not for kids. From what Candy understood, she did some equine therapy work with veterans. But most of her kids took group lessons.

However, Libby made an exception for a very special little boy whom Candy simply adored, Owen Davenport. Owen was autistic, and he was a solemn little thing most of the time. He watched everything and everyone around him in a way that made Candy think of him as an old soul visiting from the afterlife to observe how humans were getting along. The look on his face usually said that the progress mankind was making didn't impress him. But Candy knew how to make him laugh; and when he laughed, he was just like any other little kid.

She finished wiping down the counter, hoping that Libby and Owen were having a good time, and also hoping that Libby would be here before too long. Candy loved hanging out with the girls, she loved hearing about their lives, and of course their perspectives on the boys. But she enjoyed it even more when Libby was around too. It really was a novelty for her to have a close friend her own age. As much as she loved the girls, she was learning how much she enjoyed feeling like an equal more than like a mom.

Rocket came into the kitchen with a smile on his face. He didn't stop walking until he reached her and when he did, he wrapped his arms around her and lifted her off the floor, spinning her around, and making her laugh.

"Rocket MacFarland, put me down this minute!"

Rocket just laughed as he continued to spin her. She laughed with him, even as she beat her fists against his massive arms.

Eventually, he set her down and bent so that he could kiss her cheek. She wrapped her arms around his neck and pulled him down so that she could kiss his cheek before he straightened up.

"Well, that was wonderful! Was there a reason?"

Rocket just shrugged, looking for all the world like the kid he'd been all those years ago when she first met him. "I dunno, Miss Candy. I just … I'm happy you're here, and I wanted to see you smile. Sometimes, I can't help it; I just need to pick you up and make sure that it's real, that you're really here."

"Aww, Rocky. You know, for such a big guy, you're a real softy at heart."

Rocket gave her a bashful shrug and nodded. "I wouldn't go trying to tell people that, though."

Candy laughed. "Oh, believe me, I won't. I gave up trying to get people to see you the way I see you years ago. Most people are too closed-minded to see what's on the inside — and that's their loss."

Rocket shrugged again. "I wanted to check in with you before the girls arrive. I know you like seeing them, but I also know this isn't ideal. I wanted to give you the option; if you prefer, I'll take you home instead."

"Aww." She patted his arm. "You're such a good boy."

He smiled through pursed lips. "Only you, Miss Candy. Only you."

She laughed. "I know, and I'm sorry, but it's true. It's sweet of you to ask, and you're right, I'd love to go home. But it'll be fun to see the girls and to see Libby. Is it quiet out there, yet?"

"It is, it's empty. Do you want to come out, and I'll fix you a latte?"

"Yes, I've just finished up in here and if I sit in my armchair, I won't feel like coming out when they arrive."

She laughed again when Rocket scooped her up and carried her out through the front. He didn't stop until he deposited her in one of the big comfy booths at the back.

"You take a load off; I'll be back with your latte in a minute."

Candy sat, smiling to herself; life really was good. Her smile froze on her face when the door opened and the young couple who'd been here the other day came in.

The young woman looked around and froze when she saw Candy. Her boyfriend moved toward her and put a protective arm around her waist. Candy gave them a friendly smile. She was no threat to them, although the boyfriend seemed to think that she might be.

"Hey there," she called. "It's good to see you in here again."

The girl still looked wary, but she gave a small smile and nodded. "I'm surprised you remember us."

Candy got to her feet but then thought better of it and beckoned them over. "Do you want to have a coffee with me? I have to be honest and tell you that I haven't been able to forget you."

The girl looked up at her boyfriend; he looked Candy over before nodding. As the two of them approached, Candy couldn't help hoping that Rocket wouldn't come back out yet – he might scare them away.

When they reached the table, Candy held out her hand to shake with them. "I really meant it when I said it's good to see you again. Please –" she gestured to the bench on the other side of the booth "– take a seat."

They sat, and the girl narrowed her eyes. "Do you know who I am, then?"

Candy raised her eyebrows. "I think I do, but I'm only guessing."

The girl nodded. "I think you've guessed right. And from what I heard that guy say when we were here before – about the sheriff wanting to look after you – I'm guessing that I know who you are, too. But if you're still only guessing about who I am … Did you tell him?"

"No." Candy felt bad when she saw the flash of pain in the girl's eyes. "Not because he wouldn't be happy that you're here. He would — he will. He's going to be thrilled. The only reason I didn't tell him was that I wasn't certain that you were his daughter. You are his daughter, aren't you?"

The girl nodded, and Candy instinctively reached for her hand when she saw her eyes fill with tears.

"What is it, sweetheart? What's wrong?"

"You really think that he'll be happy to see me?"

Candy nodded rapidly. "I don't just think so, I know so. I don't want to say too much, I'd never try to make you feel guilty, but he misses you terribly."

The girl exchanged a look with her boyfriend that Candy didn't understand. "What would she have to feel guilty about?" asked the boyfriend.

Candy had already noticed that he was super protective, and she was glad of that. "Sorry, that probably came out wrong. I'm not saying that you have anything to feel guilty about. I just thought you might … You know, since you haven't seen that much of each other."

The boyfriend frowned. "And whose fault is that?"

The girl put her hand on his arm. "That's kind of the point, Porter. We don't know whose fault it is. All we know is what Mom said. And given how much of that has turned out to be lies lately, I don't want to jump to any conclusions. I'm here to find out the truth." She turned to look at Candy. "I'm here to get to know my dad – if you think he'd be open to it."

Candy put her hand over her heart. "Oh, my goodness, he'd be so much more than open to it. I promise you."

At that moment, Rocket came and set Candy's drink in front of her. He smiled at the young couple and asked, "Can I get you guys anything?

The girl shook her head and started to get to her feet. Her boyfriend stood up beside her and took hold of her hand.

"Wait," said Candy. "Where are you going? Don't you want to stay a while? Don't you —"

The girl shook her head rapidly and glanced at the door when it opened. Janey, Frankie, and Sierra came in, chatting and laughing loudly.

"I … I think I need to build up to it. I'm not ready to face him yet." She gave Candy a pleading look. "Do you really think that he'll want to see me?"

"I promise you. How about you give me your number? And I'll give you mine. I understand that you need a little time, but I'd never forgive myself if you left without seeing him — for his sake or for yours."

The girl – Candy needed to stop thinking about her that way. Cadence, her name was Cadence – swallowed visibly and looked up at her boyfriend once again. Candy was relieved when he nodded.

They exchanged numbers quickly, with Cadence glancing over her shoulder at the girls the whole time. Candy wanted nothing more than to hug her and reassure her that everything would be okay, but she got the impression that that would be too much, for now, at least.

The boyfriend – Porter – wrapped his arm around her shoulders once again and nodded at Candy and at Rocket, too. Candy liked him better for doing that. "We'll give you a call when Cady's ready."

Candy nodded. "Is it okay if I tell your dad that you're here? I don't want to keep it a secret from him."

Cadence met her gaze with gray eyes that were just like Deacon's. "You really love him, don't you?"

Candy didn't hesitate for a second. "I love that man with all my heart. Knowing that you're here and that he'll get to see you makes me want to turn cartwheels. Anything that makes him happy makes me happy. And I know that nothing could make him happier than seeing you here."

"Wow."

Candy raised her eyebrows.

"I'm glad he has you – that he's found someone who loves him the way you obviously do," Cadence explained. "And I'm kind of blown away that you think he's going to be happy to see me."

"Don't doubt it, sweetheart. Don't doubt it for a second." Candy smiled at her and at Porter, too. "It strikes me that you're both prepared for the worst, and I imagine that you think you have good reason to. But I want to reassure you both that this is going to work out better than you expect." She held Porter's gaze for a moment. "He's a good guy who loves his daughter, and I think you should hear what he has to say before you make too many judgments."

"Hey, guys!" Frankie appeared beside the booth with a big grin on her face. She looked up at Rocket. "We were trying to be polite, but you either have to make us coffee or introduce us." She shot a quick smile at Cadence and Porter.

Cadence gave her a tight smile and that all-too-familiar curt nod. "Sorry to hold you up, we were just leaving." She gave Candy a more genuine-looking smile and added, "I'll call you," as they walked away.

"Shit," Frankie muttered under her breath. "Sorry, I didn't mean to put my foot in it, who was that?"

Candy shook her head. "Don't worry about it. It's not a problem. Now, come on, you can come in the back with me and help me load up a basket of goodies."

Frankie was nobody's fool; it was obvious that she knew Candy was avoiding the question, but she played along and let it go.

Candy tucked Cadence's number carefully into her pocket. She couldn't wait to tell Deacon but at the same time, she was nervous for him. Porter seemed to think that Deacon was the bad guy. From what Cadence had said, that was the way Willa had painted him.

She sucked in a deep breath as she led Frankie into the kitchen. She was going to do everything she could to help them straighten it out and build a new relationship – even though she knew that the hardest thing would be keeping her opinions to herself and letting them figure it out in their own way.

Chapter Twenty-One

Deacon snapped the ring box closed and shoved it into his pocket when he heard a tap on his door. He felt guilty as hell sitting here, smiling at the shiny diamonds when he was supposed to be working.

Luke gave him a puzzled look as he came in. "Are you hiding muffins again?"

Deacon had to laugh. "Nope. You know as well as I do that Candy makes extra for you, just so that I don't have to hide them."

Luke grinned and took a seat in the chair across the desk from Deacon. "I do. She's awesome. you're not the only one who lucked out when you met her."

"Yeah. It wasn't exactly when I met her though, was it? It took a while. If it wasn't for you …" He really didn't like to think about the possibility that if it weren't for Luke, he might never have gotten his act together, and Candy might have slipped through his fingers.

Luke nodded happily. "I'm just glad that I could help. I'd hate to think of you going through life without that little lady by your side when it was so obvious that you guys are meant to be together."

Deacon pursed his lips. He really didn't want to start giving Luke a hard time today. Today was a good day — a great day — it was the day that he'd bought the ring that he hoped Candy would wear for the rest of her life. But Luke was going to have to get his head out of his ass soon if he was ever going to do it. He'd already gone through too much of his life without the woman who should be his lady by his side.

Luke cocked an eyebrow. "Why do I feel like you're about to tear me a new one?"

Deacon shrugged.

"Because you were, right?" Luke didn't give him the chance to answer before he continued. "How about we just go with not today? I don't know what to tell you, Deacon. I know what you want to say to me. I know you want to tell me to finally get my shit together and talk to Laney, and with every day that goes by, I'm getting closer to doing just that. But if you want to know the truth, I'm hanging by a thin thread lately. So, please, can we just go with not today?"

Deacon held his gaze and nodded slowly. He felt bad. He tended to assume that Luke easily blinded himself to the truth about Laney MacFarland, but from what he just said, perhaps it wasn't that easy after all.

"Okay."

Luke's eyebrows shot up. "Seriously? You're going to let me off the hook that easily? What's the catch?"

"No catch," said Deacon. "I'm not letting you off the hook completely, just for today."

"What's so special about today?" Luke looked skeptical, as though he was still waiting for the other shoe to drop.

Deacon smiled and only had to think about it for a moment before he pulled the ring box out of his pocket and set it down on the desk between them.

Luke looked down at the box, and a big grin spread across his face as he looked back up at Deacon.

"Is that what I think it is?"

"Why don't you open it and see?"

Luke reached for the box slowly. Deacon chuckled as he watched. "It's okay, it's not going to bite you."

Luke made a face at him as he picked the box up. When he flipped it open, his eyes lit up. "Holy Shit! Damn! Did *you* choose this?"

Deacon had to laugh. "What's that supposed to mean?"

Luke laughed with him. "Shit, sorry! I mean, it's beautiful. Shit. That sounds lame. I mean, it's stunning. It's just not something that I would have expected you to choose. Damn, I'm screwing this up. I'm not trying to insult you. I'm trying to say that it's amazing and unexpected. And most importantly, I think Candy's going to love it."

Deacon smiled; that was the most important part. "You really think that she'll like it?"

Luke held his gaze. "I love that that's the only part that you want reassurance about."

Deacon shrugged. "That's the only part that matters."

"Well, I don't think you've got any worries there. Is it weird to say that it reminds me of her?"

Deacon folded his arms across his chest and leaned back in his chair with a broad smile on his face. It felt good that Luke could see it too. "Nah, it's not weird. Or if it is, it must be a *Wallis boys* kind of weird."

Luke's gaze snapped up to meet his, and Deacon understood why. When they were kids, the term *the Wallis boys* had never been used in a complimentary way. Folks could've said *the scum of the earth* and meant the same thing.

He shrugged at his brother. "That's something that's been on my mind for a while now; don't you think it's time that we started to take pride in who we are? We've done pretty well for ourselves if you think about it."

Luke held his gaze for a long moment. "That's why you wanted to be the sheriff, isn't it? You wanted to rise above where we came from."

Deacon blew out a sigh. "Yeah. It is. Do you remember Sheriff Higgins when you were a kid?"

Luke let out a short laugh. "I do. He was an evil bastard, that one."

"He was. He was everything that you don't want an officer of the law to be. I hated him, even when I was a kid. He thought we were the scum of the earth. He had a point when it came to the old man, but he took it out on us, too. I once saw that man hit a woman while he was arresting her. Prostitution charges. I was just a kid, I have no idea if there was any truth in those charges, all I knew at the time was how bad it feels when someone bigger and stronger than you hits you, and there's nothing you can do about it. I knew that it was even worse when it was someone who you were supposed to be able to turn to for help and protection. Someone who was supposed to uphold the law.

"I tried to stop him from hitting her, but he hit me too. Then he tossed me aside like a piece of trash. Which is what he thought I was. It was that night, when I was sleeping on that pile of coats that we used to call a bed, that I made a vow to myself that one day I'd be the sheriff and I'd do it right." Deacon had to blink a few times and swallow to clear his throat when he finished speaking.

Luke nodded slowly. "Thanks for telling me. I've always known that there was something driving you. I guess I just thought that you wanted to be like an equal and opposite reaction to Dad. For all the bad that he did in the world, I thought you were making up for it by doing good."

"Yeah. Anyway." He shrugged and smiled at Luke through pursed lips. "I guess I'm just feeling sentimental today." He reached for the ring box, and Luke handed it back to him. He smiled as he looked down at it. "I guess buying one of these things will do that to a guy."

Luke chuckled. "Yes, I guess. But before we move on and put the moment behind us, just like you've never told me that before, I don't think I've ever told you before how proud I am that you're my big brother."

Deacon had to swallow again and couldn't manage to force any words out. Instead, he smiled at Luke and nodded.

Luke started to get to his feet. "I should probably go before one or both of us starts bawling, huh?"

Deacon let out a short laugh. "Yeah. That's probably a good idea." Just as Luke reached the door, he called after him. "I hope I've told you before, but it goes both ways, Luke; I'm proud of you, too."

Luke turned back and held his gaze for a long moment before giving him a curt nod and hurrying out.

~ ~ ~

"Candy, can I borrow some of your vanilla?"

Candy gave Libby a puzzled look. "Sure. Remind me before …"

Libby got to her feet and gave her a meaningful look. "No, we should do it now. I swear my short-term memory is failing." She looked around at the girls, who hadn't stopped chatting and laughing since they came in earlier. "You ladies won't miss us for a minute if we go in the back, will you?"

Janey and Sierra both shook their heads and smiled. Frankie narrowed her eyes at Libby. "We won't miss you, but you could've just said that you wanted a word with Candy alone."

Libby made a face at her. "Whatever. We'll be back."

She followed Candy into the kitchen and rolled her eyes when they got there. "I should've known better than to try to put anything past Frankie. She's too sharp for her own good."

Candy had to laugh. "I noticed. What's up? Is something wrong?"

"No. At least, there's nothing up with me. That's what I wanted to ask you. What's going on? I don't think anyone else has noticed, but you're not enjoying yourself as much as you usually do when the girls come in. Is everything okay?"

Candy loved that Libby already knew her well enough to notice that there was something on her mind. "Everything's okay, I think. In fact, I'm hoping that everything might be wonderful, but I'm nervous in case it doesn't turn out that way."

"You don't have to tell me if it's something personal. I just wanted you to know that I'm here for you if there's anything you want to talk about."

"I'd love to hear what you think. It's just … Cadence was in here earlier."

Libby frowned at first, but then realization dawned, and her eyes grew wide. "You mean Deacon's Cadence?"

Candy nodded. "Yep. His daughter and her boyfriend."

"Wow! And how does he feel about that? I mean, I'm sure he's happy that she's here, but … Why is she here? What's going on? Is she here to cause trouble?"

Candy's breath caught in her chest. "Why would she want to cause trouble?"

Libby blew out a sigh. "That probably wasn't fair; I don't know Cadence. I don't know who she is now, anyway. I barely knew her when she was small. Willa didn't like for the kids to hang around with the rest of us. I guess I was just thinking that if Cadence is here, Willa has probably put her up to it and is no doubt stirring trouble."

Candy shook her head. "No, that's not the impression I got. Not at all. And I can't tell you how Deacon feels about it because he doesn't know yet."

Libby raised her eyebrows. "So, if Deacon doesn't know, how do you know?"

"Because she came in here and I figured out who she was. I really don't think she's here to cause trouble. I think she wants to get to know her dad. She's nervous to see him. She thinks he won't want to see her. And from what she said to her boyfriend, her mom might have lied to her about Deacon and how he feels about her and her brother."

Libby let out a low whistle. "Wow! And how do you feel about it?"

Candy smiled. "I get the feeling that it might be messy until they work things out, but I'm thrilled for him. And I'm going to do everything I can to help."

Libby grinned at her. "See, you're just perfect for him. I've never said it to him, but I disliked Willa from the moment I met her. She was a bitch, no two ways about it. And the feeling was mutual; she looked down her nose at me from the moment we were introduced. I felt bad for Deacon when she took the kids and left, but it was still a relief to see her go."

Candy jumped and they both turned at the sound of someone clearing their throat in the doorway from the front. Deacon was standing there watching them, and from the way he had his arms folded across his chest and was leaning against the doorframe, he'd been there for a while.

Candy's heart hammered in her chest. Ever since Cadence had left, she'd been trying to work out the best way to tell Deacon that she was here. Now, it looked like he'd heard. And worse than that, he'd heard everything that Libby had to say about Willa.

A rush of relief washed over her when he pushed away from the doorframe with a smile and started toward them.

"Hey, darlin'. Don't look so worried." He glanced at Libby. "It's not news to me who Willa was or how you guys felt about her."

He met Candy's gaze and held it as he took the last few steps toward her. When he reached her, he put his hands on her shoulders and leaned down to press a kiss to her lips. "And you, little lady, I love that you're worried about me, I love that you want to help. And I'm guessing that I'm going to need your help with this one. Libby's right, you are perfect for me, darlin'."

Candy wrapped her arms around his waist and hugged him tight. "Oh, Deacon. I'm so sorry that you heard that, I mean, that you found out that way. I've been trying to figure out the best way to tell you."

His gray eyes twinkled as they looked down into hers. "You know the best way to tell me, just like I know the best way to tell you. With anything and everything, we tell each other straight. That's just how it is between you and me. I can't tell you that I'm not surprised or even that I'm not nervous that Cadence is here. But it's like you just said, no matter how messy it might get, I've got you by my side, that's all I need." He hugged her close to his chest and kissed the top of her head.

"Oh, for fuck's sake! Can you guys take it home now?" asked Libby with a laugh. "I mean, yes, it's awesome to see you both so in love. But, come on, I don't need to see it, thanks. You don't need to go flaunting that shit in front of a woman who – "

She broke off suddenly, and Candy wondered what she'd been about to say. Deacon went and gave Libby a hug, then shook his head at her. "Candy and me, we're getting a late start on our love story. You, lady, you need to get your shit together and sort yours out."

Candy was shocked that he would talk to Libby like that. She felt bad for her new friend; she knew how much she still hurt over Maverick. So, she was surprised when Libby rolled her eyes at Deacon and slapped his arm.

"Asshole! If it were as easy as you make it sound, we would've sorted it out."

"Nothing worth having — or keeping — ever comes easy, you know that, Lib." He pursed his lips. "And so does Mav."

"Whatever. My point was that Mav isn't around for me to sort anything out, but your lady here has been waiting to go home. It sounds like the two of you are going to have a lot to talk about, so why don't you take her now?"

Deacon cocked an eyebrow at Candy, and she nodded. Libby didn't seem to be upset, and she really did want to get home and tell Deacon about Cadence and Porter.

~ ~ ~

When they got back to the house, Clawson greeted them in what had become his usual manner, winding his way around both their legs in a figure eight pattern. Once Deacon had fed him, he went to Candy and slid his arms around her waist. He'd almost decided that after dinner tonight he'd take her for a drive over to Dailey Lake – before the ring burned a hole in his pocket. Now, though, he wasn't sure.

Of course, he still wanted to ask her, but the news that Cadence was here in town had thrown him for a loop. He couldn't deal with two emotional events in one day. As much of a hurry as he was in to ask Candy to marry him and to make her his wife, he wanted the day he proposed to her to be a beautiful memory that stood alone in its own right. It wasn't that Cadence being here would overshadow it, but there was no denying that the thought of seeing his daughter after all this time had his attention divided.

Candy tightened her arms around his waist and looked up into his eyes. "Are you okay?"

He smiled and pressed three quick kisses to her lips. "I'm more than okay, darlin'. I'm in love with the greatest woman I've ever known."

"Aww. I love you, too, Sheriff Wallis. I was thinking more about Cadence, though."

"I know what you meant. And I'm more than okay with that, too. I am nervous, I don't mind admitting that. I want you to tell me all about it, but before we get to that I wanted a minute with you, just to hold you, check in with you, make sure you're good."

She looped her arms up around his neck and looked deep into his eyes. "I'm better than I've ever been, thanks to you. I just want you to know that I'll do whatever you want me to when it comes to Cadence." She smiled. "Even if that means you want me to butt out, I'll understand if you do."

"No! That's the last thing I want. I love that you're the one who told me that she's here. It feels right that somehow, you've kind of ended up being the go-between. I've never managed to figure things out with her or her brother by myself. Now that I have you in my life, I believe it might finally be possible. I want your help; I need it, darlin'."

There was a time not so long ago when Deacon wouldn't have believed that he'd ever ask a woman for her help with anything, let alone something so important to him. But that was before he met Candy. Now, he couldn't imagine trying to do this without her.

Chapter Twenty-Two

As Deacon rode up the valley to work the next morning, his mind was racing. Candy hadn't been able to tell him much about why Cadence was here, or even about what she might want from him. He felt bad even thinking that, but he couldn't help it. It was sad to admit, but he didn't know who she was as a person and his only frame of reference for what she might be like was her mother. That didn't bode well, and he knew he needed to try and stop thinking of her that way.

He'd wanted to call her last night, but that was just his own impatience. Candy had told him that she'd said she wasn't ready to face him. He knew that he needed to let her take her time. It had taken all these years before she even wanted to see him, he couldn't go screwing it up now by forcing the pace.

He didn't know what to think about the boyfriend: Porter. What kind of name was that, anyway? He gripped the steering wheel tighter and blew out a frustrated sigh. It didn't matter what the kid's name was, what mattered was how he treated Cadence. Candy had said that he seemed super protective of her. On the one hand, that could be a good thing — he was aware that he could be described the same way when it came to Candy. However, he knew that there was a fine line between being protective and being controlling. He'd have to meet Porter for himself before he knew which side of that line the kid fell on.

He took a swig of coffee from his new travel mug and couldn't help smiling as he set it back in the cup holder. Candy had bought it for him. These days, when he went into the bakery in the morning, she already had it filled for him. She'd also given him his own little Tupperware container, and he flipped that open now, setting it on his lap to catch any crumbs that might fall as he ate his banana nut scone. He loved the way that she took care of him. His smile faded; he knew that she wasn't thrilled about the way he was taking care of her. Not that she had a problem with him or even with what he was doing. It was the whole situation that she wasn't thrilled with. He was less than thrilled himself.

He planned to call Saunders again today. He knew that the feds had to be thorough in their investigations, but this whole deal was taking far too long for his liking. He wanted to hear that the whole operation had been wrapped up, and the assholes who'd been using Candy's pawn shop were finally behind bars. He wanted her to have her life back. She told him often enough that she loved her life here in the valley, most especially her life with him. But he knew that her real life here couldn't fully begin until she was no longer under any kind of threat.

He loved that she'd struck up such a fast and firm friendship with Libby, but he knew that they were both the kind of women who wanted to do more than go for drives and hang out at the bakery. They'd had a couple more evenings at Trip's house, but that was as far as their social life had stretched. He wasn't comfortable with the thought of Candy and Libby having a girl's night at Chico or going up to town.

He tried to reassure her that he would love for her to have that kind of social life once the threat was behind her. He smiled as he remembered her reaction. She looped her arms around his neck and pulled him down until his forehead was touching hers. He loved the way her eyes shone with mischief whenever she did that. She'd told him that she knew damn well that he wasn't trying to control her, he was simply looking out for her, and even though she was tired of it all, she appreciated that he cared enough to keep her safe.

Then she'd laughed and taken his hand and led him to the bedroom. The memory of the way she'd pushed him back onto the bed made him hard. She'd told him that since her social life was limited to spending time at home with him, they'd just have to find ways to keep it lively. He bit down on his bottom lip as he remembered just how lively things had gotten after that.

He came back to the moment with a guilty start when his phone rang. He smiled when he saw her name on the display. As he hit the button on the steering wheel to answer the call, he was tempted to tell her what she'd caught him thinking about. But it was unusual for her to call him in the morning, especially before he'd even made it to work. So, he should probably find out what she needed before he went down that path.

"Hey, darlin'. What's up?"

"Hey, you. I know you probably aren't even to work yet, but I had to call and tell you. Cady and Porter just came in. She said that she's barely slept at all thinking about seeing you, and she wants to know if the four of us can get together this afternoon."

Deacon's heart hammered in his chest. His only plan had been to go as slowly as he could manage to, and he'd expected to have a bit of a wait before he got to see his daughter. This was better than he could have hoped for.

"Absolutely. Did she say when and where? And is that okay with you? She wants all four of us there?"

"Yes. I can find a way to get myself out of it if you like. I think it's just because she met me first with no pressure. She didn't …"

"Hell no! I want you there. I mean … if you want to be there. I don't want to force you into it if you don't …"

He loved the sound of her laughter. "Come on, Deacon. Let's not get off track now, huh? We work so well together because we always tell each other straight. Let's not start pussyfooting around now. I'll go first and say, I want to be there with you. I know you're not sure about how this will go or how to handle it. I want to be with you to help you. And I'll tell you straight as well, that it isn't just for you. I'm excited to get to know your daughter. We've talked about forever, you and me. And if that's how it's going to be for us then, of course, I want to be part of this. If that's okay with you?"

Deacon's heart felt as though it melted in his chest. "It's not just okay, Candy. It makes me happier than you know. I thought that my chance for love and family had passed me by. I feel like I was given the winning lottery ticket when we got together. You've given me more love than I knew was possible to share. And now? Now that there's a possibility that my kids might figure into my future? I'm over the moon, but it won't feel like family if you're not part of it."

"Aww, Deacon."

He had to laugh; he loved the way she said that. "Don't go making your sappy noises at me, woman. It's true."

She laughed with him. "Well, that's me told, I guess. So, if you don't want me to be sappy, would you rather I be efficient and just set this meeting up?"

"I'd love that, darlin', thank you."

"Okay, what time can you get off work?"

"I have a meeting this morning, then I'm supposed to run by the AG's office around noon. But Theo likes to keep things brief, so I should be all wrapped up with him by one, at the latest."

"So, if I say after two o'clock, we should be okay?"

"Yeah, that'll work. And if she wants to do earlier than that, let me know and I'll work something out."

"I'll talk to her and call you back. I was thinking that I could invite them to the house, but then I realized … I know it's not likely, but the last thing I want is for my trouble to somehow impact your daughter."

Hearing her say that made Deacon want to turn the truck around and go straight back to the bakery and hug her. "Shit, I'm sorry, darlin', but yeah, you're right. I …"

He could hear the smile in her voice as she interrupted him. "Don't you go apologizing to me. I'm the one who feels bad for telling you that I don't think it's the best idea for them to come to the house. I don't want you to think I'm some territorial female. I just …"

He had to laugh. "I don't. You want to know what I do think you are?"

"What?"

"I think you're the woman I want to spend the rest of my life with."

"Aww. I don't care what you say, you are a sweetheart, Deacon Wallis. But I'm going to let you go because you must be almost to town by now, and I want to go and talk to Cady and Porter."

Deacon's heart thudded to a halt. "What did you just say? What did you call her?"

"Oh, I'm sorry. Cady? I … it's what Porter calls her. I just …"

Deacon was glad when the light ahead of him turned red. As he brought the truck to a halt, he took advantage of the moment to rest his forehead on his hands on the steering wheel. "You called her Cady." He couldn't help the way his voice wavered.

"I did."

"That's what I called her when she was a little girl. Her mother hated it. She used to say that she didn't give our daughter such a beautiful name to have it corrupted."

"Well, Cady's an adult in her own right now, it's up to her what name she wants to go by." Candy's tone softened as she continued. "And hopefully it's a good sign that she wants to go by the name that her daddy used to call her."

Deacon sucked in a deep breath and pulled the truck forward when the light changed. He had to clear his throat before he spoke again. "I hope so."

"It's all going to be okay, Deacon. You'll see."

"Thanks, darlin'." It was weird; he'd thought that he'd lost any chance he had to have a real relationship with his kids, but when Candy said it was going to be okay, he believed her.

~ ~ ~

Rocket set down the last of the three armchairs he and Spider had brought into the back and looked at Candy. "What do you think? Will that do?"

"That's perfect, thanks Rocky." She went and gave him a hug, then turned to Spider, who had just come into the kitchen with a huge plate of pastries and a fresh carafe of coffee.

Once he set them down, she went and hugged him, too. "Thanks, boys. I really appreciate this."

Rocket gave her a stern look, and Spider shook his head as he said, "Please don't go thanking us, Miss Candy. You know that we'd do anything for you, and by extension, these days, that means we'd do anything for Deacon, too."

Rocket nodded his agreement. "Although, we'd do anything for him for his own sake, too. He's a good guy. And all three of us know how important it is to do what we can to keep the family together."

Candy had to swipe at the tears that pricked behind her eyes. "You know that's the biggest regret of my life, don't you? That I wasn't able to adopt …"

They both moved in on her at the same time, and she had to laugh as she ended up smushed in an awkward three-way hug.

"The adoption thing is just a piece of paper," said Rocket.

"And no piece of paper could ever make us more family than we already are," added Spider.

"I know, you're right." Candy sniffed. "You two *are* my boys, and you always will be."

Rocket swiped the back of his sleeve across his eyes, and it made her laugh. He had to be all of six foot five and he was built like a brick wall, but the gesture made him seem like the little boy who had so suited the name Rocky that she loved to tease him with.

Spider checked his watch. "They should be here any minute. Is there anything else you want us to do, or should we just make ourselves scarce now?"

Candy looked around. Inviting Cady and Porter here to the bakery had felt like the best option. It was a place that they were already familiar with. But there was no way that she wanted to subject any of them to having the conversation they needed to have out front where they could be overheard. She loved that Spider and Rocket had suggested setting up a safe, comfortable, and private space back here.

She shook her head slowly. "You boys have done all you can, thanks. All we can do now is wait for them to arrive." She smiled at them. "Although, if you want to keep your fingers crossed, I won't say no to that."

~ ~ ~

Deacon paced back and forth in front of the ovens while they waited. Cady had told Candy that she'd be here at three o'clock. So, of course, he'd been here for twenty minutes already. He checked his watch again. It was only five minutes after three, but Deacon had a nasty feeling that they would still be waiting a while yet. Maybe that wasn't fair of him – he was imagining that she would follow in her mother's footsteps and be anything from twenty to forty minutes late.

He smiled through pursed lips when he caught Candy watching him. She came to him and put her hand on his arm. "Are you okay? I'm sure they'll be here any minute."

"Yeah, I'm okay. But I won't be surprised if they're late."

They both turned when Rocket stuck his head through the door from the front. "I just saw them pull up outside."

"What does he drive?" Deacon asked.

Candy laughed beside him. "Is that really the most important detail to focus on right now?"

He shrugged and gave her a shamefaced smile. "What can I say? It's kind of a hazard of the job. The vehicle that a man chooses can tell you a lot about him."

Candy just rolled her eyes at him. "Only a man? What about the vehicle a woman drives?" She waved a hand at him with a laugh. "Never mind, forget that. If they just pulled up outside, they're going to be walking through the door any second now. Are you good? Do you want me to go out and meet them and give you a minute to gather your thoughts?"

He loved her all the more for offering to do that for him. He gave her a grateful nod and went to press a kiss to her forehead. "Yeah. Thanks, darlin'. That would probably be best."

He stood back just inside the doorway and watched her walk out into the bakery as the front door opened. His heart hammered in his chest. He hadn't seen his daughter in … He was ashamed to admit that he didn't even know how many years it had been. Too many, that was all he knew. It wasn't as though he didn't recognize her, though. He was glad to see that she'd filled out a little. She'd been a tiny, wispy little thing when she was a kid. He'd thought that she'd inherited her mom's build but seeing her now with a bit more meat on her bones, she looked more like a Wallis. That made him smile; it gave him hope. Maybe she wasn't her mother's daughter to the extent that he'd convinced himself that she was.

He loved that her shoulders relaxed a little when she spotted Candy. Although she then immediately looked around, no doubt for him. He felt bad for her that he wasn't out there, but his sense of hope strengthened when she looked disappointed to see that Candy was alone.

As Candy greeted her, he turned his attention to the boyfriend. Porter. He looked like a decent enough kid. Although Deacon had learned that appearances could be deceiving. He'd put enough clean-cut-looking kids behind bars in his time. And on the flip side, no matter how they might look, Rocket and Spider were two of the finest young men he'd ever known.

Candy was right; Porter was protective of Cadence. He didn't seem overbearing, though, and Deacon didn't miss the way that Cady kept looking to him for reassurance. When she did that, Porter moved closer to her and smiled. He put his hand at the small of her back as Candy led them toward the counter.

Deacon stepped back away from the door when she reached the hatch in the counter and let them through. His heart hammered as he took a deep breath. This was it. He was about to have the reunion that he'd longed for with his daughter. He could only hope that, with Candy's help, he wouldn't screw it up.

Chapter Twenty-Three

As Candy led Cadence and Porter back into the kitchen, she hoped that she'd done enough to reassure them that Deacon was eager to see them.

She went through the door first and gave Deacon an encouraging smile as she said, "Here they are."

She stepped aside, not feeling that it was her place to introduce Porter. The only thing she needed to do was to support Deacon in however he wanted to handle this. She loved the look on his face when he met his daughter's gaze. He was nervous, there was no question about that, but there was also no mistaking the fact that he loved her.

"Cadence." Deacon shifted from one foot to the other, looking uncomfortable.

Candy bit down on her bottom lip to stop herself from encouraging him to give her a hug.

Cadence looked just as uncomfortable as she gave him a tight smile and that trademark curt nod. "Dad." She turned to Porter, who stepped closer to her side.

Candy liked him even more when in the face of Deacon's stern look, he stepped forward and extended his hand. "Mr. Wallis, it's a pleasure to meet you, sir. I'm Porter."

Candy was relieved when Deacon smiled as he shook hands with him. "It's good to meet you too." When he let go of Porter's hand, he turned to Cadence, and Candy's heart melted for him when she saw tears shining in his eyes. He held his arms out to the sides a little way and said, "Any chance your old dad can get a hug, Cady?"

Candy had to wipe at her own eyes when Cady let out a strangled-sounding sob and flung herself at him. She turned to Porter and was thrilled to find him smiling back at her. They both looked on as father and daughter clung to each other.

It was a few long moments before Deacon stood back and put his hands on Cady's shoulders as he looked into her eyes. "Damn, I've missed you, baby girl."

Cady started to sob and threw herself back into his arms. Candy's heart ached for him as Deacon closed his eyes as he held her tight.

It was a couple of minutes before Cady managed to pull herself together. This time, she didn't let go of Deacon but instead, spoke into his shoulder. "I've missed you, too, Dad. I was so scared to come here. I didn't know … I didn't know if you'd even want to talk to me."

Deacon kept a hold of her as he leaned back to look into her eyes. "Why would I not talk to you? I love you, Cady. You're my little girl. There's not a day that goes by that I don't think about you and your brother and wish … Well, it doesn't matter what I wish. All that matters is that you're here now." He glanced at Porter and then looked back at Cady. "Is everything okay? Is there anything I can do for you? Are you in some kind of trouble?"

Candy's breath caught in her chest when she saw the look that Cady shot Porter. They both looked panicked for a moment, and Porter stepped forward. Deacon frowned when Cady moved away from him, and the frown deepened when Porter wrapped his arm around her shoulders.

To his credit, the words that came out of his mouth didn't match the expression on his face. "Whatever it is, honey, I'll help in whatever way I can."

He held his arm out to Candy, and she went straight to him as he said, "We both will."

Candy nodded emphatically. "If you guys are in some kind of trouble, we're here for you."

Cady met Deacon's gaze and bit down on her bottom lip. "It's not trouble, Dad. At least, we don't think so. It's just that … Mom …"

Candy felt Deacon tense at the mention of Willa. From what he'd told her about the woman, she understood why.

Cady looked up at Porter again for reassurance. Candy had seen enough abusive relationships to know that she really was seeking reassurance — and receiving it, too. She wasn't seeking Porter's permission to speak; it was more like she was leaning on his strength. It seemed that he had plenty of it – and not just the physical kind that his muscular frame boasted.

Porter raised his eyebrows, and Cady nodded. He looked Deacon in the eye and said, "Mrs. … Willa doesn't like me much."

Deacon nodded. "And why is that?"

Candy saw a little muscle tick in Porter's jaw before he answered. "I guess she has a bunch of reasons. She doesn't think that I'm good enough for your daughter, sir."

Deacon nodded again. "Same question again, son; why is that?"

Porter shrugged. "Cady and I met at the country club but only because I worked there."

Candy didn't miss the hint of a smile that tugged at Deacon's lips.

"I don't come from money. As a matter of fact, I come from a fishing family up in Alaska. I don't have a trust fund and I don't even have a degree. I don't make a ton of money; I work as a fitness trainer. So, according to them, I should never have had the audacity to darken their door. They think that Cady is too good for me." He tightened his arm around her shoulders and smiled down at her as he said, "I happen to agree with that part, but since she loves me, I plan to spend the rest of my life doing my damnedest to be good enough."

Deacon's face wasn't giving anything away, but everything that she'd heard made Candy want to go to bat for Porter. She managed to keep her mouth shut while she waited to see what Deacon had to say.

He turned to Cady. "You guys have been together for a while, right?"

She nodded. "Yes, a couple of years now."

"So, why now? What happened that after a couple of years you want to see me, and you want me to meet your boyfriend?"

Cady looked at Porter again, but Deacon reached out and touched her arm. "You can tell me yourself, honey," he said in a gentle tone.

Cady nodded slowly and sucked in a deep breath. "You remember that summer when you didn't come to see us?"

Candy felt Deacon tense and ran her hand up and down his back in an attempt to soothe him.

"You mean when you and Callum said that you guys didn't want me to come?"

Tears started to roll down Cady's face as she nodded. "We wanted you to come. I mean, yeah, I know we were both always busy back then and we didn't always make the time to call you, but Mom said that you were sick of us not making the effort to keep in touch." She sucked in another big breath before she continued. "She said that you decided that it would be better for everyone if we just didn't keep making the trips back-and-forth. I know we were just kids, and we weren't good at calling you, but we thought that was okay because we knew you loved us. When Mom told us that it … It sounded like you didn't really love us, that you thought you'd be better off without us. And, of course, she and Philip told us that we were better off without you, too. I know now that I was stupid to believe her, we both were."

She held Deacon's gaze as she sniffed again and said, "I'm sorry. I should've tried harder."

Deacon stepped forward, and she threw herself at him once again. "No, honey, I'm sorry. I'm the one who should've tried harder. I'm the adult. I'm your dad. I never gave up, but I thought I was giving you what you wanted by staying out of your lives."

Candy met Porter's gaze. She was seething. She'd love nothing more than to get on the next flight back to California and give this Willa a piece of her mind. But this wasn't about her. It was awful to hear what Willa had done, but the question that Deacon had asked still needed an answer — perhaps even more so now. If Willa had been lying to Cadence and her brother for all these years, what had changed recently?

When Deacon and Cady finally let go of each other, Deacon cocked an eyebrow at his daughter and then at Porter. "So, would I be right if I guessed that you guys are about to make me a grandad, and that Willa's not happy about it?"

Both Cady and Porter's eyes grew wide in shock. Candy was shocked too, but she probably shouldn't be. Deacon was a smart guy, and he'd spent his whole career figuring out what people were trying to hide.

Porter stepped forward, closer to Cady again. "Yes, sir. You guessed right. We wanted to come up here to tell you ourselves. Willa wanted … Well, she didn't want … Any of it."

Cady rested her hand on her still flat stomach. Candy felt proud of her when she stood up a little straighter. She might never have had kids of her own, but she was all too familiar with the strength a mother could summon when it came to protecting her babies.

Cady looked Deacon in the eye. "Mom wanted me to break up with Porter. She wanted me to get rid of the baby. And when I told her that I wanted to let you know that you're going to be a grandad, she flipped out. She was crazy angry about everything, but the way she was so insistent that I shouldn't get in touch with you just felt wrong. She wasn't trying to protect me in anything else, so why would she be trying to protect me from you? That was when I started to question everything, and when I started to question her, that's when the truth finally came out. If you get her mad enough, you can provoke her into screaming the truth at you."

Deacon gave her a wry smile. "Yeah, I had some experience with that myself back in the day."

Cady nodded. "I just kept pushing her and pushing her until she finally admitted that she didn't want me to settle down with Porter because that would be making the same mistake that she did when she settled down with you. I hate that I never questioned it too much before, and I'll always regret all the years that we've lost. But I'm so glad that she said that to me because it finally made me see the light. She just can't see that Porter's a good man and he loves me. And the penny finally dropped that no matter what lies she fed us all these years, you're a good man and you love us, too." Her bottom lip trembled as she looked at Deacon. "You do, don't you, Dad?"

"I do." Deacon's voice cracked as he spoke those two words.

Candy had to wipe her eyes as she watched him hug his daughter. Then he held his arm out and included Porter in the embrace.

He leaned back so he could look at Porter and gave him a wry smile. "I was prepared to give you a hard time. And I will have more questions for you at some point. But for now, I guess we can just go with if you're not good enough for Willa, then you're probably more than good enough in my book."

Candy let out a short laugh; she was loving this. Deacon met her gaze as he wrapped an arm around her and pulled her into the huddle. "It looks like we're going to need to figure out a new take on what family looks like going forward."

Cady nodded enthusiastically, and when she met Candy's gaze, she looked for the first time, like the happy, confident kind of girl she would have expected Deacon's daughter to be.

~ ~ ~

Deacon pulled his shirt up over his head and off. He'd been doing better about making sure his clothes made it into the laundry basket since Candy moved in, but tonight he just let it fall to the floor when he saw her sitting up in bed watching him with a look of lust in her eyes.

He winked at her and attempted to wiggle his ass. It wasn't a move that he'd ever tried before and he kind of screwed it up, but it didn't matter — Candy's laughter was all the reward he needed.

"You want some of this, huh?" he asked with a chuckle.

She laughed with him and threw back the covers on his side of the bed. "I do. I was wondering what was taking you so long. Get your sexy sheriff ass in here, and I'll show you exactly what I want."

Deacon didn't need telling twice, he scrambled into bed with her and slid his arm around her waist, drawing her toward him. He loved that she was just as straightforward and fun in bed as she was in the rest of their life.

Her arms came up around his shoulders as he hugged her to his chest and claimed her mouth in a deep, lingering kiss.

When they came up for air, her eyes sparkled as she smiled at him. "Wow! We already had a great day, I think you just announced that we're in for a great night, too."

He nodded happily. "Today was a great day, and it's all down to you. Thank you, darlin'."

"No, there's nothing to thank me for. Cady came here to find you, she just happened to run into me first, that's all."

Deacon pressed three quick kisses to her lips before he leaned back to look into her eyes. "Maybe, but I don't think so. I think it's more than that; she likes you, you reassured her before I even saw her. If she hadn't talked to you, she might not have contacted me. You said yourself, she was scared to death."

Candy shrugged and smiled. "You would have worked it out for yourself, there's no doubt in my mind. But I'm happy that I was able to help." She ran her knuckles down his cheek and gave him a mischievous smile. "And if you're planning on thanking me the way I think you are, then I'd be open to that."

He chuckled and slid his knee between her thighs. "You mean, this kind of open?" he asked as he slid his hand inside her panties.

"Yes," she breathed, as she spread her legs wider.

He claimed her mouth in a deep kiss while he tormented her with his fingers, teasing her clit with his thumb while he traced her entrance.

"Deacon," she gasped as he slid a finger inside her.

He nuzzled his face into her neck, breathing in that sweet vanilla scent of hers. "What, darlin'?"

She rocked her hips in time with him as he pumped two fingers in and out of her, loving how hot and wet she was for him.

She clung tightly to his shoulders as he took her closer and closer to the edge. She tried to reach for him, but he moved his hips away.

"I want you … inside."

His cock twitched and throbbed at her words, but he shook his head without breaking his pace. "And you'll have me soon enough. But first I want to watch you come for me. You're mine, darlin'. Give it up for me."

It seemed that his words commanded her release. Her fingers dug deep into his shoulders as she tensed around him. He loved that she gave herself up to him completely. She trusted him with all that she was as she let him carry her higher and higher. Her whole body quivered as she moaned his name over and over.

He brought her down slowly, finally easing his fingers out and wrapping her up in his arms. He could feel her heart thundering in her chest as she gasped in ragged breaths.

He only gave her a couple of moments before he turned her onto her back, spreading her legs with both his knees this time as he positioned himself above her.

She flattened her palms against his chest and look up into his eyes. "I think I need a minute."

He winked at her as he notched his sensitive head against her entrance. "I plan to give you more than a minute, darlin'."

She rolled her eyes with a laugh. "You know what I mean. I — oh God, Deacon!"

He didn't give her time to finish talking. He thrust hard and held deep, loving the way her inner muscles fluttered around him.

She smiled up at him as he rocked his hips, settling deep inside. "I should believe you by now, shouldn't I? I always think I won't be able to go again, but you …"

He dropped a kiss on her lips. "But I know you can. I know you want to. And I know that I want to give you as many orgasms as you can handle for the rest of your life."

He pulled back and thrust deep and hard again. She gasped his name, and that just spurred him on.

"You good with this?" he asked as they started to move together in a rhythm that had already become familiar, a rhythm that was uniquely theirs and that he planned to enjoy with her until the day he died.

"More than good," she answered as she lifted her hips to meet him.

That made him smile. He knew what she liked. He reached for the pillow beside her head and slid it down under her hips, angling her up to him. Then, he closed both hands around her ass, digging his fingers in as he tilted her back, lifting her to receive his thrusts.

At this angle, she wouldn't last long, and that was a good thing because neither would he. She dug her fingernails into his back and started to slowly scrape them down. That just made him thrust deeper and harder.

"Oh God, Deacon! Yes!"

She tensed around him, pulsating hard, gripping him tight. All the tension that had been building at the bottom of his spine spilled over. His balls drew up tight, and he grasped her ass as he thrust hard two more times before he planted himself deep and let go.

He saw stars as he came hard. Every nerve ending in his body from his scalp to the tips of his toes tingled as he gave her all that he was.

When they finally slumped together and lay panting, her hands came up into his hair. He lifted his head and looked down into her eyes.

"I love you. I'm so glad you got your daughter back."

"I love you, too. And I still think it's down to you that I got her back." He held her gaze. "And I don't want this to sound weird. I don't want you to take it wrong. But I want to share her with you. Hopefully Callum when he's ready. Remember what Luke said about us all becoming family? Well, that's what I want." He smiled at her. "I know Rocket and Spider will make you a grandma when the time is right, but I want you to be grandma to Cady's baby, too." He pressed a kiss to her lips. "How do you feel about you and me being Grandma and Grandpa?"

She kissed him back and laughed. "I love it. I really do."

"And I love you, darlin'. I really do."

Chapter Twenty-Four

Candy set her latte down and smiled when she saw Jim Sheridan come in. He nodded and made his way to the booth in the back where she was sitting.

"Has Deacon still got you sitting around here waiting for him after work every day?"

She laughed. "It's not like that, Jim, and you know it."

"Aye, I do know. He's only looking out for you. He must believe them buggers from California would really come up here after you or he wouldn't be asking you to be so careful."

Candy blew out a sigh. "He does, but I'm not so sure that I do. It was just one phone call. That man who called me was probably just trying to mess with my head. It annoys me to think that he won. He didn't have to make much of an effort, but my life has still been put on hold because of it."

Jim raised his eyebrows and gestured to the bench opposite Candy. "Mind if I sit a minute?"

"Of course, but you don't need to worry about me, Jim. Sorry, I didn't mean to whine at you. It's just getting to be a bit frustrating."

Jim slid into the seat opposite her with a smile. "Aye, I can imagine it is. But I guess it'll all be over with soon. And you know you can't be too careful. Remember what happened with Janey? I feel bad about that. I should have known that she was going over to the Moriarty place. I should've stopped her."

Candy reached across the table and patted his hand. "You couldn't have known." She smiled. "And even if you had, do you really reckon you would've been able to stop her?"

Jim chuckled. "You might have a point there. I just wanted to remind you that it doesn't do to get complacent. We might think that life is different here in the valley; it might seem that the evil in the world doesn't reach all the way out here. But it can, and it does. You just hang in there for a little while longer, and then Deacon will be the one sitting in here wondering where his lady is gallivanting off to next."

Candy laughed. "I'm not much of a gallivanter, Jim. I'd just like to be able to go home when I finish work."

Jim nodded. "And maybe go shopping or for lunch with your friends now and then?"

"Yeah, that too."

Jim checked his watch. "What time are you expecting him?"

Candy shrugged. "I'm hoping soon, but I don't know."

"Is that because Cadence is here?"

Candy laughed. "Does the whole valley know already?"

Jim chuckled. "Of course they do. You've lived here for a while now; you know how it works."

"I do." Candy frowned. "What are people saying?"

Jim smiled. "I love that you want to defend your man, but you needn't worry. Folks around here like Deacon. They look up to him, respect him. Folks are happy for him that his daughter's back. At least, they are as long as she doesn't turn out to be like her mother."

Candy tried to hide her smile but didn't succeed. "Obviously, I've never met her mother. But Cadence is a real sweetheart, just like her dad."

Jim laughed out loud at that. "I bet you call him that, don't you?" He shook his head and chuckled to himself. "Deacon Wallis, a sweetheart." He chuckled again. "And I bet he loves it."

Candy shrugged. "What can I tell you, Jim?"

Jim's eyes twinkled as he met her gaze. "You don't need to tell me a thing. I can see it, and I'm happy for you both."

He raised his eyebrows when Candy's phone rang. She checked the display and saw that it was Deacon. Jim got to his feet and touched her arm before he moved away. She liked him, he was a good guy.

"Hey, you."

"Hey, darlin'. Are you done for the day?"

"I am. What's going on with you?"

He blew out a sigh. "I … Cady called me. She asked if I'd stop and see them at the place they're renting on my way back down the valley."

"Don't worry, you should go. I'm fine here."

"But you're not, are you? Fine there, I mean. You've had a long day and you'd like nothing more than to go home, right?"

"It's okay."

"What happened to giving it to me straight, darlin'?"

She let out a short laugh. "I am giving it to you straight, Deacon. As far as I'm concerned, it's more important for you to see Cady than it is for me to get home." She looked around.

"I might ask one of the boys to go back over there with me. Will that make you feel better?"

"How about I come down there and get you first? You can come and see Cady with me."

"No, I don't want to do that. My guess is that she wants you to herself. And that's understandable. You just go and see her and don't worry about me."

He blew out a sigh. "I can't do that. I do worry about you."

"Well, I worry about you, too. And you've been taking care of me for so long now. Would you please give me the chance to do the same for you? I want you to go and see your daughter and not worry about me. Can you do that for me, please?"

"I can go and see her if you promise me …"

She laughed. "I promise. Now, hang up the phone, go and see your daughter, and I'll see you later."

"Okay. I'll see you later. I love you."

"I love you, too."

She blew out a sigh of her own after she ended the call. She absolutely wanted him to go and see Cady. But she really wanted to go home.

She looked around again, but of course, this afternoon was the one afternoon when the bakery was still busy. Several of the tables were occupied and both Spider and Rocket were busy behind the counter.

She rolled her eyes and drained the last of her latte. It was no big deal; she should be used to it by now. She started to push to her feet, thinking that she'd be better off in the kitchen in her armchair. She might even be able to take a snooze back there.

At that moment, the bakery door opened and two of Candy's neighbors came hurrying in. Rita spotted her and came straight over. Janice was hot on her heels.

"There you are, Candy. Is Deacon here, too?"

"No, why?" Candy's heart hammered in her chest.

Janice elbowed her friend out of the way. "It's Clawson, or at least, we think it is."

Candy grabbed her bag from the booth and started hurrying toward the door without a second thought. "What do you mean? Clawson's at home. Deacon doesn't let him go out by himself."

"That's what I thought, too," said Rita as the two women followed her outside. "But Clawson is the only orange cat in the neighborhood."

Candy's heart hammered even harder. "Where did you see him?" She had no idea how he might have gotten out of the house, but with that coyote still hanging around the neighborhood, she needed to get him back inside as quickly as she could.

She stopped walking when Janice put a hand on her arm. "The coyote got him, Candy."

Candy's hand flew up to cover her mouth. "No! It can't have. Clawson's too smart. And besides, there's no way he could get out of the house."

Rita held her gaze. "He's the only orange cat around, and we were sitting in my kitchen when we heard yowling. Then the coyote ran through my backyard. We went out to investigate and there's orange fur and blood in the field behind my house."

Candy shook her head. It couldn't be Clawson. It just couldn't.

Janice gave her a sympathetic look. "It might not be him. We didn't go out into the field to check. It's just ..."

Candy gave her a curt nod. "I need to go home and check." She had to believe that when she got to the house, she'd find Clawson safe and sound. And if he was missing, she'd rather learn that by finding an empty house than finding his remains in a field.

She stopped dead when she realized that she didn't even have her car here. Rocket had picked her up on his way in, just like he did whenever Deacon didn't bring her.

Rita pointed to her car. "Come on we'll take you."

It dawned on her for the first time that Deacon wouldn't be happy if he knew she was out here. But she'd just have to deal with that later. She was more concerned with Clawson's immediate safety than with some vague possible threat to her own.

Rita's phone rang and answered it even though she was driving.

"Hey, Joe. Did you find it?"

Candy gave Janice a puzzled look.

"Joe was home, too." Janice explained. "And he took his shotgun and went looking for the coyote. Everyone's been after it for weeks now, worried that something like this might happen."

Candy frowned at her. "We don't know that it has happened yet." She refused to believe that Clawson had somehow gotten out of the house. And she found it even more unbelievable that he would've been outsmarted by a coyote.

"I need to go home to check. For all we know, he's sitting right there safe and sound."

Janice gave her another sympathetic look, and Candy knew that she believed the worst. "We'll drop you off and go and meet up with Joe. I'll let you know what's going on, okay?"

Candy nodded. "Thanks. Do you want to give me your number? I'll let you know if Clawson's home. If he is, then that's some other poor creature out there in the field." And as sad as it made her, she was hoping against hope that it was some other poor creature and not Clawson.

When they dropped her off, she took her keys out of her purse as she made her way up the driveway. It had been a while since she'd had to use them. Deacon had worked things so that he was the one to come home with her as often as possible lately.

She let herself in through the front door and hurried to Deacon's door. Her heart was in her mouth as she unlocked it. As soon as she did, she let out a cry.

"Oh, Clawson, baby!" She was so relieved to see him that she scooped him up to cuddle him.

His scratchy meow sounded surprised, and he gave her a baleful stare as he suffered the indignity of being manhandled that way. It only took a few moments before he was purring and butting his head against her shoulder, though.

She turned back to lock the door behind her. Her relief at finding Clawson safe and well was quickly replaced with concern that Deacon wasn't going to be happy when he found out that she'd come home by herself. She rolled her eyes at Clawson. "He's just going to have to understand."

The way Clawson stared back at her gave her the impression that he didn't expect Deacon to be very understanding. He really was a smart cat.

She took him through to the kitchen, planning to give him some fresh water and a treat. It was too early to give him his dinner. She frowned when she spotted movement out in the backyard. And froze when she saw a man coming toward the kitchen door.

Without a thought, she scooped Clawson back up again and ran for the door. She made it out of Deacon's place and hurried to the front door. She opened it and then slammed it shut again at the sight of another man making his way up the driveway.

Shit! Shit! Shit! She recognized this guy. He wasn't one of the regulars in the pawn shop, but he did come in a few times while she was there. He'd given her the creeps then. Now, he scared the bejesus out of her.

She turned all the locks on the front door and headed for the stairs but stopped before she started up them. She'd made Deacon watch enough movies with her lately that she knew his thoughts on lots of things. What sprang to mind right now was the Lifetime movie that they'd seen where the heroine ran upstairs trying to get away from the bad guy. Deacon had rolled his eyes and said that she deserved to die. Where did she think she was going to be able to hide upstairs? And why did she go to a place from which she had no exit?

Candy had to think quickly. She'd planned to go up there because she thought it was the only option she had. But it wasn't. She hugged Clawson close to her chest as she ran back down the hallway to the laundry room. There was no way she'd be able to fit her ass inside the laundry chute, but Deacon had told her that there was a tunnel that led from the basement out to the shed. He'd even shown it to her. It gave her the creeps. It had electric lanterns on the wall, but those walls were made of earth, and she could just imagine them collapsing at any moment.

As she closed the basement door behind her and ran down the steps, she decided that she'd rather take her chances with the walls than with the man she could now hear inside Deacon's place and the one who sounded like he was bashing down the front door.

Her heart thudded to a halt when she heard a shout from Deacon's place. "You can't hide, Candy. You may as well come out and get it over with. My brother's dead – you're about to join him."

~ ~ ~

Deacon had just brought his truck to a stop in front of the cabin where Cady and Porter were staying when his phone rang. He scowled to himself as he pulled it out. He wished he were the kind of guy who could ignore it, but he just wasn't.

The door of the cabin opened, and Cady came out, followed closely by Porter. Deacon held up his phone and gave them an apologetic smile. Unless it was someone important, he planned to let it go to voicemail, but he had to check and see first.

A sense of foreboding came over him when he saw Saunders' name on the display.

"Talk to me," he answered.

"Shit, Deacon, I'm sorry. I've been meaning to call, but the day got away from me."

"What is it?" Deacon's heart was hammering in his chest now. This wasn't good news, he knew it.

"The feds wrapped up their operation overnight. They got most of them …"

"Most but not all, right? What can you give me on the others?"

"Two men were killed last night when the feds went into the warehouse they were using. One of the men who slipped through the net is the brother of one of the deceased."

"Fuck!" Deacon glanced through the windshield at Cady and Porter. They were starting to look worried, but not as worried as he felt. "What else?"

"I just got confirmation now that he knows Candy. The guy I sent in undercover as her so-called nephew IDed him as someone that he knew she'd interacted with."

"Can you send everything you've got to my office right now? My guys will get it to me. I need to check on her."

"I'm on it. And Deacon …?"

"What?" He wanted to get Saunders off the phone and call Candy. He didn't even want her going home with Spider or Rocket, he'd rather she stayed at the bakery where there were more people around.

"I'm sorry. Tell Candy that, too? And give me a call and let me know that she's okay after you speak to her?"

"Yeah." Deacon ended the call and dialed Candy's number even as he swung the door of the truck open. "I'm sorry, kids, but something urgent just came up. I have to go. I'll call you when I can, okay?"

Cady came towards the truck with a worried look on her face. "Is everything okay? You're scaring me, Dad. This isn't just work, is it?"

"No." He looked down at his phone which had gone directly to Candy's voicemail. "I think Candy is in trouble."

Porter stepped forward. "Can we do anything to help? Can I come with you?"

"No. Thanks. You kids just hang tight here. I'll let you know."

As he watched his daughter cling to Porter, he was glad that she had him. It was obvious that he was her rock. He met her gaze for a moment, wishing that they could get off to a better start, but Candy was his number one priority.

She gave him a small smile and nodded. "She's awesome, Dad. You go rescue her, and please let us know that she's okay."

He had to swallow around the lump in his throat as he pulled the truck door shut. He sent gravel flying as he turned the truck around. Then, he dialed Rocket's number.

"Hey, Deacon, what's up? I didn't think we'd hear from you guys again tonight."

"What do you mean?"

"We figured that you guys must have been in a hurry to get home, not even saying goodbye like that."

Deacon banged his fist against the steering wheel. "She's not there?"

"No. Shit! She was sitting out front, waiting for you. It got busy in here and the next thing we knew, she'd gone. We figured that you came to get her and since it was busy, you guys didn't say goodbye. I'm going to head over to your place right now."

"Right. I'm almost there. Can you tell Spider to ask around and find out what anyone saw?"

"On it," said Rocket. "I'll see you at the house."

Chapter Twenty-Five

Candy couldn't stop shaking. Her hands were trembling so badly that she struggled to bolt the door behind her. Once she'd managed it, she fumbled around, feeling for the lantern on the wall. Clawson meowed but it sounded as though he was already a long way ahead of her. She wanted to call him back but didn't dare risk it.

She finally found the lantern and pressed the switch, grateful that Deacon had shown her how they worked even though she'd protested that she didn't ever plan to come down here. All her breath caught in her chest when she heard the basement door open.

"Candy!"

She held her breath, hoping that he would think that the door to the tunnel was just a closet. Then again, he must know that she'd come down here. How long did it take to break a door open? She had no idea, and she didn't want to wait around to find out. She stumbled farther down the passageway, following Clawson.

She heard the man shout again and stopped when she heard another voice. She didn't know if Deacon would think it was stupid, but she edged her way back closer to the door, hoping to hear what they were saying.

"No sign of her down here?"

"No. But that doesn't mean she's not hiding." The first man raised his voice and called, "If you're down here, I'm gonna find you."

She brought her hand up to cover her mouth, trying to keep in the squeak of terror that wanted to escape. Why, oh why, oh why hadn't she stayed at the bakery? She wasn't even worried about Deacon being mad at her anymore. No, all she could think about was how devastated he would be if those men killed her. That poor man had done everything within his power to keep her safe, and she'd gone and blown it with one stupid decision.

The thought of what Deacon would go through if she went and got herself killed now was enough to steady her nerves. It didn't exactly calm her, but it gave her a sense of strength and determination. No way was she going to let them get her. It had taken her more than half a century to find Deacon. Just a few short months ago she'd still believed that she was one of those people who would never have a real love story. Now, she felt as though she and Deacon were just at the beginning of a great love story, and no way was she going to have that taken away from her. No way would she let it be taken away from Deacon.

She froze at the sound of footsteps approaching the door, then the door handle rattled. She was torn between staying here, hoping that they wouldn't try to break their way in and running to the other end of the tunnel in the hope that she'd be able to get out of the shed and away before they caught her.

"Come on, that's just a closet. She wouldn't be able to lock it from the inside. She's got to be upstairs."

She closed her eyes and finally let herself breathe again when she heard their footsteps retreating.

Clawson meowed again, and she stumbled after him. Just as she was thinking that her best bet might be to get the shed and make a run for it from there, she realized that she was still carrying her purse. She sagged back against the wall and slowly slid down it until she was sitting on her heels. She took her phone out with shaking hands. It only had one little bar of signal. She tried to steady herself enough to try to call Deacon but dropped the phone when she heard a commotion coming from the house.

She bit down on her bottom lip when she heard a yell that sounded more like a roar. She might not be able to make out what that voice was saying, but she knew all too well who it belonged to: Rocket.

Her heart hammered even harder as she listened to what could only be a fight. Rocket must have realized that she'd left the bakery and come to check on her. She might never have been a churchgoer, but as she listened to the shouts and bangs and crashing noises, she prayed with all her might that Rocket wouldn't get hurt because of her.

Deacon kept glancing down at his cell phone as he drove. He'd pulled up the tracker app and it showed that Candy was at the house. He'd love to believe that she'd simply had enough of waiting around and decided to go home, that perhaps her battery was dead, and he'd arrive at the house to find her apologetic. Unfortunately, he was a realist. He didn't believe that for one minute.

She was in trouble. He knew it. Every little hair on the back of his neck knew it, and the ball of dread that had settled in his gut knew it, too. He didn't know what the hell had possessed her to leave the bakery. But it didn't matter now, all that mattered was finding her and making her safe.

When he turned into his driveway, the tires of the truck screeched to a stop, and Deacon flung the door open. An icy calm settled over him, and he drew his weapon when he saw that Rocket had obviously parked in a hurry, and that the front door of the house was standing wide open.

"Deacon!"

He pointed his weapon up the stairs to where Rocket's shout came from. "Talk to me."

"Two men. I have one here, he's going nowhere. The other one got away; I think he went out the back."

Deacon swung his weapon back toward his own door even as he shouted to Rocket. "And Candy?"

"I haven't seen her."

Deacon heard what sounded like a gut punch, followed by a grunt and mumbling.

"This fucker says that they couldn't find her."

"Copy that." Deacon wanted to check his phone again to see whether it still indicated that she was in the house. But first, he needed to see if he could catch up with the one who'd escaped.

He cleared his own place quickly. They'd broken in through the kitchen door. He went out that way and scouted around the yard. It looked like they'd come in over the back fence, there were footprints back there. He moved closer to check.

Two sets of footprints, but he'd guess only one man had come that way. One set pointed to the house, the other pointed away. He grabbed the top of the fence and boosted himself up, but there was no sign of anyone back there. He knew that he should see if he could find a trail, but he couldn't make himself do it. Candy was his number one priority.

He lowered himself back down and checked his phone again. The tracker still showed that she was here. His blood ran cold at the thought that maybe the man Rocket had upstairs was lying. Maybe they'd already found her and … No, he wasn't even going to think that. He couldn't allow his mind to go anywhere near the thought of her being harmed, and the thought of losing her …? He shook his head to clear it. That just wasn't an option.

He swung around, his weapon raised, when he sensed movement over by the shed. A rush of relief washed over him when he saw Clawson strutting toward him, tail in the air, looking totally unfazed by whatever he'd witnessed in the house.

Deacon did a double take from the cat to the shed door, which was standing open a crack. His heart leapt into his mouth when he saw one finger curl around the door, only about a foot off the ground. He holstered his weapon as he rushed forward.

"Candy!"

The door opened a little farther and her head popped out at about the level of his shins. She had to be lying on the ground. Her eyes were wide, and her face was white. "Deacon?"

He yanked the door open and fell to his knees beside her, gathering her up in his arms. "Are you okay? Are you hurt?"

She buried her face in his chest as she shook her head rapidly. "We're fine. I'm so sorry, Deacon. I just … It was Clawson. Rita and Janice came to the bakery to tell me that the coyote got him. I couldn't believe it. I didn't want to believe it. I didn't even think; I just came home to check on him. I'm so sorry."

Deacon couldn't force any words out. He just wrapped his arms around her and held her tight. She was safe. That was all that mattered. She was still here.

She lifted her head, and her green eyes shimmered with tears as they looked into his. "Please don't be mad at me. I know how stupid it was. All I could think while I was hiding down there was how stupid I'd been and how terrible it would be if I went and died on you now."

He crushed her against his chest and dropped a kiss on her lips. "Don't even say it, darlin'. You don't get to die for at least another forty years. We're just getting started, you and me. And yeah, I'll be mad at you later. You might even have to put up with Grumpy the sheriff for a while, but all that matters is that you're safe."

They both looked up when Luke, Spider, and Tyler and Tanner MacFarland came bursting out of the kitchen door. Clawson let out a startled yowl and shot off up the tree.

Deacon didn't miss the look of relief on both Luke and Spider's faces when they saw Candy safe in his arms.

Tyler looked around. "Where's Rocket?"

"Upstairs," said Deacon, finally remembering that he was the sheriff as well as the man who'd been terrified that he might lose his woman. "You want to go and give him a hand? He's got one of them up there." He looked at Luke. "The other one got away." He pointed to the fence. "That way."

He watched as Tyler and Spider headed back into the house to help Rocket, and Tanner and Luke went to examine the fence.

He looked down when he felt Candy's trembling fingers touch his cheek. "I'm sorry."

He pressed three quick kisses to her lips and shook his head. "It's okay, darlin'. It's all okay. You're safe." He frowned. "And I'm going to make sure that you stay that way."

Her eyes grew wider. "What does that mean?"

"It means that those bastards don't come into my valley, into my house, try to hurt my woman, and get to walk away again afterward."

"Don't you think that they'll give up now? I mean, it sounded like Rocket taught one of them a lesson. I would think the other one would just go back to where he came from now."

Deacon held her gaze for a long few moments before he looked away. They had a deal that they told each other straight. No matter what might need to be said, they were honest with each other. But he wasn't sure that she needed to know that one of those men was out for revenge for the death of his brother. And Deacon just knew in his gut that he was the one who'd gotten away.

"Deacon?"

He got to his feet and helped her up. "I'd love to tell you that it's all over now. But I don't think it is, not yet."

~ ~ ~

Candy made a face at Libby as she slid the muffin pan into the oven. She didn't like this, didn't like it one bit. Deacon hadn't been as honest with her as he usually was when he'd said that he didn't think this was over. He told her not to worry, but how was she supposed to do that when he'd sent her over here to the MacFarland place while he and Luke took the guy who Rocket had caught up to the sheriff's office in town to question him.

Libby gave her a reassuring smile. "It's going to be okay, Candy. You know what Deacon's like; he'll make damn sure everything's okay."

"I'm not doubting him. What worries me is that if he still thinks it's so dangerous that I need to come over here and be surrounded by all these guys, who's looking out for him?"

Libby smiled. "Deacon isn't the kind of guy who needs anyone to look out for him. But he has Luke, anyway. Do you think that *he'd* let anything happen to his big brother if he can help it?"

Candy sighed and gave her a small smile. "No. Deacon's his hero." Her smile faded. "But I don't want him getting hurt either. I hate this, Libby. This is all my fault. I brought trouble here."

"Miss Candy." She hadn't seen Spider standing in the doorway to the kitchen, but his stern tone didn't surprise her.

She shrugged. "What? It's true."

He came into the kitchen and wrapped her in a hug. "I can tell you now that your troubles are our troubles. So, when you think about it, it's better — and we're glad — that you brought your troubles here rather than try to face them back in LA all by yourself."

Rocket, Tyler, and Tanner all came into the kitchen. Rocket nodded at her as he approached. "You know he's right."

"Aww, Rocky. You're going to have a black eye tomorrow."

He shrugged. "It's well worth it."

Tyler laughed beside him. "And it's nothing compared to what he did to the other guy." He punched Rocket's arm and said, "Right, Rocky?"

Rocket scowled at him, but Candy could see a smile lurking behind it. "Only Miss Candy gets to call me that."

Tyler grinned at her and nodded. "I know and I love it, but I had to get it in there just once."

Candy laughed; it was good to hear the boys joking around. It made things feel a bit more normal, even though she was only here because the MacFarland Ranch was a place where Deacon trusted that she'd be safe. It was so big that any stranger coming would be spotted a mile off, and between the brothers, Rocket, and Spider, she'd have plenty of protection.

She gave Ford an apologetic smile when he came into the kitchen to join them. But he surprised her when he came and gave her a hug. She liked him, he was a good guy. But she thought of Ford as the most distant of the MacFarland boys and he certainly didn't strike her as the affectionate type.

"I wish it were under different circumstances, but I'm glad you're here." He smiled. "We were talking about it a while back, after Luke came up with his family pre-union thing. Since Rocket married Janey and took her name, he's one of us. And since you're his mom, that must make us all family too, right?"

Candy had to blink away the tears that pricked behind her eyes as she nodded. "I guess it does." She smiled around at them all, so grateful that she had them in her life. "I love it, thank you. I just wish Deacon were here, too."

Spider checked his watch. "They're probably almost up to town by now, and I asked Luke to call and let me know as soon as they find anything out."

Candy nodded. All she wanted was for this to be over. She wanted Deacon to lock that guy up. Maybe he could find the other guy and lock him up too. Then he could come home to her, and they could put this all behind them. Part of her was almost glad that it'd happened because now they could move on from it. But she still had a bad feeling that, like Deacon had said, it wasn't over yet.

~ ~ ~

Deacon kept an eye on the rearview mirror all the way up the valley. He hadn't seen the guy who'd escaped from Candy's place, but Rocket had given him a description, and the guy driving the gray sedan behind them matched it.

"I'll give you whatever you want," said the guy in the back seat with Luke. "I'll give you everything you need to get him. He's a crazy fucker. I'm only here because he gave me no choice. He wants your woman dead."

Deacon gripped the steering wheel tight. He knew that it was just an attempt to win him over before they got to the station, and he was prepared to play the game to see what he could learn before they got there.

He glanced in the rearview mirror again and caught Luke's gaze after he checked on the sedan.

Luke nodded and turned to the man beside him. "Where is he staying? What's he driving?"

"He's driving a gray Toyota Corolla. We've been sleeping in it. We stayed in a motel in town the first couple of nights. But you guys didn't make it easy to get to her. We were running out of money, so we've been sleeping in the car."

Deacon checked the mirror again. The vehicle back there was indeed a Toyota Corolla. He didn't know if the driver intended to try to get his friend back or if he was coming after Deacon. Either way, Deacon was glad he was following them and not out hunting for Candy.

"He's lost it," the man continued. "Shit got crazy at the pawn shop the last couple days."

Deacon frowned. "You said that you two have been up here for a while. You weren't there when the feds moved in?"

"No. Vinny, that's his name, he's had it in for Candy since he found out that Tony wasn't for real. He lost it when he found out that his brother died when the feds went in. He blames her."

Deacon blew out a sigh. It was just as bad as he'd expected.

Luke met his gaze in the mirror again when he stopped at the red light coming into town. Deacon gave him a slight chin jerk, wondering if he'd be able to let him know that Vinny was tailing them without alerting this guy. "What's your name?" he asked. He really needed to get his shit together. He should've known that before now.

"Evan. Evan Smith."

Deacon doubted that was his real name. But he'd be able to run his prints once they got to the station.

The Corolla stayed with them all the way through town. As they approached the station, Deacon decided that he had to let Luke know even if it meant alerting Evan to his friend's presence, too.

He caught Luke's eye in the mirror and said, "Tail."

Luke looked puzzled for a second, but then his eyes widened, and he nodded.

"You take Evan inside when we get there, and I'll be right with you."

Luke frowned. "We can walk him in together."

Deacon scowled back at him. "I've got this."

He watched the Corolla pull up alongside the curb as he pulled the truck into the lot at the station. Whatever this Vinny's game was, they were about to find out.

"Wait there," he told Luke. "I'll come around."

He went and opened the back door, and Luke and Evan got out. As soon as they started walking, gunshots rang out, and Evan fell to the ground.

Deacon drew his weapon and returned fire, cursing himself as he did that he hadn't been prepared for this.

Luke scrambled back to him, and they both took cover behind the open door of the truck. But no more shots came. Deacon popped his head up in time to see Vinny jumping back into the Corolla.

"I'm going after him."

"I'm coming –"

"Defend this station."

"I need a weapon."

For the first time, it occurred to Deacon that Luke had been off duty when he arrived at the house. He couldn't believe that his brother had just taken fire while he was unarmed. He reached into the glove box and handed him his personal Glock.

"Take this. I'll be back." He didn't think for one second that Vinny would come back to the station; he just didn't want to risk putting Luke in danger if he came with him.

He was back in the truck and pulling away after the Corolla before Luke had the chance to argue.

He didn't need to go far. The Corolla ran the red light at the intersection of Main and Second and ran straight into the path of an oncoming pickup truck. Deacon pulled his own truck over and jumped out when he saw Vinny scrambling from the wreckage, still holding his gun.

Deacon's heart sank when he saw a woman hurrying toward Vinny, seemingly to check that he was okay. Either she hadn't noticed the gun, or she was in shock; whatever her reasoning, it wasn't going to work out well for her.

"Vinny!" he yelled.

Vinny turned wild eyes toward him and raised his weapon. "You should have just let me kill her. She's not worth it. Now, you're going to die for her. Maybe this is better. She killed my brother. I'll kill you, and she can know the pain of how it feels to live without you."

"Drop it." Deacon trained his own weapon on him as he spoke. "Drop it, and I can take you in. Otherwise, you'll be joining your brother."

Vinny just laughed and swung his arm around until he was aiming at the woman who had frozen when she realized that he had a gun.

She screamed. Deacon breathed, and the shot rang out.

His heart hammered as he watched the woman fall to the ground. He'd failed. He checked on Vinny. No, he hadn't failed. Vinny was down, too.

Deacon kept his weapon trained on Vinny as he hurried forward. A rush of relief swept over him when he heard the woman sobbing. People were rushing forward, offering to help her. He left them to it as he approached Vinny. He dropped to his knees beside him and felt for a pulse. Deacon holstered his weapon. Vinny was gone.

It wasn't the first time that he'd taken a life, but he knew without a doubt that this was one that he'd never second-guess himself over.

He looked around at the people hurrying forward, they were good people in this town. His people.

Cody from the hardware store hurried toward him. "You okay, Sheriff?"

"Yeah, I'm good." He gave him a wry smile. "I guess I'm not going to be too popular for holding up traffic on Main for a shootout, huh?"

Cody laughed. "I reckon you're going to be more than popular. They'll be wanting to give you a medal for saving Anita's life and taking down the bad guy. You're the real deal, a genuine hero."

Deacon shook his head. He was nothing of the sort, but he didn't want to stick around to argue about it. All he wanted was to go get Candy and take her home. It was over.

Chapter Twenty-Six

Candy woke with a start. She must be late; she could see the sun shining around the edges of the curtains. She started to sit up, but Deacon's fingers curled around her wrist.

"It's okay, darlin'. You're safe. It's over."

His words and his reassuring touch brought it all back; her panic over Clawson, the men coming into the house, her terror as she'd hidden in the tunnel out to the shed, and the relief that she'd felt to see Deacon after Clawson escaped from the shed and she peered out.

She lay back down and turned to face him. He was right, it was over, but she was mad at him. She couldn't believe that he'd chased after that crazy man all by himself and then gotten himself shot at in the middle of town. She pecked his lips fiercely and then slapped his arm.

He cracked one eye open and chuckled. "What was that for?"

"You know damn well what it was for, Deacon Wallis! I told you last night. You can't go stashing me away safely at the MacFarland place and then go chasing men with guns all by yourself. He could've shot you." Her chin started to wobble. "He could have killed you." She sniffed.

He wrapped his arms around her and held her head against him. "I'm safe. It's all over now."

She burrowed into his warmth and nodded against his chest. "It is, and I'm glad, but don't you dare ever do anything like that again."

She felt his laughter rumble in his chest and looked up at him angrily. "I mean it!"

His gray eyes twinkled as they looked down into hers. "I know you do, darlin'. How about this, how about we make a deal?"

She scowled at him. "I'm serious. You don't get to deal your way out of it. I was so scared when I heard that there was a shooting up in town and that you were involved. I thought … I thought I might lose you, and it scared me to death, Deacon. You don't understand … you don't know how it feels to think –"

His eyebrows drew together, and he gave her a stern look. "Just hold it there, darlin'. Let's think about how it all started, can we? Then we can talk about our deal. I do know how it feels. I imagine that you were feeling pretty much the same way that I felt when you didn't answer your phone. Maybe even as bad as I felt when I called Rocket, and he told me that you weren't at the bakery." Any trace of humor drained from his face as he added, "I hope for your sake that you didn't feel the same way I did when I got back here and saw Rocket's truck outside and the front door standing open." He looked deep into her eyes. "Don't tell me I don't understand. Don't tell me I don't know how it feels." He pressed a kiss to her lips. "It's over, and now we get to leave it behind us. We can make a deal that if you won't be mad at me, I won't be mad at you." He winked at her. "Unless you want to talk about how you promised that you wouldn't leave the bakery and then left anyway."

She smiled through pursed lips. "I really don't want to talk about that. But I do just want to clear one thing up. Well, maybe two things. First, I'm sorry. I know I shouldn't have done it, but I didn't even think. I was so worried about Clawson. I just had to know that he was okay. And secondly …" She winked right back at him. "I didn't actually promise that I wouldn't leave the bakery."

He scowled, but she put a finger to his lips before he could speak.

"I didn't. You said that you would only go and see Cady if I promised, and I promised before I let you finish the sentence. You never got the chance to say *what* I had to promise."

He smiled through pursed lips. "Yeah, but …"

"No, Deacon. No buts. I did that deliberately. I don't ever plan to break a promise that I make to you." She smiled. "So, I made sure that I didn't make a specific promise. But I do promise that I'll do my best to not be so sneaky again in the future."

She loved the way he looked when he threw back his head and laughed. "Let me guess, you're not going to make me a specific promise about that either?"

"Sorry."

"Fair enough. I vote that we put this whole thing behind us. You could be mad at me; I could be mad at you. But I'd rather not waste time on any of that. I'd rather just be grateful that we made it through it, and it's behind us."

Candy nodded happily. "I can go for that."

Clawson chose that moment to jump up onto the bed. He plunked himself down on Deacon's chest and started kneading at the blanket.

Candy had always loved how affectionate he was with his cat. It made her smile to see him reach up and scratch Clawson's ears. It made her laugh when he said, "Good morning, buddy. Are you making biscuits to let me know that it's time for breakfast?"

Clawson purred loudly and butted Deacon's hand.

"That sounds like a yes to me," said Candy. She reached out and scratched Clawson's ear. "You're a good boy, Clawson." She shuddered as she remembered how scared she'd been for him.

"What is it?" asked Deacon.

She gave him a sad smile. "I was so worried about him. I feel bad for the fox, but I'm just glad this guy was safe here at home and not …"

"Yeah." Deacon shook his head. "I guess everyone's been doing a good job of keeping their pets indoors. A coyote wouldn't normally kill a fox – not unless he saw it as competition. Too many predators, not enough prey."

Candy shuddered again. "Well, hopefully, there won't be any more predators in the neighborhood now." She smiled at Clawson. "We're not prey, are we, baby?" She pushed the blanket back and started to get out of bed, but Deacon caught her hand.

"Don't go thinking that you're making breakfast, lady. This is only the second morning since we've been together that I get to have you home with me. You take your time, take it easy, I'll see to this guy, and you can let me know whatever you want me to make you."

She leaned back toward him planning to peck his lips, but he snaked his arm around her waist and pulled her back down onto the bed with him. Clawson let out an indignant meow and ran from the room.

Deacon's eyes shone as she looked up into them. She rocked her hips and smiled at him. "Can you guess what I really want for breakfast?"

He cupped her cheek in his hand and nodded. "I'm not just guessing, I know, darlin'. It's the same thing I want."

She looped her arms up around his shoulders and pulled him down to her. "I think it's finally time for me to start taking at least one morning a week off."

She shivered as Deacon buried his face in her neck, his warm breath fanning over the sensitive skin there as he said, "You won't get any arguments from me on that one."

~ ~ ~

Deacon couldn't stop smiling as he and Candy walked hand-in-hand over to the bakery. Spider and Rocket had insisted that she should take a couple of days off after what had happened, and that suited him just fine. He had a couple of days off, too. There was always an investigation to follow up an officer-involved shooting. In this case, the undersheriff was the one who would have to ascertain whether Deacon had acted within the law. Deacon wasn't worried; he was just glad to have some time off with Candy, especially while Cady and Porter were here.

She turned to smile at him before they crossed the road. "I could get used to this."

He wasn't sure what she meant, but he was hoping … "Me too. You know, if you don't want to keep working so hard at the bakery, I can support you if you –"

She looked so shocked that he didn't even finish. Shit! It looked like that wasn't what she meant at all. He held his breath and waited to see what she had to say.

"Aww, Deacon! That's so sweet of you! It's not what I meant, but it is sweet of you. I make my own way in life. I always have. Don't you go thinking that I plan to start mooching off you."

He had to laugh. "I was thinking nothing of the kind. I was just thinking that since you live with me now …" He cocked an eyebrow. They hadn't talked about it, but she hadn't spent a night in the upstairs apartment in he didn't know how long, and he had no intentions of letting her move back up there. As far as he was concerned, she lived with him now. And if she didn't yet, he damn well hoped that she would when she married him.

"Since I live with you now, what?"

He grinned. She hadn't even questioned it. "Since we live together, you don't have rent to pay anymore. So, I figured you might want to take it a bit easier. You know, not have to go out at four-thirty every morning." He waggled his eyebrows. "We could start more mornings the way we did this morning. If you wanted."

She rested her head against his shoulder and looked up into his eyes. "You know I'd like that. We should figure something out. I don't want you feeling that you need to support me, and I don't want to let the boys down. But I would like more mornings like today."

When they were settled in the big booth in the back of the bakery, Spider and Rocket came to join them. Deacon would be forever grateful to them. If it weren't for them, he never would have met Candy. He wanted to pull them aside before he and Candy left. They were her sons in everything but blood, and it seemed right to him that he should ask for their blessing before he asked Candy to marry him. It was strange; before everything had gone down, he'd planned to have a chat with them and let them know his intentions. Now, for some reason, it seemed important to ask them.

He smiled when the bakery door opened, and Cady and Porter walked in. It struck him that perhaps they were the reason that he wanted to ask, rather than tell, Spider and Rocket that he wanted to ask Candy to marry him. He felt certain that Porter was planning to ask him for his blessing.

His heart felt like it might overflow as he watched Cady hurry toward Candy and wrap her in a hug.

"Oh my gosh! I was so worried about you. When Dad left our place yesterday, I just couldn't settle, I was so scared that something might happen to you."

Candy hugged her back tightly. "I'm fine, sweetie, thank you. And I'm sorry that you were worried. You don't need any stress." She stepped back and smiled at her. "You've got the baby to think about."

Porter came and shook Deacon's hand. "Good to see you, sir."

"You too, son. Is everything okay?"

Porter glanced over at Cady, but she was still chattering with Candy. "We have something that we'd like to talk to you about when Cady's ready." He held Deacon's gaze and swallowed visibly before he added, "And I'd like a word with you in private when you can as well, please."

Deacon took pity on the kid and smiled as he nodded. It seemed that Porter had the same thing on his mind that he did. "We'll find time before the end of the day."

Just as they'd all settled in again, and Spider had brought drinks for Cady and Porter, Luke came in. He made his way over to the booth with a big grin on his face.

"Hey, family!"

Deacon didn't know how much more his heart could take when Cady greeted him with a "Hi, Uncle Luke."

Luke leaned in and kissed her cheek, before doing the same with Candy. Then, he slid onto the end of the bench next to her and grinned around at everyone. "I guess we can start calling them family reunions now, can't we?" He nodded at Cady. "I'm so glad you're back. How long do you guys plan on staying?"

Deacon looked at his daughter. That was a question that he'd planned to ask them when he went to the cabin to visit them. But of course, he hadn't even gotten out of the truck.

Cady looked up at Porter before she answered. Deacon wasn't sure how he felt about that. He could see that they had a good relationship, but it bothered him that his daughter was so unsure of herself.

Porter caught his eye before turning to answer Luke. "That's something we wanted to talk to you guys about."

Deacon leaned forward, wondering what he was about to say. He had to smile as Candy gripped his hand in hers and asked eagerly, "Are you going to stay here? Please, say you are. That would be so wonderful."

Deacon wouldn't have dared ask, but he was glad that Candy had. He held his breath as he waited for their answer.

Cady met his gaze. "We wanted to talk to you first, Dad. I didn't know if …" She stopped and sucked in a deep breath before she continued, "I didn't know if you'd want …"

Deacon couldn't it take anymore. He shuffled out of the booth and made everyone else do the same so that he could get to his daughter. Once he did, he wrapped her up in a hug. Cady clung to him, and he could see Candy beaming at him from behind her.

"You want to know what I think?" he asked.

Cady's big gray eyes looked up into his as she nodded.

"There's not much that would make me happier than having you move back here. I'd love it." He looked at Porter. "And I'll see what I can do about helping you find work."

Luke laughed, and Deacon let go of Cady. "What's so funny?"

Luke grinned at him. "I already talked to a couple of people. Steve's been talking about hiring another trainer at the gym up in town. Wade said that as long as he can figure out the insurance issues, he'd be happy for Porter to use the fitness room at the guest lodge to do personal training. And Ford said that, if nothing else, he can always use another pair of hands on the ranch." He turned to Porter. "So, finding work shouldn't be an issue."

Deacon grinned at his brother. They didn't talk much about Cady and Callum, but he'd always known that Luke longed for family.

"How come we weren't invited to the party?" He turned to see Ace and Trip standing there, grinning at him.

He shook his head. "Probably because I didn't know it was going to turn into a party."

Trip laughed and grasped his shoulder. "I'd say that's a theme that you might want to get used to."

Deacon scowled at him. "If you're planning on throwing me a party …" He made a face. "Can you at least give me some notice?" He'd been about to say, *you can forget it,* but he wouldn't go that far. That might be his personal preference but, he smiled – he had his family to consider now.

Trip just laughed again. "Not me, Chief. Sharon Anderson."

Deacon scowled. "Why in hell would that woman want to throw me a party?"

"It's not exactly a party," said Ace. "It's just a little get together. You know what she's like – she wants to get you in front of the press. She wants to do the whole hometown hero sheriff story before it blows over."

Deacon rolled his eyes. "It's already over."

He knew that his fate was sealed when Candy came to stand beside him. She slipped her arm around his waist and smiled up at him. "You should do it."

Deacon shot an evil look at Ace and Trip. "What do I have to do?"

Trip winked at him. "We can talk about it later." He turned to Cady. "For now, we're just a couple of long-lost uncles who are hoping that our niece is back to stay."

Deacon loved watching the two of them hug on his daughter. He couldn't help hoping that soon his son might come, too. Even if it was just for a visit.

Candy enjoyed every second of that afternoon. It seemed that everyone she knew came to join them in the bakery, at least to stop by and check on them. Although many folks stuck around to join them.

Jim Sheridan was thrilled to see Cady and Porter. Apparently, he'd had a soft spot for Cady and Callum when they were kids. Even if he hadn't had much patience with their mother.

Things had quieted down a bit now. Most folks had gone home to get on with their evenings. Jim was still there, as were Ace and Trip, who were chatting with Deacon, teasing him about the little get together that Sharon had set up for him.

Candy knew that he wasn't thrilled about that, but she was pleased for him. He might not need any public accolades for himself, but she loved that Cady would get to see it.

She smiled when the door opened, and Libby came hurrying in. "How are you doing? Sorry, I would have been here sooner if I'd known that you were all getting together. I ran into Frankie in town just now; she told me that everyone was here." She turned to Spider. "She said to tell you that she'll be here as soon as she can, but she needed to stop to see Owen on the way."

Candy hugged her tightly. "I'm fine, thanks." She glanced over at Deacon. "And he is, too. And now, thank goodness, I don't have to hide anymore."

Libby laughed. "Well, halle-freaking-lujah for that! When's girls' night?"

Deacon narrowed his eyes as he came toward them. "I was wondering how long this would take."

"What would take?" Libby attempted an innocent look, but didn't quite pull it off.

Deacon slid his arm around Candy's waist. "I'm guessing that the two of you are going to be living it up now that you're free to get out and about, right?"

Candy smiled up at him. "You're guessing right."

Cady came over to join them and smiled at Libby. "It's good to see you again. I always remember you being kind to us when we were kids."

Libby nodded at her. "You were good kids, and I probably shouldn't say this, but I always felt sorry for you. How long are you here for? Are you planning to stay?"

Cady nodded slowly. "We'd like to … but …"

"But what, sweetheart?" asked Candy. "What details do you need to figure out?" She glanced at Deacon. "We'll help with whatever we can."

Cady shrugged. "The first thing we need to do is find a place to stay. I mean, we have the cabin until the end of next week. But we didn't know how this was going to go, so we didn't want to plan for anything more than that."

Candy beamed at her and then nodded at Deacon. "I think we have a solution for that, don't we?"

Porter had come to join them too, and she grinned at him. "You guys could take the upstairs apartment at Deacon's house. It's free now."

Her heart sank when she didn't get the kind of reaction she'd expected. It seemed perfect to her. She was living with Deacon now. The apartment was empty. They needed a place to stay. But no one else seemed to be thrilled with the idea. Cady looked at her dad and shrugged.

Deacon just nodded. "We'll figure something out. For now, how about we take this back to the house?" He jerked his chin toward Rocket and Spider, who were cleaning up. "I bet these guys are ready to get out of here."

As they walked hand-in-hand back to the house, Candy was glad that he wanted to have everyone over, but she was puzzled why he didn't seem thrilled about giving Cady and Porter the apartment.

She looked up at him to ask him, but when he met her gaze and smiled, she forgot about everything except the fact that she was here. She knew how lucky she was to be living this life with this wonderful man and to now be free to fully enjoy it.

Chapter Twenty-Seven

Deacon ran a finger under the collar of his shirt and made a face at Trip. He was wishing that he hadn't let his friend talk him into this. He didn't need it. Didn't need half the town showing up to see him get presented with some award. He didn't deserve it. He hadn't done anything out of the ordinary. He was the sheriff, for fuck's sake. And besides, it wasn't as though he'd been doing his duty for the public good.

Anita might have gotten in the way and put herself in danger, but Deacon had been there on personal business. Taking Vinny down had been all about keeping Candy safe. That was all there was to it. He'd tried to explain that to anyone who would listen. But folks wanted to make a big deal out of it; it seemed that people wanted to believe there were still heroes in the world. He wasn't one, and he knew it. But if they wanted to parade him around for a night, he'd do it. He had to smile; he wasn't sure that he'd do it if Candy and Cady weren't here, but still …

He looked out at the crowd. There were way too many people here for his liking. He couldn't wait to get this over with and take Candy home. He closed his fingers around the box in his pocket. Well, he wasn't going to take her straight home. Tonight was the night that he was finally going to ask her. He'd had his chat with Rocket and Spider, and they were good with it — more than good, they were happy about it. He'd talked to Cady about it, too. She was thrilled for them. He loved that she'd gotten to know Candy in her own right first. He could see the two of them building a solid relationship going forward.

He knew that the two of them would grow close, especially with the baby on the way. But he was glad that Cady had been as unenthusiastic about taking the upstairs apartment as he was. He loved having her back, but he didn't think that having her and Porter, and soon the baby, living under his roof would be the wisest move. He wanted his family to be close – but not that close. He smiled, remembering the look of relief on Porter's face when he'd explained that to him – he hadn't wanted them thinking that he didn't want to help.

His smile turned into a scowl when he saw a news crew at the back of the room. He turned to Trip, who was hanging out back here with him. He enjoyed all this community stuff and had volunteered to be the one to introduce Deacon – more like talk him up a bit – before he said as few words as he could get away with.

Trip raised an eyebrow and came over. "What's up, Chief?"

"I thought you said there weren't going to be any cameras."

Trip laughed. "And I thought you said you were going to wear something nice."

Deacon looked down at himself. He thought he looked pretty sharp, but what did he know? He made a face at his friend. "Candy likes it."

"Jesus, Deacon. I'm just yanking your chain. Loosen up a bit." Trip gave him a puzzled look. "Are you nervous?"

It was Deacon's turn to laugh. "No. I'm not. At least, not about this whole deal." He glanced out at the gathering crowd again and smiled when he saw Candy chatting happily with

Libby and Cady. He chuckled when he saw Frankie, Janey, and Sierra making their way toward them. He knew Candy would love that. "I'm just impatient to get this over with." He touched the ring box in his pocket again. "I've got more important stuff to be doing."

Trip grinned at him. "Are you finally going to ask her?"

Deacon smiled. "Yeah."

"I like it," said Trip. "What's the plan? Are you going to do the whole big deal, public proposal while everyone's here to see?"

Deacon looked at him as if he'd lost it – he must have if he thought that he'd want to do that. "Hell no! I plan to get her out of here just as soon as we can. I'm going to ask her when it's just the two of us."

"I like that even better. That's more your style. I was going to say good luck, but you don't need it."

"I'll take it if you're offering," said Deacon when he saw Sharon gesturing for them to come out onto the platform where she was bustling around getting ready to announce them. "You know I hate doing this kind of shit."

Trip grasped his shoulder and walked him out onto the big stage in front of the crowd. "I know you do, brother. But that's why you're so damn good at it. Folks don't want to see the kind of man who would be happy to stand on a stage and preen in front of them. Folks need heroes, Chief, to give 'em hope – so smile, would you?"

Candy clapped her hands together when she saw Deacon walk out onto the stage with Trip. He was a good-looking guy no matter what he wore, but when she'd seen him all dressed up tonight, she had joked that she wasn't going to let him leave the house. Looking like that, she wanted to keep him home — in bed.

Cady moved closer and linked her arm through Candy's. "Doesn't he look great?"

"Doesn't he just?!" Candy said with a laugh.

"Is he okay with this? I mean, I guess he's probably changed over the years, but when we were little, he used to hate being in the limelight."

Candy squeezed her arm. "He's not changed that much. It's just that this is something important. Not that it's so important to him, I thought he was going to try to get out of it at one point. But I'm glad he didn't. People around here look up to him, and I think they're glad to be able to do something to recognize all that he does for them."

Cady nodded. "I wish Mom could see this. Don't get me wrong," she added hurriedly. "I wouldn't want her to be here. But I just wish that she could see him the way everyone else does." She smiled at Candy. "Then again, I'm glad that she was never able to see him that way. He would never have met you, and I'm so glad that he did. You guys are perfect for each other. And in case I haven't said it already, thank you. Thank you for making it easier for me to make things right with him."

Candy squeezed her arm again. "You have nothing to thank me for. I didn't do much. But I would have moved mountains to help make things right between you if that was what it took. And I still wouldn't have needed your thanks then. Family is important to me; it always has been."

Cady rested her head against Candy's shoulder as they listened to Trip introducing Deacon. "Well, I'm happy that we're family now." She rested her hand on her stomach. "And I can already tell that you're going to be the best grandma to this little one."

Candy had to wipe away the tears that threatened to fall as she nodded. "I'm going to do my best, sweetheart."

At that moment, Porter came and stood on the other side of Cady. Candy let go of her when Deacon started to speak. She knew that he planned to say as few words as possible and get off the stage as fast as he could. He managed to pull it off, too. Trip had spoken for longer than he did.

As he came to the end of his short speech, Deacon looked around at the crowd, meeting people's gazes and nodding here and there. When he found Candy, he smiled. Her heart felt like it melted in her chest. That smile! Damn!

"I want to thank you all for being here tonight," he said. "I appreciate it, even if I'm not sure I deserve it. All I can tell you is that I was doing my job. I think you all know that I love this job and I plan to keep doing it and looking out for you all for as many years as I'm able." He looked around again and grinned. "But you know what? It's Saturday night. And I'm not on shift; Undersheriff Townsend is on duty. He's the one who's looking out for you good folks tonight. So, I'm out of here." He caught Candy's gaze and winked. "It's my night off, and I want to spend it with my lady."

With that, he gave the crowd a nod which was nowhere near as curt as usual, then made his way down the steps from the stage as people laughed and slapped his back as he passed.

Libby laughed beside Candy. "Well, that was typical Deacon."

Candy laughed with her. "They did well to get that much out of him, they should be grateful."

"Oh, they are. Believe me, they are. I was surprised that he agreed to do it."

"I may have done a little talking him into it."

Libby raised her eyebrows. "Really? Why?"

"Don't look at me like that. I couldn't care less whether he does stuff like this. It doesn't matter to me." She jerked her head toward Cady, who had a big smile on her face as she watched her dad make his way through the crowd toward them.

"I thought it was important for her to see, to understand, how folks around here see him."

Libby looked puzzled. "I thought they were doing well. I thought she was just as happy to be around him again as he is to be around her. Are things still a bit rocky?"

"No! No, it's nothing like that. It's not that their relationship needs healing, so much as he needs healing around the way he thinks his kids see him." Candy put her hand over her heart as she watched him reach Cady. She threw herself at him, and Candy had to swallow as she watched Deacon squeeze his eyes tight shut as he held his daughter close.

"You really do understand him, don't you?" said Libby beside her.

"I do. I understand him and I love him."

When he let go of Cady, Deacon said a few words to her and then met Candy's gaze. He held it all the way as he walked toward her. She couldn't wipe the smile off her face. He put his hands on her hips and drew her to him as he pressed three quick kisses to her lips.

"You ready, darlin'?"

She laughed. "Don't you need to do the rounds and talk to people?"

"Nope." He shook his head adamantly as he took hold of her hand. "I gave these people what they wanted from me. Now, it's my turn. I meant what I said up there. It's my night off, and I want to spend it with my lady."

He cocked an eyebrow at her as he started to lead her away. "Unless what my lady wants is to stay here and hang out with these folks?"

She shook her head just as adamantly as he had. "No, thank you. I wanted you all to myself the minute I saw you dressed like that." She let her gaze travel over him and waggled her eyebrows. "Take me home."

He chuckled as he made a beeline for the door. He didn't stop to chat with anyone, just smiled and nodded and kept moving. Candy had to laugh, she loved it. She was glad that he'd done this tonight, but she was even more glad that they were getting out of here.

Deacon smiled to himself as the truck ate up the miles. They were almost back home now. Candy had chatted away at first, telling him how proud she was of him, which did more to boost his ego than the whole deal with the award tonight — or any award, for that matter — could ever do.

She told him how happy Cady had been, and how proud of him she was, too. He'd choked up over that. Not so long ago, he didn't think that he'd have a real relationship with his daughter again. No way would he have believed that she would come to live here in the valley. To hear that she was proud of him made his heart swell in his chest.

He looked down at Candy's hand where he held it on top of the console. Their fingers were linked together and after tonight, their lives would be linked together forever. He knew that she would say yes. There wasn't a single doubt in his mind. He wasn't even nervous about the ring anymore. He'd shown it to Cady when he told her what he planned to do. She'd fallen in love with it and said that she just knew that Candy would love it.

Candy squeezed his hand when she saw him glance down. They'd been riding in companionable silence for a while now. "Are you okay?"

He winked at her before turning his attention back to the road as he said, "Never been better."

He tried to hide his smile as he drove on past the bakery and the turnoff to the house. Last time he'd done that after a night out she'd been happy to go wherever he wanted to take her. He hoped that she'd feel the same again tonight. She made it clear that she was in a hurry to get him home to bed, and he was eager to get there too. But by the time they did, he wanted her to be wearing his ring on her finger.

She laughed when she realized that they weren't going home.

"Problem?" he asked.

"Nope. No problem at all. I know by now that whatever you do, you mean to do it. You didn't turn off the highway, so you're not planning to go home. I'm happy to just sit back and relax and see what you have in store."

That was just one of so many things that he loved about her; she'd proved over and over again that she trusted him. She never grilled him with a dozen questions about where they were going – or about anything. She just accepted what he said, and she accepted what he did, and she had enough faith in him to trust that he would always do the right thing.

He couldn't think of anything more right than what he planned to do next. He couldn't think of anything that he'd ever done in his life that was more right than asking her to marry him.

She turned to smile at him as the truck bounced over the bumpy gravel road. "I know where we're going this time."

"That good with you?"

She nodded happily. "I think it's perfect. It's like we said last time. It's enjoyable to be around a bunch of people." She rolled her eyes at him and added, "Don't look like that, it can be, and you know it — especially when those people are our friends and family. But it's really special to be able to come out here where it's just the two of us." She looked out the window at the golden moon that hung low in the sky. "It's so beautiful.

I've never been anywhere so beautiful before in my life. And I love that you share this place — your place — with me."

He brought the truck to a stop next to one of the picnic benches that stood by the water's edge. He hadn't thought of Dailey Lake as *his* place before, but she kind of had a point. The whole valley was beautiful; there were a thousand spots that a guy could escape to when he needed some solitude in nature. But Dailey Lake had been one of his haunts, even when he was a kid. He'd come out here when he wanted to escape the world, whether it was his dad when he was young, or Willa when he was married to her, or just after a long hard week dealing with the less desirable element of the community. It hit him that in all his life he'd never come out here with another soul.

She squeezed his hand. "Are you okay?"

He smiled at her and nodded. "I'm better than I've ever been. I'm with the only person on this Earth who I've ever trusted enough to truly be myself with." He pressed three quick kisses to her lips. "I'm with the woman I love. And I'm going to take her for a walk in this beautiful place and ask her a question that I've been wanting to ask her for a while now."

She made to open her door, but he gave her a stern look. "Wait right there, I'll be around."

He jogged around the hood of the truck and opened her door for her. He set his hands on her hips and lifted her out. Then he backed her up against the side of the truck and claimed her mouth in a deep, lingering kiss.

She looped her arms up around his shoulders, and her eyes shone as she smiled at him. "Wow! I like where this is going, Sheriff Wallis." She glanced behind her at the bed of the truck. "I'm up for it if you are. I'm not even going to ask if there's a law against it; I don't want to know."

He threw back his head and laughed. Here he was, trying to build some magic, some romance; he didn't know what it was supposed to be, but he wanted to try, and she was joking about getting it on in the bed of his truck like a pair of horny teenagers. He wasn't against the idea, not in principle, but he had something more important to do right now.

He shook his head at her and led her to the back of the truck. Once he let the tailgate down, he lifted her up and sat her on it. As he stood between her legs to kiss her again, he couldn't deny that the idea of climbing in there with her was more than tempting. She rubbed herself against him and moaned into his mouth.

"I have to tell you that I've wanted to do this for a long time now." She waggled her eyebrows at him. "I know you're not serious, at least, I don't think you are." She pressed herself closer, and added, "But just in case you're considering it, you should know that I'd be happy to."

He leaned back so that he could look into her eyes and smiled through pursed lips. "I wasn't serious, but now you've got me thinking about it."

She laughed. "I promise I won't tell if we do."

He chuckled. "I'm not worried about that. It's just …" He felt around in his pocket for the ring box, and when his fingers closed around it, a sense of peace came over him. This was right. This was who they were. It didn't need to be about creating some magical moment out here, any more than it needed to be a staged moment with a hundred people around up in town.

"I told you I was going to take you for a walk and that I have something to ask you. It looks like we're skipping the walk, and I'm moving straight to the question."

She waggled her eyebrows again. "Ask away; I think we both know that whatever you ask of me, I'm going to say yes."

She was still joking, but Deacon had never been more serious in his life. "Okay," he said as he dropped down to one knee. He hadn't thought this out very well. With her sitting on the tailgate and him kneeling, he was at eye level with her crotch. But then again, it made her laugh, so it worked.

She stopped laughing when he held up the ring box. One hand came up to cover her mouth while the other gripped his tightly. "Oh my God, Deacon!"

He squeezed her hand and smiled. "Don't tell me your surprised, darlin'?"

She shook her head slowly. "No. I mean, I am. But only the timing. I … Yes!"

He had to laugh. "I'm tempted to go with just sliding this sucker on your finger and taking your yes as good. You know I'm not great with words. But I thought about this, and I want to ask you properly. If you're okay with that?"

She nodded rapidly.

He sucked in a deep breath and blew it out slowly. "I didn't have the greatest start in life, and I know you didn't either. I didn't choose well when I got married the first time, and I know you didn't either. But I've done a lot of learning and growing over the last several years, and I know you have, too.

"When I first met you, I thought that I was past the stage in life where I'd get to have love and family." He smiled. "I told you once before that I tried to resist you, but that was a mistake, and you turned out to be irresistible.

"I'd say that we both got most of our mistakes out of the way in the first half of our lives. And now, I want to ask you to spend the second half with me. If you do, I promise you that I'll do everything I can to make all the years we have left the best years of your life."

He had to clear his throat as he held the ring box up for her to see. "Will you marry me, Candy?"

Tears rolled down her cheeks as she nodded. "Yes, Deacon, I will. I'll marry you, and I'll love you, and I'll do everything I can to make the rest of your life the best of your life, too."

He got to his feet and slipped the ring onto her finger.

He threw his head back and laughed when she looked down at it and squealed. "Deacon! It's beautiful!"

He cupped her cheek in his hand and moved in closer until his forehead rested against hers. "I wanted it to be special, just like the lady who's going to wear it." He traced his finger over the huge diamond that was circled by a dozen smaller ones. "That big one in the middle? That one's you. You're this sparkling, shining beauty." He traced his finger over the smaller diamonds. "These ones are the rest of us. Me, Rocket, Spider, and the girls, Luke, and now, Cady and Porter, and their baby, and all the babies to come. You've drawn us all together in a circle around you. You've made us a family, and you're the center of it."

He tapped the ring again and looked deep into her eyes. "You're the center of our family, and the center of my heart."

She pressed a kiss to his lips and nodded. "You're the center of my heart, too. I promise you, Deacon, I'll love you forever, and I'll hold our family together. The best of our lives has just begun."

As he wrapped his arms around her and hugged her to his chest underneath the big Montana sky that twinkled with a million stars, he knew she was right. And he couldn't wait to see what their future would hold;

;

A Note from SJ

I hope you enjoyed Deacon and Candy's story. The next MacFarland Ranch book will be Luke and Laney's story. You can get more details as they become available on my website at "The Cowgirl's Inevitable Love". I can't wait to share that one with you!

Next up, it's back to The Hamiltons and Napa for Bentley and Alyssa in "Bourbon and Bluebells". Even though this will be book seven in the Hamiltons series, these two meet in Summer Lake. They've both gone to visit their parents – Alyssa has gone to see her dad, Russ, and Bentley's there to see his mom, Ria. Neither of them sees a problem in hooking up with the hot stranger they meet at The Boathouse, but the next day when they go off to meet up with their parents they each discover that their one-night stand is also their soon-to-be step-sibling.

Check out the "Also By" page to see if any of my other series appeal to you – I have the occasional ebook freebie series starters, too, so you can take them for a test drive.

There are a few options to keep up with me and my imaginary friends:

The best way is to Sign up for my Newsletter at my website www.SJMcCoy.com. Don't worry I won't bombard you! I'll let you know about upcoming releases, share a sneak peek or two and keep you in the loop for a couple of fun giveaways I have coming up :0)

You can join my readers group to chat about the books or like my Facebook Page www.facebook.com/authorsjmccoy

I occasionally attempt to say something in 140 characters or less(!) on Twitter

And I'm in the process of building a shiny new website at www.SJMcCoy.com

I love to hear from readers, so feel free to email me at SJ@SJMcCoy.com if you'd like. I'm better at that! :0)

I hope our paths will cross again soon. Until then, take care, and thanks for your support—you are the reason I write!

Love

SJ

PS Project Semicolon

You may have noticed that the final sentence of the story closed with a semi-colon. It isn't a typo. Project Semi Colon is a non-profit movement dedicated to presenting hope and love to those who are struggling with depression, suicide, addiction and self-injury. Project Semicolon exists to encourage, love and inspire. It's a movement I support with all my heart.

"A semicolon represents a sentence the author could have ended, but chose not to. The sentence is your life and the author is you." - Project Semicolon

This author started writing after her son was killed in a car crash. At the time I wanted my own story to be over, instead I chose to honour a promise to my son to write my 'silly stories' someday. I chose to escape into my fictional world. I know for many who struggle with depression, suicide can appear to be the only escape. The semicolon has become a symbol of support, and hopefully a reminder – Your story isn't over yet

Also by SJ McCoy

Summer Lake Silver

Clay and Marianne in Like Some Old Country Song

Seymour and Chris in A Dream Too Far

Ted and Audrey in A Little Rain Must Fall

Izzy and Diego in Where the Rainbow Ends

Manny and Nina in Silhouettes Shadows and Sunsets

Teresa and Cal in More than Sometimes

Coming Next

Dalton and Taryn in Can't Fight The Moonlight

Summer Lake Seasons

Angel and Luke in Take These Broken Wings

Zack and Maria in Too Much Love to Hide

Logan and Roxy in Sunshine Over Snow

Ivan and Abbie in Chase the Blues Away

Colt and Cassie in Forever Takes a While

Austin and Amber in Tell the Stars to Shine

Summer Lake Series

Love Like You've Never Been Hurt

Work Like You Don't Need the Money

Dance Like Nobody's Watching

Fly Like You've Never Been Grounded

Laugh Like You've Never Cried

Sing Like Nobody's Listening

Smile Like You Mean It

The Wedding Dance

Chasing Tomorrow

Dream Like Nothing's Impossible

Ride Like You've Never Fallen
Live Like There's No Tomorrow
The Wedding Flight
Fight Like You've Never Lost

The Hamiltons
Cameron and Piper in Red wine and Roses
Chelsea and Grant in Champagne and Daisies
Mary Ellen and Antonio in Marsala and Magnolias
Marcos and Molly in Prosecco and Peonies
Grady and Hannah in Milkshakes and Mistletoe
Jacob and Becca in Cognac and Cornflowers
Coming Next
Bentley and Alyssa in Bourbon and Bluebells
Slade and Willow in Whiskey and Willow
Xander and Tori in Vodka and Violets

The Davenports
Oscar
TJ
Reid
Spider

Remington Ranch Series
Mason
Shane
Carter
Beau
Four Weddings and a Vendetta

A Chance and a Hope

Chance is a guy with a whole lot of story to tell. He's part of the fabric of both Summer Lake and Remington Ranch. He needed three whole books to tell his own story.

Chance Encounter

Finding Hope

Give Hope a Chance

Love in Nashville

Autumn and Matt in Bring on the Night

About the Author

I'm SJ, a coffee addict, lover of chocolate and drinker of good red wines. I'm a lost soul and a hopeless romantic. Reading and writing are necessary parts of who I am. Though perhaps not as necessary as coffee! I can drink coffee without writing, but I can't write without coffee.

I grew up loving romance novels, my first boyfriends were book boyfriends, but life intervened, as it tends to do, and I wandered down the paths of non-fiction for many years. My life changed completely a few years ago and I returned to Romance to find my escape.

I write 'Sweet n Steamy' stories because to me there is enough angst and darkness in real life. My favorite romances are happy escapes with a focus on fun, friendships and happily-ever-afters, just like the ones I write.

These days I live in beautiful Montana, the last best place. If I'm not reading or writing, you'll find me just down the road in the park - Yellowstone. I have deer, eagles and the occasional bear for company, and I like it that way :0)

Made in United States
Orlando, FL
26 August 2023